I was beyond mad—my internship gone, my career over…all because of Spenser.

I ran from 21, jumped in the first cab I could, then made the poor cab driver run through a red light, and almost knocked over a lady to get back to my internship as fast as I could. It was pointless, though. Carmen was standing in my path to the back door.

"Don't bother," were the only two words she said before, "your stuff is all here." She pointed to the bag at her feet. "Don't come back tomorrow. We've already contacted your school, so you might want to touch bases with them. Have a nice life. I hope he was worth it all," she said, holding her hand out.

She was waiting for me to place my badge in her hand, and it killed me. It was like ripping my own heart out and handing it to her.

I grabbed my bag after she went back into the building. The thick metal door slammed shut behind her, making me jump. I had lost everything I had worked for my whole college career. Without my internship, I had nothing. My future plans to work there had been pulled out from under me. My degree was likely not going to happen, because I'd refused to intern anywhere else.

All of this happened because I wasn't focused. I had always been so focused before. All it took was one night at a club that I should never have gone to in the first place. There wouldn't have been notes and flowers, lies, or paparazzi. *My god!* My life would have been so different, if I hadn't gone to that damn club. Everything I had worked for was ruined.

Elizabeth:

My heart had just been splintered by the man I thought I was in love with. Betrayed by one, mislead by another. My twisted triangle of a nightmare was over. It should be a walk in the park now…right? That's what I thought when the clock struck twelve. I was in the arms of the man I knew I should be with, and I was ready for a new year, a new me, and a new love. But this wasn't the fairy tale I thought it was going to be. I'd stepped into a completely new field, and it wasn't full of daisies. It was a field of landmines, secrets, lies, and more heartbreak. Is any of this worth saving?

Simon:

I love her. That's never going to stop, and I don't want it to. I'll make her see…

KUDOS for *Mended Hearts*

In *Mended Hearts* by M. E. Gordon, Elizabeth Monroe has just learned that Simon Sullivan, a man she believed loved her, has been lying to her all along and using her. In fact, she doesn't even know his real name. As the story opens, she's shattered and has turned to the other man she'd been dating before choosing Simon, Spencer Salvatore. He's everything a girl could want—handsome, rich, and thoroughly smitten with her. But can she trust him? After all, he hasn't been completely honest with her either. But at least his real name is Spencer, and he doesn't work for the tabloid that has been hounding Elizabeth since she met him, like Simon does. It's now the new year, and Elizabeth is ready to start fresh with a new love and leave the heartaches of the last year behind her. But she quickly discovers that it's not quite that easy. For one, Simon, whose real name is Nick, won't go away. He still loves Elizabeth and is determined to win her back, certain that Spencer is only using her. Like he has room to talk! And for another thing, Spencer might not have lied about his name, but there's a lot he hasn't told her that she needs to know. Told from Elizabeth's, Nick's, and Spencer's POVs, the story is fast-paced, tense, and sexy—with some very spicy love scenes. I loved it and couldn't put it down! ~ Taylor Jones, Reviewer

Mended Hearts by M. E. Gordon is the story of a love triangle with an innocent young woman caught in the middle between two dynamic, handsome, charming, secretive, and manipulative men. Elizabeth Monroe is a size-twelve beauty with a serious self-confidence problem. Because she's not a supermodel size two, she's not comfortable in her body, and she's suspicious when, not one, but two gorgeous men start vying for her attentions.

In the first book in the series, *Torn Hearts*, Elizabeth is torn between her feelings for Simon, who she believes is a freelance photographer, and Spencer, a rich entrepreneur and a partner with her brothers in opening a night club. Both men claim to love her. Even though she has very strong feelings for Spencer, she doesn't trust his feelings for her because, after all, "men like him don't fall for girls like me." Believing that she and Simon are a perfect match, she convinces herself that she loves him, even though her feelings for him aren't as strong as her feelings for Spencer. But just as she makes her decision, she learns that Simon works for Fame, the tabloid that's ruining Elizabeth's life, and that he's been spying for them all along. Devastated, she throws herself into Spencer's arms, which is where book two opens. But even though Simon is now out of the love triangle, Elizabeth's new life with Spencer isn't as quiet and peaceful as she imagined. The paparazzi still follow her everywhere and threaten her internship at the Library of Congress who don't want all the people and cameras there. Spencer is still being secretive, even though he promised no more lies, and his mysterious trips, explained by "doing this to protect you," make her think he's cheating on her. In addition, Nick (AKA Simon) keeps calling Elizabeth, trying to convince her that Spencer is a dangerous man and will only hurt her. Confused and angry, Elizabeth makes a lot of bad decisions and her life spirals out of control. But worst of all, someone is out to get Spencer, and they don't seem to care who gets caught in the crossfire. Mended Hearts is intense, passionate, fast-paced, and suspenseful, and has plenty of very hot love scenes. This isn't your grandmother's romance, but you'll want to read it over and over again. ~ *Regan Murphy, Reviewer*

ACKNOWLEDGEMENTS

Mended Hearts has been a labor of love. I'd known how Elizabeth, Spencer, and Simon's story was going to end from the very first few words I wrote in *Torn Hearts*. All I had to do was sit down and write the middle.

This book was close to a four-year process and there are a few people I'd like to thank who helped me to finally get it done.

As always I'd like the thank Black Opal Books and Lauri for accepting the story before it was even finished and having faith that I would get it done. Speaking of Faith, my editor did a great job of keeping me on track and again teaching me so much about writing.

My cover designer, Melissa at The Illustrated Author did an outstanding job again! It's a simple, feminine, refreshing cover and I wouldn't want anyone else working with me. I can't wait to continue to work with you on upcoming books!

To my kids and husband, thank you for letting me get lost in my writing and sometimes forgetting to clean the house. I love making up stories in my head and without all of your patience they would never get written down.

Also from M. E. Gordon

The Hearts Series:

Torn Hearts
(Black Opal Books, 2015)

Mended Hearts
(Black Opal Books, 2017

Opposite Hearts
Coming soon

One Night Stand Series:

Make Me Stay
Black Opal Books, 2016)

Not My Type
Coming soon

Bring Me Back
Coming Soon

Mended

HEARTS

M. E. GORDON

A Black Opal Books Publication

GENRE: CONTEMPORARY ROMANCE/WOMEN'S FICTION

This is a work of fiction. Names, places, characters and incidents are either the product of the author's imagination or are used fictitiously, and any resemblance to any actual persons, living or dead, businesses, organizations, events or locales is entirely coincidental. All trademarks, service marks, registered trademarks, and registered service marks are the property of their respective owners and are used herein for identification purposes only. The publisher does not have any control over or assume any responsibility for author or third-party websites or their contents.

Dedication

To my love Shaun,
it's only loosely based on you.

Chapter 1

Elizabeth

I sat upright in bed. Sweat beaded on my upper lip, and my hair stuck to the back of my neck. My heart was pumping overtime to keep my blood circulating.

Spencer—

I looked to either side of me. I was alone. The room was still dark, the curtains still drawn. The clock read 3:06 am. My fantasy had become my very own twisted nightmare. Six hours ago, my life had flipped upside down. The man I thought I loved had been lying to me. Simon Sullivan wasn't at all who he said he was. *Who knows if that's even his real name.*

It turned out Simon was the reason why my life was on public display for all to see. It was he who had betrayed me like no one ever had. I trusted him, loved him, and he was just using me.

Spencer had brought me home that horrible night. He stayed with me and reassured me that he wasn't going anywhere. He comforted me in my time of need, and I was grateful. The moment my head had hit the pillow, I let exhaustion take over. I remembered Spencer lying next to me, combing his fingers through my hair. I hadn't wanted anyone but him lying next me. Sure, we had lots to work through, but I was ready to finally accept that what we felt toward one another was real and not imagined.

Holy shit—what was that? Someone else was in the condo. I had clearly heard another man's voice from the living area. I got out of bed and moved toward the voices. Stopping just before the hallway ended and the open floor plan of my cozy DC condo began, I scanned the room. Hidden by the darkness of the night, I watched a looming figure pace, while another stood, solid as sculpted marble.

"What do you want me to do, S?"

The pacing figure stopped moving and ran both hands through his hair. It was Spencer.

"I can't tell her, not now. You have to stall. I need more time. Do whatever's necessary to keep it underground. Fuck! So many years and they choose now to start digging around."

"I'm not sure how long we're actually going to have, but you know I'll do my best, S."

"Thank you, T. I'll be in touch with you sometime tomorrow," Spencer replied.

"No problem. Hey, bro, we're going to get through this, just like everything else." The sculpture named T moved closer to the door then turned back. "Happy New Year, S."

"Yeah—happy New Year."

The door closed, but nothing else moved. I went back in my room, jumped in bed, pulled the covers up, and waited.

I felt like I was in a Telemundo soap opera. All we needed was a secret marriage and an evil twin to show up. *Scratch that. I don't need any more drama than I al-*

ready have. My family was slowly shrinking. My best friend was in love with both my brothers, plus she was mad at me. *Let's see, what else? Oh right, the man I thought I was in love with was totally using me. Let's not forget about the striking man pacing in my living room with a temper problem. Who, might I add, seems to have more secrets than an award-winning novel.* Truth be told, I knew nothing about the man who was pacing in my living room.

I had no idea why he was interested in me. I wasn't famous or anywhere close to the company he was use to keeping. I was simply Beth Monroe, plain Jane, curvy, and stubborn as a mule. He, on the other hand, was a thirty-one-year-old, highly sought-after man, with the world at his feet. He ran his businesses with an iron fist and was good at it, so good he had become rich beyond his years.

The floor creaked slightly as Spencer came back into my bedroom. I faced away from him, trying to steady my breathing, to make it look like I was still sleeping. I could feel his presence standing over me. The bed dipped and the covers moved as he slid in. I wanted to turn to him, have him hold me tightly. I wanted to know who he was. I wanted to ask him a million questions, but I didn't. I just lay there and played dead.

His hand snaked around my waist, pulling me closer to him. Then he moved the hair that lay in the crook of my neck. His warm lips kissed me, as his hand wrapped around my stomach, pulling me still closer to him. *Suck it in, Beth.* I felt his lips smile on my neck. Bastard. He told me once before to stop doing it, but it was habit. I wasn't a twig, I never would be, and I'd probably never stop doing it. I dared him to say something.

He nuzzled my neck inhaling deeply. "I'm not like him," I heard him whisper softly. "I won't hurt you. I will not be like him."

He must have been talking about Simon. The urge to look at him took over. I needed to see him. I needed to make sure it was all real.

I moved my body, as if waking from sleep. Turning in his arms, I found myself face to face with him. His breathtaking features were laying on *my* pillow. His black hair was messy but still looked perfect. His eyes were out of this world, blue as the most beautiful sea. His eye lashes were dark and long. He had strong cheekbones, and divine, sexy, stubble grew along his strapping jaw. I stared at him, in awe of his beauty, as he stared back at me. I would have loved to known what he was thinking then. Smiling at him, I decided to throw it all out the window. My need to figure him out overruled the need to stare at him in silence. I wanted to learn about his past, learn about him.

"What are you thinking?"

His hand moved down my back, finding its way under my shirt to my bare skin, as I asked my question. "I was thinking about you. How I need you." He paused. "Elizabeth, I'm scared out of my mind right now. I've never felt this way about someone before."

This wasn't the usual Spencer, the Spencer who knew exactly what he wanted and how to go about getting it. He looked vulnerable and truly frightened.

"I won't lose you," he said fiercely, staring right into my eyes. "I'm not like him."

There he was, the demanding Greek God who knew what he wanted.

"Spencer, I know you're not like Simon, but you have to talk to me."

He touched my face and let his thumb run along my bottom lip, tugging it to one side. God, that drove me wild. Holding the back of my neck so that I couldn't move, he crashed his lips to mine. It was as if he couldn't hold back any longer and, honestly, I couldn't either. His tongue slipped between my lips, exploring my mouth, as mine fought against his.

My hands went to his hair, and I held on tight to the roots. I felt his chest against mine. His heart raced against me as if he had just been running a marathon.

"I need you," he said, pulling back, waiting for me to say something. "Elizabeth, I need you"

I nodded my head vigorously because, I couldn't form any words. He crushed his lips to mine again, pulling me up to rip my T-shirt and shorts off. I lay underneath him, naked as a new born baby. I sat up on my elbows to get closer to him. Taking my neck in his fingers, he pulled me closer, not rough or hurried, but carefully, sensually. I was Jell-O in his hands. The best part was, he knew it. He knew the effect he had on me, and he was taking full advantage.

I felt safe with Spencer, safe from everything. His words echoed in my mind. *'I won't hurt you.'*

I had been hurt, and now I just wanted to be happy. But could Spencer be the one to do that for me? We had our differences, but I needed him as much as he said he needed me.

A hand moved between my legs, his fingers falling right where I needed them most. Before I had the chance to beg for more, he was sinking them inside. I arched my body as he claimed me, my vision going dim in ecstasy. Those magical fingers, that had me losing it on my father's desk in a matter of minutes, were at it again. I moaned in pleasure, clutching at his chest.

I had a feeling my nails were moments away from drawing blood, but when he touched me like that, he deserved it.

"Spencer—please, I need you—I need more."

He stopped moving and looked me in the eyes. The

early morning light was starting to show through the closed curtains.

"Say it again," he demanded, caressing my cheek with his thumb.

"Spencer."

The words wouldn't come out as fast as he wanted them to, so he asked again, "Say it, say you need me. Tell me you choose me."

His expression changed as I took my time figuring out if this was what I really wanted, or was it just what my sex-crazed body wanted.

Even through all the madness going on around me, I was always drawn back to Spencer. It was more than the animalistic pull I thought it was when I first ran into him on the side walk outside of my brothers' soon-to-be night club 21.

Before, I had pushed Spencer aside for Simon's sake, but now Simon was gone, and I was free to let my heart choose, without feeling guilty.

I took in his beautiful face, every inch of it. I ran my fingers through his hair, around his ear, and let my hand rest on his cheek. I had never seen Spencer look more nervous. He wasn't the multi-millionaire, demanding, hot shot right now. He was just Spencer, a man, putting his heart out on the line for me—again.

"Spencer, I—" I was finding it hard to say. I knew exactly what I wanted to say, but it scared me to jump in head first after everything that had happened with Simon. I thought I had known him. I didn't know anything about Spencer, but the one thing I definitely did know was that I falling for him faster than I had thought possible. I used the simplest of words. "Yes."

"Yes? Yes, what? Elizabeth, I'm not going to do this—" His face fell and he shook his head, as if in disbelief.

"Spencer, look at me!" I interrupted him. "Yes, I choose you, only you."

He had such a great smile, and I was determined to see more of it, a lot more of it. I had made a decision. I wanted Spencer Salvatore and, by some miracle, he wanted me too.

"You're sure?" he asked, after kissing me.

"Yes, I'm sure. But you have to promise me, no secrets. You need to tell me everything, I mean it, Salvatore."

"Making demands of me already, Miss Monroe? I'm glad to see that your stubborn ways are still intact. It will make for some very interesting conversations."

I rolled my eyes, a little disturbed that he knew me so well.

"Don't roll your eyes."

I looked at him and cracked a smile. "And I see your domineering ways are in full swing. Like you said, it's going to be fun ride."

Smiling back at me, he kissed my lips.

A moment later, he was on his knees, spreading my legs and making room for himself. He slid his boxers off and leaned over me, kissing my lips, neck, and breasts. He kissed around my navel, and my hips flexed in response. Of course, I sucked it in. Did he really expect anything else?

"Stop that. You don't have to do that." He was inches from my stomach, looking up my body.

"Spencer, I can't help it. You're just going to have to deal with it," I said, practically panting, as I waited for him to put those lips where I really needed them.

"Don't take this wrong way, but shut the hell up and don't do it again." He grinned up at me before kissing me just below my navel. He sat back on his knees and held himself, teasing me. "You still on something, you good?"

he asked, as the tip of him was on the verge of entering me.

"Yeah, I'm good—you?"

My question took him off guard but I wasn't trying to get an STD from some bimbo pop star.

"Baby, I've been good since the night I met you."

Look at that, I'm already getting to know him. This could work out.

"Good."

He leaned over me, his lips finding mine as he gently filled me.

I had forgotten how tight he made me feel. It was mind altering. I moved my hips with him as he kept kissing me. Grabbing his back, I dug my nails in, to anchor myself to him.

He sat up holding my legs wide. Spencer was a sight for my very sore eyes. His body was flawless as he moved in and out of me. I had to touch him. I had to make sure he was real, that all of this was all real, because it could have easily been just a fantasy that I had made up in my mind. I touched his abs and let my fingers make their way up as he slowed his movements to watch as I touched him. My fingers went from one muscular pectoral to the other. They grazed over the large scar that ran down the middle of his chest. I froze over it, it was longer than I had remembered it being the first time I had noticed it. Spencer was still moving slowly, when he grabbed my wrist with one hand. When I tried to place my other hand over the scar, he grabbed that one too. Holding tight, he pushed my hands above my head, keeping them there. His lips curled before he moved faster. I think he was trying to distract me and, fuck, if it wasn't working. *Scar? What scar?* All I could think about was my building release as I tightened around him.

"Let it go, baby."

I was unraveling at his words as I called out his name in a sweet release. He gave me a few more deep thrusts before he lost it as well. Thank god, for birth control. We did not need to add a baby—*Baby? Did he call me baby?*

He collapsed over me, moving slightly to the side so as not to totally squish me, although I wouldn't have minded at all. Breathing heavily, we lay there in silence, looking up at the ceiling.

We turned our head sat the same time. Our eyes met and, if the smiles that were upon our faces weren't an indication of how happy we were to be exactly where we lay, then I didn't know what would have been. I moved closer to him and laid my head on his chest. I wrapped my arm around his damp body. He held me tightly as he kissed the top of my head. This was going to be a great year. All the bullshit from before was over, and I was happily in Spencer's arms. The rest of the world was just going to have to deal with it.

Chapter 2

Nickolas

W hat are you talking about, Natasha? What do you mean a murderer?" I sat across from my boss, waiting to hear what she had to say for herself.

"Poor little naive Nickolas, always wanting to see the best in people. Don't fool yourself or me. I know you want this just as bad as I do. I want you to help me uncover all of Mr. Salvatore's dirty little secrets."

"I told you—"

"Cut the crap, Nick. You're my best guy." She smiled wickedly from across her large glass desk. "We can take Spencer down together."

"Enlighten me, Natasha. What are you going to get out of all of this?"

She sat back in her seat. Her wicked smile fell from her face and anger replaced it. She stood from her desk and went to stare out the window. She always made everything so dramatic. I leaned forward, shaking my head at the pile of files on top of files of famous people. One caught my eye, an unknown, new celebrity Francis Phillips. The poor girl was surely in for it if she had her own file on Natasha's desk.

Natasha must have turned back around and seen me eyeing up the files on her desk, because she quickly moved the file of her newest victim to the bottom of the stack. She slapped both her hands on the files and narrowed her eyes at me, "Let's just say I have a feeling that Spencer Salvatore doesn't deserve anything he has. I believe that he hurt people, lots of people, to get to where he is today, and he needs to pay for what he's done. Plus, it will make for good gossip. Everyone loves a scandal."

I was the first person on board to take Salvatore down, but the way she was talking about him "paying" made it sound even more personal than my fucked-up situation.

"What else are you going to do, Nick? You can't quit. You need the money. Mommy and Daddy cut you off and out of their lives, remember? You can win Elizabeth back. Once she sees Spencer is bad news, she's not going to stick around. And you'll be there to comfort her."

Dammit, she had a point. There was a reason why Natasha was so good at what she did. She taught me everything, from how to use a camera to befriending celebrities and getting all their juicy gossip. Elizabeth wasn't the first person I had betrayed. She was just the first person I cared about. Having to use her and betray her was the hardest thing I had ever had to do in my life. I told Elizabeth I wasn't going to give up on us, and, if this was the only way, then I had no choice.

"Fine, I'll help you, but I have conditions this time around."

Natasha sat straight in her chair smiling over at me. She gestured for me to go on.

"First, you leave Elizabeth out of this. We are going after Spencer. I don't want anything bad posted about her."

"Okay, I can stick to that."

I rolled my eyes. I had heard that one before.

"Second, you are going to pay for me to open a gallery, because after I help you with this, I'm walking, for good."

"Nick, come on—"

"Natasha, I'm done after this. I'll help but you have to let me walk after."

She pouted her lips and, for a few happy moments, I thought of my Belle and her tantrums. God I missed her.

"Nickolas, you are free after we bring Salvatore down, I promise. As far as your gallery goes, consider it done."

Her fingernails clicked together rhythmically. I knew she had a dark side, but that day she looked like the ultimate evil villain. She'd better just keep her claws to herself, because if she even thought about hurting Belle, I was done.

Chapter 3

Elizabeth

The sound of the front door closing startled me from my peaceful slumber. I rolled from Spencer's chest to my back, hoping I could drift back to sleep. It was the loud voices that woke me up enough to sit up in bed. Gia was home and not alone. I didn't want her barging in and yelling at me for being with Spencer, especially because I was still buck-ass naked. I had heard enough the night before. She'd gotten her point across loud and clear.

Gia blamed Spencer for ruining her relationship with Teddy, and she didn't approve of the way Spencer had treated me in the past. I knew she meant well, but it was different now with Spencer. I heard her bedroom door open and then slam shut, followed by giggling and furniture moving against the floor. *I guess she brought the party back here.*

"They sound like they're having a good time," Spencer said as he brushed my bare back with his fingers.

It sent a chill up my spin, making my body shiver. I turned around to look at him still lying down. The covers were low on his hips, and I was a little more than excited to see his bare chest in the light of day. He looked even better than that first night we spent together. Every muscle was cut and just perfect.

Holy hell, I need to go to the gym, like yesterday. I quickly pulled the covers over his flawless body. I couldn't concentrate with all that out in the open, especially that early in the morning.

I looked over at my alarm clock, only eight-thirty. I was sure it should have been later. I lay back down next to Spencer, pulling the covers up to my chin. I didn't need him to see my naked body in the bright morning sun, not after looking at his. I still couldn't get over the fact that Spencer Salvatore was in my bed. I knew it shouldn't have mattered, that I should have just been happy, but curiosity was a bitch, and I wanted to know why he found me attractive.

"Why me?" I kept my eyes looking at the ceiling as I blurted out my question.

"Are you really asking me this right now?" There was irritation in his voice.

"Yes, I am. I need to know" I said, crossing my arms. I waited for an answer. I didn't care if he was mad that I asked or not. I wanted to know.

It was quiet for a few seconds before he propped himself up on his elbow and leaned over, looking down at me. I averted my eyes from his, afraid that he'd see the desperation in them.

"If you'll look at me, I'll tell you," he said from beside me.

I let my eyes find his and waited for him to go on.

He shook his head and smiled. "Honestly, I don't know."

Not really what I was hoping to hear, and the little laugh/smile didn't help either. "It's not funny, Spencer.

There are hundreds of beautiful woman out there willing to throw themselves at you. Yet, you don't date, you make sure to keep your distance from them, but you let the freaking paparazzi have a field day, letting them think you're 'smitten' with me." I crossed my arms tighter and looked back to the ceiling. "I need a better reason then 'I don't know.' So let's hear it."

"God, you're feisty. What do you want me to tell you? It's the truth. I am smitten with you." His voice was harsh as he lowered his head. He continued on in a normal voice. "You took me by surprise, Elizabeth. I was content in my life. I stayed out of the gossip as much as I could, because I have a lot of demons, and I didn't want them getting out. But you changed all of that. The first night I saw you at Mood, you stood out over every woman I'd ever met. I was drawn to you like a moth to a light. I couldn't stop moving in your direction. I didn't care who saw or what ramifications it was going to have. I just needed to be closer to you."

I uncrossed my arms and glanced over to him. "And what about now? Do you still want this—me? You have to see it from my side. You're the hottest bachelor out there, and I'm—I'm just me."

His brow shot up to the ceiling and the side of his mouth curled. "I'm not a bachelor—not anymore, and you're beautiful. Why is it so hard for you to believe me that I want you? All of you. All the time," he said, shaking his head as if it was the most obvious thing in the world.

"Because this," I said, gesturing between the two of us, "doesn't happen to girls like me."

I couldn't look at him, embarrassed with myself for needing so much reassurance. I claimed to be a confident, strong-willed woman, but with him by my side and the media following me, I just needed to fight a little more for that confidence I thought I had in the bag.

"It's happening. You're just going to have to get over it. I'm not going anywhere. You're not going anywhere. You're mine, and I don't care who knows."

That one statement brought butterflies to my stomach and my confidence to the forefront. "Well then, I guess we should make a public appearance. Coffee?"

If we were really doing it, then we were getting out and letting the world know.

"Are you asking me out on a date, Miss. Monroe?"

I guessed I was—our first date. I was giggling like a school girl on the inside. "Yes, I am, Mr. Salvatore. Join me for breakfast?"

"I'd love to, but first I want something else."

He tossed the covers off of us. I screamed. He laughed. I tried to cover myself back up. He tore them off again.

"I don't think so." His voice was deep with that dominant tone that set a fire inside me. He took my arms and spread them out to either side of me. "Look at what you're doing to me. Sometimes I don't even recognize myself when I'm around you."

"Really? Because you look the same to me." *Yes, yes, you do—demanding, hot, and sexy as hell!*

eↄeↄ

I took a quick shower before we left for our first outing together that wasn't an awkward run in. We rode the elevator down to the lobby with smiles on our faces and hands held tightly together. The doors opened and we made our way to the front entrance.

"Um—isn't your car around back?" I asked, pointing toward the back entrance.

"Nope, not anymore, I had one of my guys bring it

around to the front while you were in the shower. We're doing this all the way. So make sure you smile for the cameras."

He took my hand in his and kissed the back of it. I held onto his arm with my other hand.

"Are you sure about this?" I asked, digging my heels in to the tile floor before he could open the door.

"I'm sure," he said with a curt nod.

He was so confident and I was so…terrified seemed to be the appropriate word for what I was feeling. I was scared shitless that I was going to get stoned, or worse, have food thrown at me. I took a shaking breath and clutched onto his arm as tightly as I could.

He held the door open as we walked through. I couldn't believe all the people who were standing in front of my building. Not only were there over a dozen people with cameras, there were also regular people standing around. Most of them were woman, screaming and calling out for Spencer. I squinted, in preparation for flying objects, but they never came.

"Hold that beautiful head up. This is just the beginning," he whispered in my ear before leaving a kiss on my cheek.

As I scanned the crowd in front of us, they were all staring up the front steps and watching intently. They were waiting. Waiting for me to fall? Or for me to run back inside, maybe even for Spencer to leave me?

Not a chance in hell on that last one. I held his hand tightly as we went down the steps. Spencer took an extra step down and turned back to me. I was eye level with him. I wrapped my arms around his neck and kissed him with as much passion as when our lips had first met in my father's office. The cameras erupted, and the people standing around cheered. *I can't wait to see these pictures on Fame! Eat your heart out!*

Chapter 4

Nickolas

Natasha's computer started making an annoying ringing sound. Looking over at it, she clicked a few buttons then smiled widely at me. "Seems my new guy is fitting in just fine." She turned the computer screen around for me to see. "Looks like the little vixen has become what we intended for her, after all. She sure didn't waste any time getting over you."

Cold. She was the coldest woman I had ever met in my life. I glanced at the computer screen to see my Belle wrapped in the arms of that fucking Salvatore dog.

It was all the fuel I needed to bring Spencer down. I stood, grabbing my bags from the floor. "Where am I going Natasha?" I snapped at her.

She laughed to herself as she turned the screen back around. "Ooo, I love a jealous man ready for revenge. If only I was younger and wasn't disgusted by you."

"Natasha, where am I going?"

"Calm down, tiger. You're going to Las Vegas. Well, outside of Las Vegas, The Salvatore homestead to be exact," she said, sneering.

"Fine. What am I looking for, and who am I getting close to, to do it?"

"I have it on good authority that his family is covering up a huge secret. I heard that his father paid a lot of money to shut a few people up. Your job is to simply find out what they're hiding. There are a few different ways to get close. He has three very attractive younger sisters around your age," she said, winking at me.

"No, I'm not doing that again."

"What, are you afraid?"

"No, I'm just—I can't do it right now," I said, a little defeated and humiliated.

"Aw, how cute. He's heartbroken. Well, I don't care how you do it. Just get it done. I suggest going to the courthouse. Stir things around a bit. Someone will start talking."

"Anything else?" I asked, putting my bag over my shoulder.

"Yes, one last thing." She tossed me a manila envelope. "Everything you need to know is in here. Report back to me as often as you can. I will be working another angle, so we need to stay connected at all times."

I opened the envelope and peeked inside. It was the usual—papers, ID, job information, money, plane tickets, back story. Closing it back up, I placed it under my arm. I turned to leave but stopped before opening the door. "Remember, Natasha. Spencer, not Elizabeth."

"I know, you only want to see good things. Don't worry."

I rode the elevator down to the lobby. The streets of New York were bustling with people getting a jump on the New Year. I grabbed a cab and made my way to the airport. I was headed to Spencer's home town, and I was hell bent on destroying him.

Chapter 5

Elizabeth

We found a small dinner that was open outside of DC. It was quiet, and no one was taking our picture. It was perfect. Of course, people were still ogling over Spencer. He had the same suit he had on last night, but he kept the top few buttons and tie un-done around his neck. It was taking all I had not to jump over the table and assault him.

"What would you like to do today, Miss Monroe?" he asked, sipping his coffee after we had finished our meal.

I want to lick every square inch of your body—eek, maybe not the most appropriate thing to say at nine-thirty in the morning in a public dinner. "I don't know. This is a little weird. Actually spending time together. I honestly never thought this far in advance. Usually, right about now, I'd be getting a phone call, or we would start fighting, so I'm open for anything that doesn't involve the later."

He sat back in his seat. That aggressive look he got when he was getting angry appeared on his face, and I knew I had probably just stepped on a land mine.

"Your phone better not start ringing and, if it does, you'd be smart not to answer."

Why does he have to do that—make such a nice morning go to shit with one smart ass statement? "I don't know if you know this or not. I mean, we are still only on our first date, but I don't like to be told what to do. And that smart ass comment you just made makes my blood boil."

He flashed a devilish grin over the rim of his coffee cup.

Don't give in, Beth. He's trying to seduce you with those sultry blue eyes and long dark lashes.

"Well, I don't know if you know or not, but I can get rather jealous. And now that you are mine, I don't want you to talk about anything related to your…what did you call him?…your Beast? Very appropriate, I might add."

"That's not fair, Salvatore, and you know it." I sat back to stare out the window. "I guess it was inevitable that we would end up fighting with each other," I said, before sliding from the table and walking back to the restroom in a fit of rage.

I heard him calling my name, but I ignored it, as I walked into the empty restroom. I choose the last of the three stalls, slamming the door behind me. I grabbed some toilet paper and wiped the angry tears that had welled up in my eyes on the way to the restroom. The door to the restroom swung open, making a loud bang on the tile behind it.

"Elizabeth!"

Holy crap, he followed me—into the girl's bathroom? Is he crazy?

"I know you're in here." He slammed the first stall open then the second. His well-polished shoes were on the other side of the thin stall door.

I grabbed the top of the door, opening it to see his perfect body standing in front of me. The sexual charge he was putting off almost made me fall over the toilet. He took a step closer to me as I backed up farther into the stall. He kept coming closer and closer. The door swung closed behind him as he leaned over, centimeters from my face.

"Sorry," he said in a seductive, low voice.

I hit the back of the stall as I stared into his eyes, trying to read them. It always seemed to come back to me wanting to touch him. My chest rose and fell faster the closer his lips came to mine. Suddenly, he lifted me, pressing me up on the wall. I wrapped my legs around him, as he kissed me hard on the lips then down my neck.

I'm angry at him, remember? Angry, mad, upset, rage, boiling hot—very hot—sexy hot. Dammit!

It was useless. My body always won those battles against my head. I kissed him back, holding him tightly around his neck. My fingers ran up the back of his hair, as his slid up my shirt, finding my bra and moving it to up under my chin.

Letting me down, he placed his fore head to mine, "I'm sorry," he said again.

"Okay," was all I could get out as I caught my breath.

I felt the smile on his face, followed by his hands sliding across my stomach to the button on my jeans. I sucked it in. He looked at me, smiled, and shook his head, but continued on with his mission. He had gotten my pants unbuttoned and down my legs before I even had time to realize what was happening. My back was against the wall as I gripped the railing. When he came back up to me, I returned the favor undoing his pants in a hurry and pulling them, as well as his boxers, down. Lifting me back up, he fucked me against the wall of a bathroom stall, and it was perfect.

I had had sex in a bathroom stall with Spencer. I almost drew blood as I bit down on his shoulder to keep from screaming in ecstasy.

If that was going to happen after every fight, then maybe I shouldn't be too quick to complain about it. I pulled my pants on with a smile that stretched from ear to ear.

I went to open the stall door, but he held it shut.

"Elizabeth, listen. I'm sorry I said that. I was just—"

"Jealous?" I answered for him, leaning against the closed door.

He sighed. "Yeah. I care about you, and jealousy isn't easy for me to control."

Letting go of the door, I straightened up. "Spencer, it's hasn't even been a day. We're going to need a learning curve. Just be honest with me, and I will try to understand and not be so quick to take offense." I cupped his face in my hand. "I chose you, remember? You have nothing to be jealous about." I guess we both needed reassurance. "Now, I'm going to leave and go back to sit down at our table. Wait five minutes then come out," I said, backing away and walking out the stall.

"Why do I have to wait?"

"Because, unlike you, I care what little old ladies sitting in a diner think, and I don't need it public knowledge that I just fucked the sexiest man alive in a bathroom stall."

I heard him chuckle as I walked out of the bathroom. I almost ran back to him but, this time, my head was in the right place. I sat in our booth, taking a sip of my now lukewarm tea. On cue and five minutes later, Spencer came out, making sure to adjust his belt and tighten his now tied tie. He kissed the top of my head before sitting across from me.

"You just had to come out like that, didn't you?"

"What? I had to use the bathroom, figured I may as well freshen up a little."

His megawatt smile melted my frustration, and I could do nothing but laugh back at him.

"So, as I was saying before, what would you like to do?"

I made sure to choose my words carefully this time. As much as I loved having sex with Spencer, I could do without the fighting. "Well, I'm sure that you could use a shower and a new change of clothes."

"Are you trying to tell me I'm dirty?"

"Yes, you're a little dirty—like bathroom-stall-sex dirty," I said, holding a straight face—until I couldn't.

"In that case you are just as dirty. How about we go to my place and get cleaned up? Give us some time to work on that learning curve."

"Sure, that sounds great."

We left the diner hand in hand and headed to Spencer's place.

We pulled up to a large historic townhouse, the kind you'd see in movies. It was beautiful, with a brick front and black iron bars. There was a large tree in front and a little garden under the windows. He parked the car in front of the house and got out, coming around to my side.

"Wow, Spencer, this is beautiful."

Spencer nodded. "It's one of my favorites."

"How many homes do you have?" I asked, turning from the what had to be four story townhome.

"A few. Come on, let's get inside. It's cold out."

He took my hand and led me up the stairs. We walked through the small mud room that separated the door to outside to the one that entered into the house.

He opened it then turned to me. "Welcome to my temporary home."

Stepping aside, he let me enter first. It was breathtaking. It was exactly as I had thought from the street, like a movie set. Everything looked antique. It almost reminded me of the club. Maybe it was more Spencer than either of my brothers. I walked past a living room with Victorian couches and a beautiful fireplace. The stairs were to my right. The floors were a beautiful dark wood. The kitchen was amazing. I turned around and saw that Spencer was following me as I walked through his house.

"You live here?"

He laughed and ran his fingers through his hair. "Yeah, for now, I do."

"What do you mean, for now? Do you rent it out while you're not in town?" I turned back to see the cozy sitting area off the kitchen, complete with large TV and fire place.

"No, I usually sell, but I might hold on to this one."

I put my bag on the large island that separated the kitchen from the sitting area. "You'd better not sell this place."

I couldn't help but see the differences between this place and the one in New York. They were polar opposites.

He held his hand out for me to take. "Come with me?"

I didn't have to hesitate about whether or not to go with him anymore. I would go anywhere with him. I took his hand as he led me back to the stairs. There were three doors, all closed when we got to the top of the steps. Opening the farthest door, he led me into the sprawling room, his bedroom. The huge king-sized four-poster bed sat in the middle of the room. The decorations in here matched the rest of the house perfectly. Everything was right out of a Victorian movie. I walked over to the massive bed and quickly figured out you needed stairs to get in it. "I'm going to take a shower, please make yourself at home."

I watched as he undid the tie around his neck. "Do you mind?" I asked, pointing to the bed.

"Are you really asking me if you can get in my bed, Elizabeth?"

I shrugged my shoulders. "Well?"

"You don't have to ask, make yourself at home."

Spencer turned and walked through the door leading to the bathroom. I heard the water come on and decided it was safe to jump up onto the bed. I kicked off my shoes and pants, leaving my underwear and shirt on. I moved all the decorative pillows, getting right down to the sheets, climbed up the bed, and got under the covers. I layback, resting my head on the pillow.

I was in Spencer's bed. So many women had dreamed of that, yet there I was. I pulled the covers up around my chin. They even smelled like him. I turned on my side, feeling the soft sheets under my hand. I inhaled again, thinking about him sleeping here every night, perhaps thinking about me. I closed my eyes and let my tiredness take over. I was drifting away, the softness of the bed, the smell of Spencer all around me, the hum of the shower, and the quiet of the room. It didn't take long before I was out.

I woke up relaxed and well rested. I was alone in the massive room and alone in the bed. Looking around, I saw a piece of paper folded on the night stand with my name on it.

> *Elizabeth,*
> *You have no idea how amazing it is to see you sleeping in my bed.*
> *Come find me when you wake up.*
> *S.*

I lay there, smiling from ear to ear as I pressed his note

to my chest like a school girl. I couldn't help how happy I was. This was really happening to me. Spencer was in the process of sweeping me off my feet. I couldn't help but think how things would have been if Simon would have never entered my life. Would Spencer and I have been together all this time? Would I be living with him? But if that were all true, I would have never of met Simon and, even though he was working for the enemy, I had some pretty strong feelings for him. Strong enough to try to ignore Spencer, and I thought that said a lot for how I felt about him.

I rolled out of bed and put my jeans back on, excited for my treasure hunt. I heard mumbling coming from down the hall and decided to follow it.

The closer I got, the louder Spencer's voice became. He was yelling at someone, but I couldn't tell who. The room he was in had the door cracked, so I peeked inside. Sure enough, Spencer was sitting at a large desk, talking on the phone. There were papers scattered all over the desk. He was still on the phone, his head hung low, his fingers rubbing over his eyes, as if he had a headache.

I should leave, I shouldn't be snooping. But it looked serious and, if it even remotely involved me, he promised he would tell me. I hesitated before opening the door all the way. I didn't want him to get even more upset, but he did tell me to come find him.

I let a deep breath out. I opened the door and stood in the doorway. Spencer immediately looked up from his desk and dropped the hand from above his eyes. He smiled over at me, looking relieved to see me standing in the doorway to his home office.

"Let me call you back. My sleeping beauty just woke up and is standing in my doorway...Yeah, that one...Thank you, T. I'll make arrangements as soon as I can."

He hung up his phone, placing it down on the desk. He never took his eyes off of me.

He was dressed casually. I had only seen him like this one other time and, unfortunately, I was covered in mud. He wore a gray T-shirt and had black sweat pants on, no socks, and his hair was as wild as his eyes while they drank me in.

He stayed sitting in his chair but backed away from the desk. "Come in," he called.

I walked over to him, noticing the large bookcases on either side, filled with what looked like antique books.

"Got your note." I held it up, turning it between my fingers before sticking it in the pocket of my jeans.

"I'm Glad. You know I love leaving them."

This was true. Even though some of his notes were confusing, I did enjoy receiving them, and I was glad it wasn't just a hook.

"Who were you talking to?" I knew the man he was talking to. T was the same man in my condo last night, but as far as Spencer knew, I'd been sound asleep.

"A friend."

"You seemed really upset talking to him. Is everything okay?" I stood at the end of his desk, rocking on my heels and putting my hands in my back pockets nervously.

Asexual prowl danced across his eyes. "Come here."

I walked around the desk and stood in front of him.

"Did you sleep well?"

Way to change the subject, Salvatore. "Yes I did. What were you talking to T about, Spencer? No secrets, remember?"

He grabbed my hips, pulling me closer to him. His face was just below my chest. God, he smelled good. I didn't think he could smell any better, but damn. He tugged me down. I sat on his lap, wrapping my arms around his neck for stability.

"Spencer, stop trying to get around this. Just tell me what's worrying you."

His face turned up as he sighed. "You are relentless. T is a friend of mine from long ago. He's helping me with something."

"Long ago, like New York long ago?"

Spencer froze under me. The hand that was suggestively running up and down my spine stilled as he looked at me, confused. "How do you—"

"You told me, remember? On the car ride home when I hurt my ankle." He sat staring up at me, as his hand once again moved lovingly over my lower back. "Spencer, what happened in New York?"

That was it—the straw that broke Spencer's back. He stood abruptly, placing me on the ground. Turning away from me, he faced the window.

"I'm sorry, I was—"

"Dammit, Elizabeth! I'll tell you, just not yet. I can't tell you yet."

I didn't think it was that serious. He was mad and trying as hard as he could to keep his temper in check.

"Okay, tell me when you're ready."

He stood looking out the window then turned back to me. Moving in one swift action, he held my upper arms tightly, looking me straight in the eyes. "I will tell you. I'll tell you everything, I promise."

His grip on my arms was getting tighter as he spoke, passion and fire burning behind his eyes.

I winced as his hands dug into my arms. "Spencer— you're—"

He let go quickly, backing a few steps away from me, running his hands through his hair.

I wasn't frightened, more taken off guard. He'd been rough before, but that was sexual. This was different. He looked momentarily crazy but, the minute he heard my voice, he snapped out of it. I took a step toward him, but he backed away. I took another step and, this time, he didn't move. I reached for the hand that was by his side. I brought it up to my lips, palm up, and kissed it. "You told me you would never hurt me. I trust you. I know these hands could never hurt me." I kissed his hands again.

Was this what Teddy was always worried about?

"I'm sorry. I—"

"Spencer, don't take this the wrong way but shut up and kiss me."

I stared up at him, waiting for his smile to appear. It took a little longer than usual, and that scared me, but he came around. Whatever that was, it was over and I thought it scared him more than it did me.

I kept my head on his chest. "I was thinking maybe we could sit on that cozy couch of yours downstairs, maybe talk or not talk?"

"That sounds great," he said as he took my hand and led me down the stairs and into the cozy sitting area.

We sat closely together on the couch. I snuggled up against him, as Spencer's arm wrapped tightly around my body. I felt safe, and nothing or no one could touch me. He turned on the TV, and we just sat together. Nothing needed to be said. Of course, I wanted to ask a ton of questions, but it could wait. We were both just happy being close to one another. There would be plenty of time to talk.

Time passed and soon it was dark outside. I hadn't told anyone where I was, and it didn't seem like anyone cared. I wondered what Gia was doing, who she had brought home from the night before, how my brothers were.

My stomach made the most embarrassing sound ever, just as the TV went silent between shows.

"Hungry?" Spencer asked, smiling down at me.

Cute very cute. "Yeah, my stomach has a mind all its own sometimes."

"I'm kind of hungry too. What you in the mood for?" he asked.

I stretched to relieve the ache in my back from sitting for so long. "I don't care."

"I'll get you anything you want."

He started naming all these expensive sounding foods, and I suddenly felt totally out of my element.

"What about pizza?"

Here he was, offering elegant foods, like roasted chicken with a red wine demi glaze, braized short ribs, and tuna tartare. And I just asked for pizza.

"Pizza sounds great. I'll call some in." He sat up and kissed my temple before making his way to the kitchen.

I turned to follow his beautiful physique. *Maybe pizza was a bad idea. I should have said salad. Tomorrow. Tomorrow, I'm getting a gym membership.*

My attention was pulled back to the television as the entertainment part of the news came on. *Wouldn't you know it?* There I was on the six o'clock news. At least the story was nice, talking about how Spencer and I met each other at Mood and how fate kept bringing us back together. Cue all the embarrassing pictures from the past five months.

The story ended with the picture from this morning on the steps of my building. I couldn't help the smile that crept over my face. We looked good together. I actually thought I was holding my own next to the Greek god.

Spencer came back over to sit next to me, a menu in his hands. "You see, that's why I get jealous," he said, pointing to the television screen.

There was a picture of me from last night standing in the dress he bought me.

"You have no one to blame but yourself. You bought it for me."

"Touché, Miss Monroe." He winked. "Do you have any idea how hard it was to see you in all those pictures they posted of you? I almost took you over my shoulder the night you came to Mood wearing that damn sheer blouse."

"Why didn't you? That could have been exciting."

He turned to me brows creased.

Oh, Simon. I had forgotten about that for a second.

"When you were yelling at Terry to let you in the VIP, I was dying. Watching you stomp your feet, it was entertaining. You really are a hot little thing when you're riled up. I was going to let you keep yelling at him, but I felt bad for the poor guy."

I snatched the menu from him, a little miffed that he let me verbally abuse someone for his amusement. "You were watching me that whole time? Where were you? I didn't see you anywhere."

He winked again. "I'll never tell."

I glanced back at the menu, laughing at the stupid expression on his face.

Our pizza was delicious. I laid my head on his lap after eating. It felt good to have food in my belly, but now I was tired again. Spencer turned on some movie. I tried to watch but fell asleep instead.

I shifted as Spencer tossed a cover over my body. He ran his fingers through my hair. The soft touch ignited my insides. I stared up at him, while he continued to play with my hair.

"Elizabeth, will you stay with me tonight?"

I wasn't planning on leaving, so I nodded.

Chapter 6

Nickolas

I woke up late Sunday morning. Still in disbelief, I knew Elizabeth and I had a few issues to work through. I knew she was entrapped in Spencer's web, but I had faith that we would be able to work it out. The past month had been just as amazing as our first. It was a true do over, and I was falling more in love with her. I had even convinced Natasha to back off, put the focus on her brothers rather than her.

If it weren't for Natasha persuading me to go after Salvatore, I'd have been on a plane back to her, with my tail between my legs, begging my parents to take me back. One of my father's clients got mixed up in some incriminating circumstances, and it just so happened that Natasha assigned me to it. Once my father found out I was the one ruining his client's life, he told me I wasn't his son anymore and that he didn't want to be around the person I was turning in to. *Right now, I don't even want to be around me.*

I always made sure to keep a distance, to not make things personal. I treated everything simply as a job and

kept my feelings out of the way. When I first saw Elizabeth, I had no idea how much she was going to change
me. I thought I was going to have a chance at a regular
relationship with a beautiful girl. I just didn't expect
Spencer Salvatore to want the same damn thing with her.

Chapter 7

Elizabeth

The next day was just as wonderful as the day before. I spent the morning cuddled in bed with Spencer. I became acquainted with his shower and figured out why he smelled so damn good. We made breakfast together. Everything was perfect.

Night was slowly approaching, and I knew I was going to have to ask him to take me home. I had my first day of my internship tomorrow, and I didn't want to start off on the wrong foot. This weekend with Spencer was more than I could have asked for. Minus the few fights in the beginning, it was ideal. I was getting us a drink when my phone started ringing from my bag.

Spencer turned from the couch to look over at me, a puzzled look on his face. I was sure it was crossing his mind that it might be Simon calling.

He tried to stay calm, keeping an unaffected face but he was Spencer and, try as he might, he obviously couldn't hide the hint of jealousy. Hell, I was a little worried it might have been Simon too. What would I have even said to him?

I pulled out the phone and looked to see who was calling. I was a little shocked to see who it was, and that tipped Spencer off to start questioning me.

"Who is it?" he asked, standing up from the couch and making his way to me.

I looked up from the phone and smiled. "It's Charles. I wonder what he wants. He usually doesn't call me."

"Well, answer it." Spencer's body language did a one-eighty the moment he found out it was my brother and not my ex-lover.

"Hello?"

"Hey there, baby girl, where the hell have you been?"

In all my years, I would have never have thought Charles would be calling to find out where I was. "I'm with Spencer, why?"

"Ooo. So, you think it's cool to just disappear for two days and not let anyone know where you are? Gia, Teddy, and I have been going crazy, trying to find you. You couldn't answer your phone all weekend?"

"Charles, I don't know what you're talking about. My phone hasn't rung once."

"Really? Check your messages."

I pulled the phone away from my ear to check if there was any real truth to his accusations. My eyes widened as I saw the twenty new texts and twenty-six missed calls. "Charles, I'm sorry. I didn't see or hear any of these messages."

"Yeah, that's what we figured. Tell that ass Salvatore to answer his phone too."

I looked over at Spencer who had sat back down on the couch to watch TV.

"Anyway, do you need a ride home? I'm close to Spencer's, and I can give you a lift back to your place.

I was so confused. "Yeah, that's fine. You come get me."

"Okay, I will be there in about fifteen or twenty minutes."

"Thanks, Charles, bye."

Spencer turned back to me when the call ended. His face was pained, as if I had punched him in the stomach.

"Charles said to answer your phone. They have been calling us all weekend, but I didn't hear my phone go off, or yours." I put my phone back in my bag, and noticed Spencer's expression begin to change.

"Why is he coming to get you? This is why—" His voice was low as he ran his fingers through his hair.

I was learning that that was his tell. He did it every time he was mad or frustrated. "Did you know that they were calling me?" I asked.

"I didn't want you to leave. I wanted you to myself."

"Hold up. Did you turn my phone off so I wouldn't hear it?"

"I only wanted it to be us, no interruptions," he said, as if that was a logical explanation.

I slammed my hand so hard on the counter it stung. "Spencer! Did you turn my phone off?"

It wasn't how I pictured leaving him. In my mind, I pictured a longing kiss at the door, a million little good-byes, maybe even a little begging for me to stay. Here I was, dumb enough to think that we wouldn't fight again. I was scolding him and couldn't have cared less about kisses and hugs goodbyes at that point.

"I may have turned the sound and vibration off, but I did it for us."

"Spencer, you can't shut me off from the world because you want me all to you yourself. They were worried about me, about us."

"I thought you'd be happy to be left alone for once."

It was nice to be left alone, but not at the expense of my family thinking I had disappeared, or run away, or was lying in a ditch somewhere bleeding to death. That wasn't it. There was more to this that he wasn't saying. He liked my brothers and wouldn't ignore their calls. This was all because of Simon.

"I don't believe you," I said, crossing my arms as I moved to stand in front of him.

"Believe it," he said composedly from the couch.

"Nope, now I definitely don't believe you. You're lying to me. You told me you weren't going to lie and, here you are, lying straight to my face."

He stood up from the couch and stared down his slightly crooked nose at me.

There was no way I was backing down from this.

He let out a loud and frustrated sigh. "Fine, it wasn't the only reason."

I cocked my head, still glaring at him. "Let's hear it, Salvatore."

"Simon—okay? I didn't want Simon calling you so I turned your phone off at the diner, when you went to the bathroom. Then I turned it back on while you were in the shower today. Sue me. I wasn't willing to share this weekend."

I stared at him. He gazed off toward the TV. I figured he didn't want to see how I would react. I didn't know *how* to react. I should have been pissed. Unfortunately, my jumbled heart was singing a completely different tune. *He wanted me all to himself, this gorgeous man wanted me—aww.*

"You weren't kidding when you said you get jealous, were you?" I waited for him to say something back, but he didn't. "Next time, you want me all to yourself, just ask me, so we can avoid all this ridiculous fighting." I grabbed his jaw and turned his face to mine. "Mess with my phone again, Salvatore, and I won't be so forgiving. You got me?"

His lips curled up and his blue eyes seamed to sparkle at my warning.

The doorbell rang as I held Spencer's jaw tightly in my hand. *That was not fifteen or twenty minutes.* I suddenly regretted telling Charles to come pick me up.

"That's Charles. I'm going to run upstairs and grab my clothes. Is it okay…" I trailed off, feeling the clothes that hung on my body.

"Take them, I have plenty more."

I smiled up at Spencer, kissing his lips quickly before turning to run upstairs. Unlike last time, those clothes were not hiding in the back of my closet. I planned on wearing them to sleep every night. The doorbell rang again, and then there was a knock at the door.

"Spencer, don't just stand there, let him in. It's Charles, not the Unabomber."

I watched from halfway up the stairs to make sure he was going to let my brother in. As he walked over to the door, he smiled up at me before opening it. Damn, I loved that smirk of a smile of his.

I ran around Spencer's room, collecting my scattered clothes. My pants were by the door, my shirt was under a chair, one sock was on the dresser, the other was on the floor next to the dresser, and my bra was on Spencer's night stand. My underwear—*Shit, where is my underwear?* I searched through the covers and pillows on the floor but didn't see them. I could hear my brother and Spencer talking, and then I heard footsteps coming up the stairs. I turned to see Spencer standing in the door way. He leaned on the doorjamb, grinning as he watched me run around his room.

"Where did you put my underwear?" I asked, kneeling at the side of his bed after looking under it.

He simply shrugged his shoulders and chuckled to himself.

"Not funny. If you know where they are, you better give them up," I demanded, looking through the sheets again.

"Why are you leaving?"

I stopped rustling the sheets. "Spencer, I have to go home."

"Why can't you just stay here? You said you were going to stay with me."

"No I didn't. That was last night, not tonight. Besides I have no clothes—"

"I'll buy you new clothes."

I rolled my eyes. "Right. I don't think so, Christian Grey."

Spencer chuckled and adjusted his body against the door frame. "I've heard I'm compared to him. Should I just tie you up to the bed so you can't leave?"

He had been compared to the leading man, but Spencer was in a league all his own. Where Mr. Grey was slender and lean, Spencer was massive, broad, but, most importantly, Spencer was real and all mine.

"Spencer, you can't keep me locked up here. I start my internship tomorrow. I need to rest and get ready for it."

"You can't do that here with me? You didn't tell me you had an internship."

He was right. I hadn't told him. Between all the sex, sleeping, and cuddling, we really didn't do much talking. "I need this, Spencer. This internship is a dream come true for me. It's what I have been working toward my whole college career. I'm counting on this."

"Where is it at?"

How do you explain to someone so popular and business savvy and—for lack of better words—hip that you are interning at a library? Basically it was the total opposite of what he did for a living. *Opposites attract, I guess?*

"I start interning at the Library of Congress tomorrow morning at eight. I'm hoping to turn my internship into a job. That's why I need it so bad." I couldn't look at him. I was embarrassed enough telling Mr. Sexy Entrepreneur that I was in school to become a librarian. I shuffled through the sheets again so as not to look up at him.

"Library...of Congress?" He said it slowly and thought about it a moment. "That sounds interesting."

I stopped moving the covers. I suddenly felt silly for thinking he would make fun of me. He wasn't my brother or my sometimes-judging friends. He was...*my boy-friend?*

Spencer seemed to care about me differently than anyone else at the moment. Even Simon joked around when I first told him, which was okay at the time, because— well, he had a way of saying anything and making it sound sexy or funny.

Spencer, on the other hand, just looked over at me with nothing but admiration.

"Beth! Let's go! I'd like to get home sometime tonight," Charles yelled up to me.

Spencer looked behind him and down the stairs then back to me. "Give me the go ahead, and I will tell him to hit the road."

I laughed, shaking my head. "No, it's okay. I'm sure there will be other times for you to kick him to the curb."

"Beth!"

"Chill, Charles, I'm coming," I yelled back as Spencer laughed at my frustration toward my brother. "Where is my underwear?"

"You don't have them on?"

I cocked my head because he knew damn well I didn't. "No—you know, I don't. Hand them over, Salvatore. You already have a trophy pair." *Did I really just refer to my panties as a trophy? Now he's laughing at me.*

"How do you know—"

"My father's office, my panties mysteriously went missing. Don't get me wrong, that's sexy as hell that you kept them, but I'd like to take this particular pair home to wash."

"I honestly don't know where I threw them last night. I promise if I find them, I'll wash them and give them back to you."

I narrowed my eyes at him. "You better."

"*Beth*!"

I stomped my foot angrily and walked past Spencer to head down the stairs, but was pulled back by the arm wrapped tightly around my stomach.

"What time are you done your internship tomorrow? I want to pick you up," Spencer breathed in my ear.

I found myself gripping the doorframe to keep from falling. "I'm not sure. Can I call you when I find out?" I said, turning in his arms.

"That works," he said.

I reached up on my toes to kiss him. I was going to miss having him so close and at my beck and call. The past two nights and mornings waking up in his arms were better than I could have ever imagined.

"Finally! Let's go," Charles gripped. "Do you have any idea how many people are camped outside?"

"I can only imagine," I said and sighed as Spencer and I walked over to the front door.

I pulled back the small curtain on the side of the door, to see all the paparazzi standing on the sidewalk, and hugged Spencer tightly.

Nestled against my neck, he spoke so low, only I could hear him. "You don't have to leave. I can take you home later or early in the morning when no one will be out there."

I pulled away, seriously contemplating Spencer's

proposition. It took all I had to turn him down. "I'll call you before I go to bed, okay?"

"And first thing in the morning. If I can't touch you, I want to be able to hear you."

There was no doubt I was going to make sure that that happened.

Charles cleared his throat. "I don't mean to sound rude—eh, maybe I do. You two might be taking this a little fast, considering."

Spencer and I both shot a warning look at Charles.

He held his hands up in surrender. "It's just a little weird," he said, moving to the door to open it.

Spencer turned from me in one fluid motion and slammed the open door shut. He was face to face with my brother. Charles seemed a little more than shocked to see his business partner be so aggressive toward him. Not me, this was simply aggressive Spencer. I'd encountered him a few times.

Charles stood his ground as Spencer towered over him.

"Listen, Chuck, I like you. You're a good guy—a little cocky for my liking, but I'm falling for your sister and, for your own good, you need to stay out of our relationship."

Charles just glared up at Spencer through narrowed eyes. "Huh. I never believed much of what Teddy told me about you. I always stuck up for you. Maybe I should have listened to my brother." His gaze came my way before going back to Spencer.

"Teddy and I are fine. He gave us his blessing, and you'd be smart to do the same," Spencer threatened.

"I don't have to give you shit, Salvatore. This is my sister were talking about, not some business deal." Charles turned to me, grabbed my arm, and pulled me closer to him. "You have one minute to say goodbye before I make a scene for your fan club out there." He let go of my arm, walked around Spencer, and went out the front door. Smiling and waving, he took to the sidewalk and got into the SUV that waited by the curb.

The door was still wide open as I turned to Spencer. "I'll talk to him. He doesn't like to be told what to do. I'm sure you can understand that."

Spencer nodded down at me, wrapping me tightly in his embrace. "I see now why you two don't get along. Bit of a jerk, that one."

That was Charles, my cocky jerk of a brother. But for all his flaws, he was family, and I appreciated him sticking up for me, even if it was to Spencer. "I better go. He wasn't fibbing when he said he'd cause a scene."

I had to stretch up on my tippy toes to reach Spencer's lips and, as I did, the storm of cameras went off.

"Elizabeth, you better call me when you get home. If you don't, I'll come over there."

I ran my hands down his chest, laughing at his threat.

Chapter 8

Nickolas

Early Monday morning, I was awoken by my cell phone ringing. *Seven-thirty? Way too early for Natasha to be calling me, especially for a Monday morning.* Reaching over for my phone, I rubbed my eyes to focus on the screen. *Chuck Monroe?*

I sat up in bed, staring at the phone as it continued to ring in my hand. Chuck and I had exchanged numbers the weekend of the charity event. We never used them, but it was a comfort to know I had another way of getting in touch with Elizabeth. For the briefest moment, I thought that maybe it was her calling me on his phone, but I knew, thanks to Fame, that the love of my life had spent the weekend with someone else.

Today, she started her internship. I had thought about calling her last night to wish her luck, but a lustful picture of her leaving Salvatore's house put a little bit of a damper on my mood. I answered, hoping deep down that it was her, anyway.

"Hello"

"Simon?" the voice was deep and sharp,

Not Elizabeth. "Yeah, it's Simon. What do you want, Chuck?" I figured it would be better to keep the fake name until I could explain everything to Elizabeth.

"I need your help."

"You need my help?"

"I'm still fucking pissed at what you did to my sister and to our family, but I've seen you guys together, and you can't fake what I saw. So, yes, I need your help." He paused, so I took the opportunity to apologize.

"Chuck, I'm so sorry. I wish I could take it back. I was blackmailed. There was nothing I could do."

"Save it, Simon, I'm sure you had a reason for what you did, but I really don't give a fuck right now. It's Salvatore I'm concerned about. Now that I know you work for Fame, I know that you and your associates are known for uncovering the truth and making sure the public knows everyone's dirty little secrets."

What is he getting at? Does he know something about Salvatore? "What do you want from me, Chuck?"

"Before we became partners, Teddy did an extensive search on Salvatore's history. Teddy is paranoid about everyone we work with. He came back with few findings, but a lot of question marks. That's why Teddy didn't want Beth getting involved with him."

"Wait, what did Teddy find?" There was another long pause. "Chuck, if it's something that can hurt Elizabeth, you need to tell me. There are lots of different ways to deal with this, but if Elizabeth could get hurt because of it, I'm going to do whatever is necessary to report it."

"I know. That's why I called. Something happened last night that made me believe everything Teddy told me, and I don't think I could live with myself if—"

"Chuck, what did Salvatore do?"

"All I know is that Teddy found a blip of an article about Spencer being charged with assault. He tried looking deeper, but everything was wiped clean. No records, nothing. It's like someone erased it."

Something bad must have happened to make him turn to me for help. "What happened last night?" I asked again, needing to know if Elizabeth was involved.

"Off the record?"

"Yes"

"Let's just say I saw his aggressive side firsthand, and it was a little more than intimidating. He looked crazy, dude. I'm worried he's going to flip on Beth. You know how stubborn she is. And that, mixed with his temper…you've seen some of the pictures of him grabbing her arm. Something just doesn't add up. I'm worried about my sister being with him."

I have to call her. I needed to hear her voice, make sure she was okay. It was taking all I had not to punch the wall. If that asshole laid a hand on her—If she knew this, knew about his past, maybe she would leave him. I had my mission for the day—digging. "Listen, Chuck, I love your sister, too. I would never lay a hand on her and, now that I have a place to start, I will find out exactly what happened."

"I need your word that you will tell me everything that you find. Leave me out if it. From now on, I'm simply a reliable source. If Beth and Gia knew I was helping you, they'd never talk to me again. I'll work from my side, see if I can find anything. I know you care for Beth, so I have faith that you won't screw us over again."

"I won't, Chuck. Now I need to know where Teddy found this partial article."

Chuck gave me everything I needed to start my search for Salvatore's secrets. In a few hours, I would make my way over to the courthouse to see what I could dig up. It was one thing to have someone look into something, and a completely different thing when you had access to records that no one else did. Once again, Natasha was a master at her craft. I had my badge to investigate in any part of the courthouse, except the judge's chambers. If there was something hiding there, I was going to find it.

Whatever Salvatore did in his past, it happened his senior year in high school, so I made sure to get information on his father's lawyers during that time. There's no way a seventeen-year-old could erase an assault charge without the help from Daddy and Daddy's lawyers.

ℰↃℰↃ

I sat in the back of the town car on my way to the courthouse. It was later than I wanted it to be. I had originally planned to call Elizabeth before her internship began, but it was now closer to noon. We had talked about her calling me during her first lunch break, before things went to shit. She told me to wait by the phone from noon till one, because she didn't know exactly when she would get a free second to walk out of the building to call. *What's the worst that can happen if I call?*

After talking with Chuck, I was even more worried about her being with Spencer. I had to make sure she was okay, even if all she did was yell at me or hang up. At least, I'd get to hear her voice.

I waited while the phone rang and rang. *She's not going to answer.* It was just wishful thinking that she would.

"Hello?"

Holy fuck, she answered. My heart pounded in my chest, and I swore the driver could here because he looked back at me through the rear view mirror.

"Simon?"

There were so many things I wanted to tell her, needed

to tell her but, mostly, I just wanted to hear her voice.

"Hey, Belle."

I couldn't call her anything else. She was my Belle, my beauty, and lately, I had lived up to being the beast.

"Simon, why are you calling me?"

She didn't sound mad or angry and I was so thankful for that.

"I just wanted to wish you good luck today. I know how important this is for you." There was such silence on the other end. "Belle? Are you still there?"

"Yeah, I'm here."

"I need to explain to you why I did what I did—I—" I needed to tell her. I needed to just tell her I was black-mailed, even if she didn't believe me. It was supposed to end on New Years. I was supposed to find her waiting for me. I was going to tell her everything, quit Fame, and work on my photography. Instead, I walked in on her with Spencer. "I need you to know that I loved you—I still love you. I didn't have a choice. I was being black-mailed—"

"Simon, please just stop. I can't do this right now."

"I'm so sorry. I wish we could have met under different circumstances. Please don't write me off yet. I'm not the bad guy in all of this. I know it looks that way, but I'm not. I'm doing everything I can to fix what I have done."

I could hear her sighing through the phone then a few mumbled voices in the back ground.

"Simon, I have to go."

"Yeah, sure. I—um—I'll talk to you soon."

"Goodbye, Simon."

"Bye, Belle."

I held up my phone. The front screen was her picture, the one I took on our first date. I wanted to kick myself for not telling her that night. I was being selfish. *How did*

I ever let it get this far? I hit my head repeatedly on the back seat for being stupid enough to let someone like Elizabeth slip through my hands. I turned, looking out the window. We had arrived at the courthouse and, apparently, had been sitting for a few minutes.

"We're here. Whenever you're ready to get out, sir."

"Thank you. I just need a minute. You don't have another client to get, do you?"

"No, sir. You're the only one today. We can sit as long as you like."

I could hear the compassion in his voice. He was obviously listening to my phone conversation. You could get shot for less in New York. I could attest.

⊱⊰⊱⊰

I was finally on to something. After digging around in lost files for most of the day, I was more than ready to abandon the crusade. Natasha's cover was one of her best yet, so I hunkered down and continued my search. I was now Collin Hayes, sent over from the higher ups to make sure all the files in the vault were being properly handled. Not one person stopped me.

This was almost becoming too easy. A nice red-haired secretary came down to help me after a few solitary hours.

"So what are you looking for, again?" she asked, flipping through a box.

"Nothing in particular. Just making sure everything is filed the correct way. This is a small town, right?"

She nodded.

I tried my hardest to turn on any sort of charm I might have left in me. "Have you ever heard of the Salvatore family?" I glanced up and caught the girl turning as red as her hair.

"I do know who they are. I went to school with Spencer."

Maybe I won't have to keep digging in this vault for much longer. "What do you know about Spencer?"

"I wish I could say I knew more. Unfortunately, I was on a scholarship to Channing School, home of the rich and richer."

Why would I think anything less from that family?

"I hear a little hostility in that statement, not the all-around good guy he perceives himself to be nowadays?"

Chuckling over at me, she shook her head. "Ha, good guy? When he first came, maybe. He actually talked to me back then. I always ended up with the desk or locker right next to his. Salvatore, Salvine—got to love alphabetical seating charts and locker handouts."

"First came? What do you mean?"

"Yeah, he was adopted when he was eight."

How did I not catch that? How did Natasha not catch that—unless she did and just didn't tell me?

"He had this funny New York accent the first year he was here. I mean, when he would actually talk. It was weird. As soon as we went to high school, something changed in him, like he realized how hot he was and how rich. He started playing sports and dating the popular girls, well only one girl."

I felt like I should have had a pen and paper to take notes. *This is unbelievable. Where do I even start?* This girl was wealth of knowledge.

"I see now why you're so hostile toward him."

Sighing, she placed the file in her hand down on the table to look over at me. "I'm not hostile. I just hoped that someone I saw every day from age eight to seventeen would at least remember my name."

Shit, what's her name? I need this lead. I can't lose her trust now.

Luckily, her badge was hanging from her neck. *Maggie Salvine*.

"Why are you interested in the Salvatore family? I thought you were just checking files."

Why do they have to be pretty and smart? The girl was on to me, but I had a feeling I would be able to charm her. *This is going to suck.* I took a step closer as she began to blush. "Can I tell you a secret, Mag? Can I call you Mag?"

"Sure, I—yeah—"

"I'm not here to check up on the files. I'm here to find dirt on Spencer Salvatore. I'm a reporter."

Gasping, Maggie took a step back and covered her mouth. "I knew it! I knew you were too hot to be working for the system. Oh my god, I said that out loud, didn't I?"

"It's okay, Mag, but I need you to not tell anyone, or my cover will be blown."

"This is about senior week, isn't it?"

This girl is just getting better every second. I might have to take her out to dinner as a thank you.

"I'm not sure. That's what I'm here to find out. Would you like to help take down the man who couldn't even bother to remember a name as beautiful as Maggie Salvine?"

I took her hand in mine and kissed the back of it. I saw all I needed to as her lips curled up in pure vengeance. Salvatore better watch out. I didn't think he had a clue to how many people he had pissed off in his life, and, lucky for me, they were all on my side.

I quickly let her hand go and backed away as footsteps came closer to us. I placed a finger over my lips. She nodded and smiled in agreement.

"Maggie, are you down here?"

"Yeah, I'm back here."

A man who could have easily been Spencer's twin

came from around the corner. Looking me over curiously, he turned back to Maggie.

"The phones are going crazy up there. Would you mind?"

"Yeah, just give me a second. I'll be right there."

"Hey, man, finding everything in order? I really don't need to be written up this year." The man looked to be in his early thirties and an almost replica of Salvatore.

"Yes, everything is going perfect so far, finding everything I need."

"Great." Turning, he left us as fast as he came.

"Who was that?" I whispered, moving closer to Maggie.

"That's Christopher Thomas. He's the sheriff. He and his father moved here soon after Spencer arrived, actually. His dad was a cop. He took over the family business, I guess you could say."

"You call him Thomas?"

"Yeah, I've known him forever. We didn't go to school together, but I lived a few houses down from him. We're both from the other side of the tracks. Everyone calls him Thomas or T."

Strange, never known a sheriff to be so informal. Then again, this is a small town, small but rich. Can't be too many crimes.

"Well, as cool as Thomas is. I should get back to my work. Someone might have wrecked their Bentley." In a whirlwind of red hair, Maggie turned and headed for the stairs.

"Hey, I thought you were going to help me."

"I will, but it's going to cost you. I'm thinking dinner should get you all the information you need."

Damn, I might have underestimated this chick. "Where should I pick you up?"

"I'll give your driver all the information you need.

Keep digging, Collin, remember your cover story."

I think I should introduce this girl to Natasha. They'd make a hell of a team. "Thank you, Maggie Salvine. I certainly won't forget your name."

"You'd be smart not to." She winked before leaving the room.

The minute she walked out, I gasped a sigh of relief and held my stomach tight. *That was painful, flirting with someone when you care so much for someone else. Dinner is going to excruciating tonight.* I had to keep a straight head. I couldn't stop. Spencer needed to be knocked down a few pegs, and this girl might have all the ammunition I needed to take him down. The faster it all happened, the faster I could get back to a regular life and, hopefully, back to my Belle.

Chapter 9

Elizabeth

E lizabeth, we need you to go to the back room and finish the new cataloging."

I turned back to the middle-aged woman who was in charge of me. I still didn't know how to take her. Most of the morning, she seemed more annoyed that I was there, and then, out of the blue, she could be sweet.

"Sure, Carmen I'll get right on it."

What did I expect? That they would have me researching or acquiring information for a prestigious writer or politician? Of course not. They stuck me in the back out of view and buried in files and files of card catalogs.

I walked back to the dungeon, replaying the conversation I'd just had with Simon. I was happily sitting in the lunch room, eating my soup, when my phone started vibrating from inside my bag. I figured it was Spencer, but was more than stunned to see Simons name flash up. I wasn't sure why I answered.

Maybe I needed closure but, after talking to him, that wasn't what happened. I did my best to be strong but, after not hearing his voice for a few days, it was comforting. The sound of his voice always seemed to comfort me.

What he said didn't surprise me, telling me he loved me still and that he was trying to fix what he did. For the life of me, I wanted to believe him. I wanted to believe he was a good guy, but the evidence against him was substantial, and he couldn't deny any of it. Maybe in a few weeks, or months, I could talk to him and try to understand the situation, but everything was still so raw. I still had feelings for him, not as strong as before, but I loved him, I cared about him, and I couldn't shut that off cold turkey. My feelings for Spencer were stronger than I expected them to be so soon. *Oh, shit, Spencer. If he finds out I talked to Simon, he's going to blow a gasket.*

I'd never had to lie to Spencer before, not about something as serious as another man. I had lied about wanting to be with him, but he and I both knew the reasons I did that—Simon. *How am I going to look at his face and not have it written all over mine?* I only had two hours left before my day was over. This specific internship lasted from eight to three, so that I would be able to take the three classes that remained in order for me to graduate. I had two hours to get my act together before Spencer would be parked outside the library, waiting for me.

I thought about calling him and telling him not to come pick me up today. But that would only raise red flags. I wanted to call Gia, ask her opinion, but that was out of the question. This morning, when I was getting ready, she came out of her room, got some coffee, and went right back in. I figured I'd give her a few days to cool off, and then I'd try to mend things.

"You did a great job today, Elizabeth. Usually, the interns we get beg us for something more important to do, but I was pleasantly surprised with you. You seem to have your head on right. I like that."

"Thanks, Carmen. I know how lucky I am to have received this internship. My classes don't start until mid-January. If you need me to, I can stay longer and help out wherever I'm needed." *Please let me stay. I don't want to face my hot ass, hot tempered boyfriend right now.*

"I'll keep that in mind, but it's your first week. Don't want to wear you out just yet. Have a good evening, and I'll see you tomorrow at eight."

I walked out the front door, and there he was, leaning against his SUV. *Shit, why does he have to look so good?* He had his dress jacket on and a scarf wrapped around his neck, his dark hair blowing in the wind. He stood up from the car when he saw me walk out. It was then that I noticed the shift of people standing around him. The sea of cameras turned from him to me as I walked down the front stairs. *Tomorrow, if he picks me up, it will be around back.*

I held on tightly to the bag over my shoulder as I walked closer.

Spencer acted like the dozen people around him weren't there. I loved his confidence. I, on the other hand, still wasn't use to it. So I covered my face as the cameras went off around us. I was a few steps from the SUV when Spencer opened the door. I didn't say anything to him, only smiled as I got in the car. He slid in beside me, closing the door.

It was toasty warm inside as the driver drove off and away from the people clambering around.

"So how was your first day?" he asked from beside me.

I found myself fiddling with the bag on my lap to keep from looking over at him. "It was good."

"Tell me about it, what did they have you doing?"

"Oh, nothing interesting, just boring intern stuff, that's all." I glanced up quickly to see him watching me intensely. His eyes were piercing me as I shifted in the seat.

"Are you okay? You're acting a little weird."

"Yeah, I'm fine, just a bit overwhelmed. You know, first-day jitters." I made sure to look at him this time. His beautiful eyes looked down at me, questioning. "How was your day?" I asked, trying to take the heat off of me.

Spencer sat back in his seat, looking out the window. Suddenly, it seemed that I wasn't the only one who was having an uncomfortable ride home.

"Spencer, are you okay?"

He turned back to me, a hint of anger etched in his brow. "I have to leave town for a few days. Something came up at home that I have to deal with."

"How long are you going to be gone?" The desperation in my voice was something that I couldn't even begin to hide. I knew what his leaving was going to do to us, and I didn't want to lose what we had, even if it had only been one weekend. It was my turn to be selfish and demand for him to stay.

He reached over for my hand. "I don't know. Hopefully, only a couple days."

I took my hand from the seat so he couldn't touch me. "Well, you can't go. Not now. I just got you—you can't leave me."

"Trust me, I don't want to, but I have no choice. I'm leaving tonight."

With as much money and as many people as has working for him, why couldn't he just have someone else do this? *Dammit! He can make me so angry.* "You know who you sound like, right now? Simon. That's the same shitty line he used to pull on me every time he had to 'leave.'"

"Don't compare me to him. I am nothing like that asshole. What I am leaving for is going to protect you."

"Protect me? I don't believe you. You're lying again.

If you really want to protect me like you say, then don't keep secrets from me, Salvatore. Tell me the real reason why you're going."

The atmosphere intensified. Neither one of us seemed to be willing to compromise, and the longer we were confined in that back seat, the more I wanted to smack him—and then kiss him. *Ugh, he's so frustrating.* I never thought that arguing with someone could be such a turn on.

"I told you, why I have to leave. I don't think I need to repeat myself. If you're that worried about my intentions, then come with me."

Go with him? To his home? Like to meet his family?

"You know I can't leave."

"Really, you can't leave? Is something physically keeping you here? You plan on meeting up with Simon or something?"

I was sure he meant for the comment to be passive but the minute he said it, I could feel the color drain from my face. My heart began to race in overtime. I tried to make a recovery but it was too late. He'd see my reaction.

"You've got to be fucking kidding me, Elizabeth." He ran his fingers through his hair and stomped his foot on the back of the seat in front of him hard enough I could feel the vibration.

"Spencer, no. I'm not meeting him. I wouldn't do that, not now."

"Oh, but maybe later on. Jesus, you talked to him today, didn't you? That's why you couldn't look at me."

I sat silently as he stewed next to me.

"You know that whole not lying and keeping secrets works both ways, Elizabeth."

He was right. I was just as bad as he was. I should have just told him. He would have understood.

No. No, he wouldn't. What am I saying? He would

have freaked out, just like he's doing right now.

"I wanted to tell you, but I knew you would get angry, just like you are now. Sorry if I didn't want to upset you."

I crossed my arms and turned to look out the window. I stared out the window wondering where in the hell were we going anyway, it certainly wasn't to my place.

The mound of tension beside me spoke up. "What did he want?"

I turned back to see Spencer watching my every move. "You really want to know? I guess you can't get any angrier than you already are. He was wishing me good luck on my first day. He apologized, told me he was blackmailed. Oh, and he told me he still loved me." I glanced up at the roof of the car and thought hard before glaring back at him. "Yup, I think that was all."

Spencer waited a beat, before asking, "Do you?"

"What, Spencer? Do I what? Accept his apology? Do I believe him? What do you want to know?"

His elbows were on his knees as he bent over to rub his temples. "Do you love him?" he asked from the same crumpled position.

"Spencer, I want to tell you no so badly. But I said I wouldn't lie to you. I did love him, and as much as I want to make myself stop, I still care about him. Not like I care about you. It took me months and months to realize I was in love with him. It took me one weekend to realize that it was different with you. Shit, I was probably falling in love with you long before this past weekend. Spencer, I don't think I can live without you. I don't think I would be able to function without you. But I was able to function when Simon was gone. I should have known then that he wasn't what I wanted, because the whole time I was with him, I was thinking about you. And when I'm with you, I don't want anyone else."

I prayed that what I had just told him made sense. It

sounded good in my head, and it was all true, every word of it. I felt freed telling him, I felt like a weight had been lifted.

"I did something terrible when I was seventeen." Spencer rose from his bent position and rested his back against the seat before going on. "Someone is poking around, trying to figure out what it is that I did. My father made sure to make it look like nothing happened, but whoever is digging around is getting close to figuring it out. If it does come out, there's a chance I could lose everything, and that includes you. That's why I have to leave."

Although it wasn't a detailed explanation, I couldn't deny that Spencer was trying.

His cool blue eyes were asking me to trust him. "I was a different person back then. I don't want you to know that part of me, not if you don't have to."

"Spencer, you can't keep trying to protect me from everything. Trust me, I can handle it. My past wasn't daisies and happy-ever-afters, either. Everyone has a past. It makes us who we are. It took me a long time to understand that, but I wouldn't be who or where I am today if it wasn't for who I was back then."

I placed my hand on the middle of the seat between us, a peace offering of sorts. He accepted it and laced his fingers between mine. We sat in silence, letting all that had been said sink in. He began removing his fingers from between mine. Then his long thick fingers wrapped around my wrist. He squeezed it tightly then moved them to my elbow. Pulling me across the seat and closer to him, he grasped the back of my neck, urging me toward his face.

"The truth is, I'm pretty sure I'm in love with you," he confessed. "Please, let me handle this my way. Maybe one day, I will find the courage to tell you but right now, I can't do that to you."

"Truth?" I asked.

He smiled, shaking his head at me.

"I'm pretty sure I'm in love with you, too."

I smiled up at him as he too smiled back. "Did we just make this 'love' official?" I giggled at the thought of an equal exchange of feelings between the two of us. For the first time, there was no guilt in the word love like there had been in the past with Simon. I was falling hard—no, I had fallen and I was in love with Spencer.

Spencer nodded. "I didn't know we had to, but if you must put a label on it, yes, we are officially in love."

The 'want-a-be' detective in me wanted to keep prying but, I didn't have the strength. I just wanted to be held after a long day of card cataloging. *I think my paper cuts have paper cuts.*

Another hour in the car, and we finally made it to our final destination—the airport.

I hadn't expected him to be leaving now. I sat up to look at him. "You're really leaving, this isn't a joke?"

Kissing the top of my head, he held my hand tightly. "You can still come with me. I may, or may not, have your underwear packed."

I gasped as I let go of his hand to punch his shoulder. "I can't call out the second day of my internship, and you actually brought my underwear with you?"

Spencer's deep laugh filled the vehicle. "I could call for you, say you're sick."

Yeah, love sick and stupid. I sat, back crossing my arms. "Okay, and then what do I say to them when they see me on the news looking healthy and glowing in the Las Vegas sun."

He winked. "Librarians really keep tabs on celebrities? I think you'd be safe."

"Ha-ha, very funny. Not all librarians are old and grouchy. I'm sure as hell not."

At least he was smiling, even if it was at my expense. "No, you are certainly not old—maybe sarcastic, stubborn, and only a little grouchy."

"That's not true. I'm not grouchy! You're the grouch. Are you sure you're not the old grouchy librarian, because you have both mastered."

"Old, huh? I'll show you old." Lunging over, he grabbed me around the waist and, pinning me down on the seat, kissed up and down my neck. The next thing I knew, I was ripping his jacket off and the divider in the SUV was going up. I grabbed his tie and yanked him down for a kiss.

I had never felt such passion as I did when I was with Spencer. I wrapped my legs tightly around him dragging our hips together. His pants bulged with anticipation as he rocked between my legs. I ran my hands down his muscular back, un-tucking his shirt. My restless hands clawed at his stomach and chest.

"Sit up." His voice was stern as he whispered in my ear.

I sat up as he backed off me, but only for a minute. He had pulled my jacket and blouse off before I was even in a full sitting position. *Thank god for tinted windows.*

Spencer's hands went straight for my skirt and hiked it up. I quickly scooted back and pulled it down again. *This—what's happening right now—is typical, Beth.* I flattened my hand over my more-than-natural stomach. *Damn you, spanks! How sexy—not! Oh, shit. I can see the bulge in his pants.* I needed him so badly. *No!* I yelled at myself. *He cannot see me in spanks. It's not going to happen, not as long as I'm breathing.*

"Is something wrong?" he asked, curiously.

"I'm…I…umm…don't have the proper attire on right now."

"I know, you don't. Why is that a problem? I'm trying to help you out of the rest of this very inappropriate outfit. You clearly have too much on."

His hand slid up between my skirt and thigh. I instantly ripped his hand out.

"Is something wrong?" he asked.

"Yes!" I covered my lap protectively with my hands and cringed as Spencer stared at me in amusement. "I mean no!" I pointed at him but quickly covered my lap again when his eyes went to my goodies. "You're the one who's—"

"Elizabeth," he sighed. "I don't care what I have to do to get you out of that skirt, but I can promise you I will have it off you in the next minute, so get over whatever it is that's bothering you. My flight leaves in thirty minutes, and I'm not leaving this car till I fuck you."

Okay, maybe I can let that whole, never seeing me in spanks thing go—thought about it and—nope, not letting it go. "Fine, just turn your head and close your eyes."

"Are you serious?"

"As a heart attack, now turn around."

Sighing Spencer reluctantly turned to face the window and closed his eyes. "What are you doing anyway?"

I tried to pull the tight spanks off as quickly as I could.

"Why is the SUV rocking?"

Shit! These things are glued on. "Everything's fine, just keep your eyes closed!" Leaning back and thrusting my ass in the air, I finally managed to pull them down and off. I shoved them deep into my purse. *Mental note: clean out your purse—again.*

I fixed my skirt and fluffed my hair. "Okay, you can turn back around."

He did so and glanced around to see what could have

changed in the confines of the once-rocking vehicle. Luckily, he got over it quick and went right back to pulling my skirt up and moving me so I could straddle him.

"You never cease to amaze me," he quipped.

He leaned forward, and I would have almost fallen off his lap if his hand wasn't firmly on my lower back. He held me there for a second as he ravished my neck and collar, his lips finally placing soft kissing along the top of my cleavage. When he pulled me back toward him, I smiled down at him. Those beautiful blue eyes seemed to see into my very soul. He took a second to look down and away from me, and, when I followed his gaze, I saw my flesh-colored spanks in his hand.

I ripped them from his hand and hid them behind my back. "Spencer!"

I wanted to die. *Right now, I want to run as fast as I can and hide under my covers.* I lowered my head, as a single tear escaped without permission, and landed on Spencer's pants. *I can't believe he—no, I can. He's a control freak.*

"Elizabeth, look at me."

"No. I can't," I said, refusing to let him see the shame I knew was written all over my face. "Why couldn't you just leave it alone?"

I went to move off him, but his hands held me tightly against him. Unfortunately, I wasn't going anywhere. *Oh god, another stupid tear.*

Typical. Only *my* fantasy of having sex in the back of a chauffeured car would end this way. I felt his hands on either cheek as he wiped away the next untamed tear. He tilted my head up but I kept my eyes, looking down.

"Look at me. Please."

I let my eyes drift up to his face.

"I'm sorry. You had me intrigued, as usual, Ms. Monroe."

"Well, you should have just kept your grubby hands out of my bag. I was only trying to protect you." I threw his line back at him, but only caught a smile on his face.

"From what? A deadly pair of underwear? I hardly think they would have hurt me."

I narrowed my eyes at him again. "No, maybe not, but it would have hurt me. It does hurt me. I'm not— Spencer, I'm not a super model. Not everything's perfect."

Oh, God, are we actually having this conversation?

"Wait, you're not a model?" he asked, sitting back in his seat, looking all cute and confused.

"This isn't funny, Spencer, not to me." I hit his shoulder in frustration. "I might seem like I have my shit together, but I'm a mess inside, especially with you. Look at you—you're beautiful, and I'm just some silly girl who actually thinks her size-twelve ass deserves to be with you. I'm crazy. I really think I'm going crazy."

He held my chin between his finger and thumb and made me look at him. His lips gently found mine. The heat that had been radiating off of us was enough to steam up the windows. His velvet tongue slid over my lips as he pulled me tightly against his hard body.

"Don't ever talk like that again. I'm the one who doesn't deserve you. You *are* beautiful, and I don't give a fuck what you wear. It's what you *don't* wear that I love."

He was right. I had been comfortable in front of him all weekend. It was the nasty girl that lived in the corners of my mind, who liked to mess with the image I had of myself, that was fucking things up. She liked to remind me of the constant judging from the media. She also liked to sneak flashbacks, of kids making fun of me, to the fore front of my mind every once in a while.

I'm going to have to have a talk with her. An eviction notice is surly on its way.

His hands slid up my thighs and pushed my skirt up so it wrapped around my waist. "You are crazy, crazy for thinking that I want anything other than what is in front of me right now."

"Spencer, all this kind of killed the mood, don't you think?"

I jolted up as his fingers found their way inside me.

"Doesn't feel like it to me," he purred.

I couldn't help the faint sigh that escaped my lips as a warm calm came over me. *Fucking magic fingers.*

"You wasted thirteen minutes. Now you only have seventeen minutes left to get my pants down, I suggest you get started."

I didn't know how he did it, but fuck he could take me from enraged and embarrassment to turned on in mere seconds. I tossed the spanks on the floor of the SUV wishing to god they'd just melt into it, as I begin working on his belt.

Seventeen minutes later, and I could proudly scratch another fantasy off my list. The cool winter air was welcomed as Spencer cracked the window. Sweat beaded off both of us as I collapsed against his chest. I had managed to make it through another embarrassing obstacle with Spencer. Doubt girl was definitely getting evicted. I didn't need her anymore. I had Spencer, I felt comfortable in my skin and I was ready for the world to know it. *I dare anyone to say something.*

Chapter 10

Nickolas

The driver pulled up to the apartment complex. Taking a deep breath, I opened the door and made my way up to Maggie's front step. *I can do this, just dinner. No feelings are involved.* I needed to make her feel good, get all the information she had, call it a night, and then call Natasha.

Before I could knock on the door, it opened. Maggie stood there with a hand still on the door knob, and the other on the door frame protectively. She stuck her head out and looked in either direction. There was a paranoid expression on her face, which instantly put me on edge.

"Are you okay, Maggie?"

Her eyes locked on mine, and she shook her head. Grabbing my hand aggressively, she pulled me inside and slammed the door shut, locking it behind her. *All right, now I'm really starting to get anxious.*

Clearly something had spooked her. She was still in the same clothes she wore earlier in the day, her eyes were puffy as if she had been crying, and her hands were visibly shaking.

Sitting next to her on the couch, I took her hands in mine to offer what little comfort I could. "Maggie, what happened to you?"

"They know—they know you're snooping around, and that you aren't who you say you are."

My heart caught. *Shit, my cover has never been blown this fast.* "Who knows?"

"I don't know. They had their face covered, but they threatened me, told me I would lose my job if I told you anything."

Fuck, I needed this girl to stick with me. I can't lose the only lead I have. "You're still going to help me right?"

"Simon? That's your real name right?"

I nodded over at her, another lie to cover my ass.

"I thought you looked familiar, but I didn't put everything together until I was threatened. You're in love with Elizabeth Monroe, aren't you? And all of this is a way to get back at Spencer for stealing her from you, isn't it?"

Damn, I did not come here prepared for all of this. I was done with lying. The only way Maggie was going to give me anything was if I was honest with her. "Yes, I'm in love with Elizabeth, and I am going to do everything in my power to make her see Spencer for the bad guy that he really is. Elizabeth is only going to be hurt by him, and I don't want to see it happen. She belongs with me. I screwed up, and I'm trying my best to fix it the only way I know how." I paused racking my brain as I tried to figure out how to save this fucked up situation. "Listen, Maggie, you are the only one who can help me with that."

Standing from the couch, I turned away, facing the door. *God, just thinking about Spencer's hands all over my Belle makes me sick.* And to know that this woman sitting behind me could have everything I needed to win her back. I was desperate. I kneeled in front of Maggie, taking her hands in mine, looking deep into her eyes. "Please, you have to help. I can't lose her, not when I might be so close to winning her back."

Maggie's brows scrunched together, and she bit down on her lip, as if fighting a battle in her own head over whether to help me or not. "Okay, I'll tell you what I know, but it's going to be he said, she said, and I do not want my name in it. I'll tell you everything, but you're on your own for proof, because I'm pretty sure there isn't any."

"That's fine, anything will help."

I sat back next to her on the couch and readied myself for whatever was about to leave her mouth.

"It was the end of our senior year, and Spencer had been with this one girl the entire year. They were always together. They genuinely seemed like they were in love with each other. One night, some guy had a huge end-of-the-year party, invited just about everyone. You can imagine the kind of party it was—rich kids with an unlimited amount of money to waste. Well, to make a long story short, I wasn't invited. So I picked up a shift at the police station where I was learning the ropes of secretarial work. It was early only seven when a group of people came in the station. Three cops had Spencer in restraints. Even in the restraints, he looked like he was going to break free from them. Anyway, I overheard them saying he nearly killed a kid. Later, I found out that he had walked in on his girlfriend sleeping with some other guy. I guess he snapped. Tossed the girl off the guy. She hit the wall so hard she broke her arm, and then he nearly beat the guy to death, until someone pulled him off."

So Mr. Goody Two Shoes nearly killed a man, beat a woman, and his father made sure to make it all disappear.

"What happened to the kid? His parents didn't press charges?"

"Nope, he was from my side of town. I heard a rumor that Spencer's father paid them off big time, along with the girlfriend. It's like as soon as it happened, everything disappeared. No one talked about it, no one reported it, and Spencer walked out less than an hour after being brought in."

"What happened to the kid he beat, did he make it? Or?"

"Oh, he made it through his injuries. He ended up marrying the girl. Supposedly, she had been seeing him for a long time. She was just embarrassed that he was poor, but once he got his hush money from the Salvatore's, I guess she was more than happy to make things work."

"Thank you so much, Maggie. I won't tell a soul I got any information from you." I stood from the couch, pulling her to stand with me and hugging her tightly with appreciation. "I just want to see people pay for what they have done.' It's not right for him to get away with everything just because he has money. He might have changed over the years, but someone like that can't hide their demons forever."

I kissed her cheek and headed for the door. I let myself out and walked toward the waiting car. My hand was inches from the handle and a chill went down my spine. Not one to question my instincts, I turned around to see a figure leaning against the door of a very expensive Mercedes.

"Simon Sullivan—Or is it Collin, maybe Nick? When are you going to get it through your head—I won."

"Trouble in paradise so soon, Salvatore? If there isn't any yet, there will be." I took a step toward him. I wasn't afraid of him. I was younger, probably in better shape, and if he tried anything, I wouldn't hold back. Elizabeth wasn't there to stop me.

"Did you find what you were looking for?" he asked also moving from the shadows of his car closer to me.

"Oh, you mean the fact that you nearly killed someone because they were sleeping with your girlfriend, who was cheating on you long before you caught her in bed with another man?" *Laughing? He's laughing about this?* "You're a real class act, Salvatore, hitting women—"

"Shut up. You don't know what the fuck you're talking about."

"You sure about that? What do you think Elizabeth's going to think about it after she finds out who you really are?"

Before I could react, Spencer had me backed up against the car, his fists curled around my jacket.

"Do it." I spit the words at him, tempting him to take his rage to the next level. "I'm sure Elizabeth is just going to love hearing that you beat me to a pulp, after discovering who you really are. And your daddy isn't going to be able to pay me off like he did that poor kid."

His face fell and his hands slid from my body and into his hair. "If this was fifteen years ago, I would have killed you. But that's not who I am anymore. You might not believe this, but I am doing all I can to *not* be that guy."

I didn't believe him for a second. His shitty "woe is me" bull crap might work with Elizabeth, but he didn't fool me. "Soon your secret will be out. I'm playing for keeps and the thought of Elizabeth being with someone with your temper and a history of hitting women—I'm sorry, I can't let that happen. I still love her, and I will not stand by, knowing you could potentially hurt or kill her because you have a bad day."

The sound of flesh hitting flesh rang in my ears and I

fell back against the car. I brought my hand up to my face and tasted blood on my lower lip. Licking my bloody lip, I looked over to Spencer. *That fucking asshole actually punched me.*

Spitting the hot iron blood from my mouth, I stepped closer. "You're done, Salvatore. Even if she doesn't believe me, I have faith that you'll screw it up all on your own. You don't deserve her. You're nothing but a spoiled little rich kid stuck in a thirty-year-old's body. She'll resent you for ruining her life, because you know you will, and you better believe I'll be there to comfort her." I spit again, just missing his perfect shoes.

Chapter 11

Elizabeth

"Gia?" I called loudly as I walked through the door. "Hey, are you here?"

I knocked on her door but heard nothing. When I called her cell, it went straight to voice mail. I couldn't believe she was acting like this. I knew she was upset, but this was a bit dramatic.

Getting comfortable, I sat on the couch to watch TV. An hour later, the door opened. It was Gia. She threw her stuff on the table before walking past me.

"Hey," I said, sitting up straight from the couch.

"What?" she spat back, irritated.

"What's your problem? I get that you're upset things didn't work out with Teddy, but *you* kissed Charles. You can't blame that on Spencer." I watched as she grabbed a bottle of water and shrugged her shoulders.

"I'm moving out. I guess this is my two week notice."

I stood from the couch, tossing the blanket I had over my lap down. "You're moving out over this? Gia, come on, talk to me, don't be ridiculous."

She shrugged again. "My internship in New York

wants me to come early. They're helping with my living arrangements, and I can't turn it down. Plus, I need a change of scenery."

I stared across the room at her. Her expression was vacant. We had gone from doing everything together to—hell, after that weekend, I felt like I didn't even know who she was any more.

"Well, I'm sorry to see you leave early. I thought that we'd have another month to hang out."

"Oh, you're sorry to see me leave? I guess you'll have to find another shoulder to cry on when Spencer leaves you again."

"Why can't you just be happy for me? Are you jealous?"

"Ha, that's rich. Me, jealous of you? I don't think so, darling. Never been, never will," she said, taking a swing of her water.

"Are you sure they don't need you to be in New York tomorrow?"

"If only," she said under breath but loud enough for me to hear.

"If I wasn't such a nice person and remembered how great a friend you could be, you'd be living on the street tonight, honey! You keep that in mind while you're sleeping in that nice plush bed that I bought. And when you hear the crisp cold wind blowing against the window, you remember who pays for the heat that's keeping you all nice and cozy while you sleep. Try to remember who's kept the sturdy roof that's over your head while you drift off to dreamland. So please, try to keep all that in mind after you slam your door in my face again." I walked past her and into my room, slamming my own door before she could do the same to me.

I sat at my desk and tried to calm my nerves. I wanted to go out there and slap her back to normal. My phone started buzzing from the pocket of my sweat shirt. Simon was calling again. I didn't have the patience to talk to him then. Eventually, I was going to have to, but not yet, I wasn't ready. Hitting the end button, I placed my phone back in my pocket.

ϾϿϾϿ

The week went on, day in and day out. Spencer came home two days after he'd left. We established a nice routine together. He'd pick me up from interning, we'd go to his place and have dinner, and then he'd bring me back home. Gia was keeping her distance from me and the condo. We hadn't spoken since the night she told me she was moving out. Boxes started piling up in her room as she prepared to move up north to New York.

Standing outside her room a few days later, I watched as she threw some books in a box. I didn't believe for a second that her internship wanted her to come early. No one else was asked to leave early. She was lying. I'd come to the conclusion that she hated me so much that she was going to throw away all her savings to move to New York a month early.

"Gia," I called, gaining her attention.

She looked up from the boxes in front of her, but quickly went back to packing.

"Why are you doing this? I know that you don't have to leave yet. You can stay here, we can work this out." I had hit an all-time low, I was begging.

Tossing another book in, she glanced up at me. Moving her hair off her face, she sighed. "Beth, I need to move on. I can't live here. I see your brothers everywhere. I miss Teddy too much—I just need to start over," she confessed, finally revealing the real reason why she was packing and moving to New York early.

"I'll tell them they can't come over anymore. Please don't leave because of them," I begged.

"I'm sorry I said all those nasty things. I guess I am jealous of you. I'm jealous that you and Spencer are together and happy. I wanted that with Teddy, and I took it out on the easiest people I could, you and him."

I walked into her room and sat down next to her and the boxes. "It's okay, I know it's tough, and I understand that you need to get away." I sighed and looked around at the mess in her room. Clothes were everywhere, books were scattered, and boxes were only half packed with things hanging out the sides. "So, how much more do you have to pack?" I asked, smiling at her.

Hitting my shoulder with hers, she gave me a relieved smile back. "I know. It's pretty bad in here. But on a positive note, now that you're going to help me, it should be a cake walk," she said, wiggling her eyebrows.

ℰℐℰℐ

I held Gia in tight bear hug. "Remember you can come home anytime you want. Your room will be waiting for you. Call me when you get settled in. I'm coming to visit in three weeks, don't forget."

The day had arrived. Gia was getting ready to get on the plane that was going to take her to New York and her fresh start. She had found a nice loft that was close to her internship. She had showed me pictures, and it seemed right up her alley. Close to everything—shops, food, clubs. She was making her dreams come true.

"I know, I know. All right, I'm officially on my own when I walk down there," she said, pulling back from me as she looked down the hallway that would lead her to her plane. "I love you, Beth, thank you—for everything."

"I love you too! I'll see you in three weeks!" I pulled her back to me and hugged her tightly.

I'd never had a best friend till I met Gia freshman year of college. I was a loner before I'd come to college, but when I opened up to her that first semester in our crappy dorm room with no heat, I knew that I was going to have a friend for life. I watched as she pulled her bag down the long corridor. She was starting a new chapter in her life, and so was I. I was going to have to embrace being in the spotlight when I was with Spencer and use it for good. I was scared but I knew between my family, friends, and the man I loved, I was going to be fine.

I turned in the opposite direction and started making my way back to where I had entered. Rounding the corner, I ran right into Charles.

"What the hell are you doing here?" I asked, taking a step back.

"I—umm—I just wanted to make sure she—I mean, you—got home okay," he stuttered.

Raising a questioning brow at him, I wrapped my arm around his and started walking. "Un-huh, sure ya did. Come on, Romeo, let's get some coffee."

He didn't have an option really. He was coming with me whether he wanted to or not. We sat down at a table in the large eatery inside the airport.

"Charles, I told you she's leaving to get away from you, to start over," I said, sipping my drink.

"I know you said that, but it doesn't mean I have to listen to it. She's making a mistake in leaving," he said, matter-of-factly.

"Oh, brother of mine, what am I going to do with you?" I glanced around the large space and noticed that a few people were staring at us. I brushed it off and tried to act normal.

"I'm moving back to New York," he said out of the blue.

Immediately I turned back to him almost choking on

my drink. "You're what?" I asked with my jaw practically on the table.

"I'm moving back."

"You can't do that. What about your work here? What about the club? It just opened. You can't leave."

I knew what he was thinking. He thought that if he could get Gia alone, then maybe he could rekindle whatever little spark they might have had.

"Someone needs to be at the other office. Shit's falling apart up there, so I volunteered. Teddy is going to stay here and run the club and look after you—that, in itself, is a full time job, and one that I don't want. We both decided that I should go. I was going long before Gia ever decided to leave. We just wanted to wait till after the club opening to tell you."

"I'm not that bad, Charles," I grumbled, sitting back and crossing my arms.

He chuckled. "Really, you're like a toddler, let's not pretend any differently."

"Well, when are you leaving?" I asked.

"I'm heading out later this week. I'll let you know before I go. I know how you can't function without your cool brother around." Tapping the top of my hand, he made a pouty face at me.

"You're so funny. It might be nice with just Teddy and me. We're the perfect children."

He sat back, laughing. "Yeah, perfectly dull."

My phone was sitting on the table, and we both turned to it as it began ringing. It was Simon, again.

"Why's he calling you?" Charles asked, strangely nervous.

"I don't know. He's been calling every day for the past two weeks. I just can't talk to him yet."

Charles relaxed in his chair, and I'd swear I heard him sigh with relief.

"Besides, if Spencer found out I was talking to him, he might strangle me." I said it only in jest, but Charles was seeing red.

"What do you mean by that?" he asked, sitting up in his seat getting serious.

"Nothing, I was just being sarcastic. Come on, you're telling me you wouldn't be mad if your girlfriend was talking to their ex?" I asked.

He relaxed back into his chair and nodded in agreement.

"Excuse me, can I have a picture?"

We both turned in unison to a girl in her late teens, holding her cell phone out in front of her. Charles gave her a disgusted look and then turned back to me. She was short and clearly nervous. Her face was round and spattered with freckles. She wasn't ugly, but I'm sure like most people they only saw her figure. I knew exactly how she felt, as she covered her stomach with her bag. I smiled up at her and she relaxed with a warm smile.

"Sure," I said standing from the table. I adjusted my clothing and ran my hand through my hair.

"Beth—are you kidding me?" Charles deadpanned.

I stood next to the girl, a good head or more taller than her. "No, now stand up and smile."

Reluctantly, my brother got up from his chair and stood next to me. She held up her phone up, and we all smiled for the picture.

"Thank you so much, Elizabeth, you're such an inspiration."

I knew my cheeks were red. I could feel the heat coming off them. "Oh, I'm really not. But thank you," I said, shaking the compliment off.

The girl kept staring at me as if I was a grade-A celebrity. "You are, to a lot of people," she said, before turning to leave.

"Does this mean we're going to have to have auto-graphed signings now?" Charles asked from next to me.

I hit him in the ribs before grabbing my bag. "You don't have to be so nasty. She just wanted a picture."

"Yeah, well, you know how that works. One picture leads to more—look," he said, pointing down the long corridor.

"You know, I really hate it when you're right."

There, coming down the corridor were at least fifteen grown-ass men with cameras.

Chapter 12

"Spencer, I can't be late again," I said, pathetically. He was lying on top of me, kissing up and down neck. "Spencer please, I'm already on probation for being late."

I had managed to get myself on probation the first three weeks of work, and it was all Spencer's fault. The first time I was late, he wouldn't let me get out of the car, the second time, he held me captive on the kitchen table. The third time, he told me he was taking me to lunch and we somehow ended up in a hotel room. Other than him making me late for work, things were great.

Thirty minutes. I had thirty minutes to get my ass in gear if I wanted to make it in on time. I tried my best to wiggle free and push him off of me.

"Spencer, I'm not playing around anymore. If you don't get off me right now, I'm going to—to—Oh, God!" I yelled as I gripped the pillow to my left.

As he came up from under the covers, I was greeted by his devilish smile. "What were you saying? I missed that last part," he asked from hooded eyes.

I hit his shoulders and managed to push him off of me. I jumped out of the bed, grabbed a loose cover, wrapped it around my body, and backed away from the bed. I made sure to walk backward so I could keep an eye on him.

"I said, I have to get ready to leave. You know I can't be late again."

"But I wasn't finished."

His cocky grin made my knees buckle a little. Luckily, I was at the door to the bathroom. "You can finish all you want tonight, playboy." I winked at him before stepping in the bathroom and locking the door behind me so I could get ready.

Six minutes, I can do this! I was running up the stairs two at a time. I'd rushed through the back entrance of the library and was racing down the hall. I took the corner hard, almost falling on my ass as my dress shoes slipped on the slick tile floor. I ran right in to the locker room and threw my bag in my locker. Next, I ran to the time clock. *Shit,* standing at the time clock was Carmen, my supervisor.

"Elizabeth, you just made it," she said, looking up at the clock.

"I'm so sorry." I chewed on the inside of my cheek nervously.

"I can't keep turning a blind eye. There are hundreds of other people who wanted this position. If you're not ready or uninterested, then we can always let you go and give it to someone else," she threatened.

"I know, Carmen, I'll do better."

I moved to walk around her, but she stopped me by placing a hand on my shoulder. "Another thing, Elizabeth. The department and building managers are concerned about all the traffic that's coming through. We're a library, not a night club."

What did she want me to do about that? I couldn't make those people go away. I'd tried, and it only made things worse. "Carmen, I can't make those people leave," I said, turning back to her.

"We know that, but we *can* make you."

I stood there, boiling on the inside, as she patted my shoulder like a child. This was my dream, to be here working and learning everything that I could. It took all I had not to say something back to her but I held it in and kept my cool.

"Well, get to work, don't just stand there," she said, shooing me off.

I was at a loss for words. Well, that wasn't technically true. I had a lot of words. I just didn't want to get fired for saying them. I smiled the fakest smile I could before I turned and went off to paper-cut hell.

Hunkering down at my desk, I started the task of entering data into the computer. I'd swear they had me doing all the brunt work. Then again, I guess that was what happened where you were at the bottom of the food chain and not on the payroll. Twelve-thirty finally hit and, to be honest, I thought lunch would never get here. I needed to get out of the building before I ran into Carmen and said something that I'd most likely regret.

I grabbed my bag and snuck out the back. I wanted to call Spencer and tell him everything but that would only lead to more problems. When I had let him know all the issues that I was having with Carmen, he flipped out. He tried to convince me to let him talk to her, like that would do any good. I wanted to confide in him, but he would just take it one step too far. I just wanted him to listen and agree with me, but I knew that was never going to happen.

I walked to a small café and got a sandwich. Sitting at one of the tables, I settled in and tried to enjoy my hour break.

Looking up from my phone, I watched a man walk inside the café. I'd have known that frame anywhere. It was Simon. My heart sank in my chest. He stood in the middle of the café for a moment then turned right to me. Part of me wanted to get up and run, but the other wanted to stay and see what he had to say for himself.

"Hey," he said, walking up to my table.

"Hi, Simon."

He looked around the café then back at me. "Can I join you?"

"I—umm—oh—whatever, have a seat," I said, gesturing to the seat across from me.

Spencer was going to kill me if he found out, but I couldn't keep on avoiding this. I had questions, and I wanted to close that chapter of my life.

Sitting down, he leaned back in the booth and examined me. "How are you?" he asked, placing his hands in his lap.

"I'm—I'm good."

Cocking his head, he gave me a skeptical look. "That's good. I'm sorry for surprising you like this, but I needed to talk to you. I need to get some things off my chest."

I simply nodded. I needed to hear it all, from the beginning.

"First thing I want to say is that I'm sorry—" He messed with the table, and his breathing was all uneven. "Okay—man, this is harder than I thought it was going to be," he said, adjusting himself in the seat again.

"Simon, just start at the beginning. I'd like to know everything." Catching his eyes, I saw the fear in them. Maybe I said it a little too harshly.

"Well, first off, my name's not Simon, It's Nick."

Holy hell, maybe I don't *need to hear all of this.* It hit me then as he sat across from me that I had been in love with a complete stranger all along.

"My name's Nick Holsen. I'm twenty-seven, like I told you. I did grow up in California. My parents disowned me, and that's how I got involved with Fame. I needed money, and they paid really well. Other than my job, everything I told you was true," he said, leaning over the small table.

"No, no it's not. You lied to me. You're name isn't even Simon. You used me, for what? Money?" I asked. I was getting more and more upset with every word that came out of his mouth.

"Elizabeth, it's not like that."

"Yes, Nick, I think it is." I should have gotten up or walked away, left him, and never looked back, but I held my ground, sat there, and tortured myself.

"All right, fine. I *was* using you—in the beginning. That first night at Mood—yes, I blatantly used you to get to Spencer. I saw the way he was acting toward you, and I took advantage."

"Jesus, Sim—I mean, Nick. How many times have you done this to people. How can you live with yourself?"

"Look, I'm not proud of my past. I had to do what I did to get by, but I never let my feelings get involved. That is until you came along. Elizabeth, you changed me. After that first day we spent at the café talking, I knew this was different, you were different. You didn't make it easy for me at all, and I really liked that about you.

"That first date, I told my boss that I didn't want to do it, that it felt wrong. I should have walked away, then and there, but I didn't. The more time I spent with you the deeper my feelings grew.

"Soon my boss found out and used it against me. She was blackmailing me. If I didn't get the info and pictures she desired, then she was going to tell you exactly who I was. I tried so many times to tell you, but I was sacred you'd leave, and I didn't want to ruin what we had."

"What we had? What we had was fake! It wasn't real," I clarified for him.

"Yes, it was real. Don't sit there and tell me you felt nothing. The only thing that changed is my name and my job, everything else is the same." He seemed desperate for me to understand, and to forgive him. He reached across the table and held my hand. "Elizabeth, please believe me. I might have been portrayed as the bad guy, but I'm not. I'm in love with you, the kind of love that doesn't go away."

Taking my hand from his, I placed it safely on my own lap. That simple act of him touching my hand brought back a flood of memories.

Sadly I knew how he felt. I still cared about him. I thought back to all the fun times we had, how easy going our lives had been that last month and the first. It was simple back then, now it wasn't. He had a hand in changing my life. I never wanted to be like my brothers and be in the spotlight, but there I was, the talk of the town, the latest "it" girl. Just when I thought that they were going to leave me alone, something always happened, and I was being thrown right back into it.

"Si—Nick, ugh, sorry it's going to take a few to get that right," I said snidely. I studied his face. Nick. I kind of saw it now. He did resemble a Nick more than Simon, the longer I stared at him. He was still well built, his shoulders broad. The long dark stubble on his face told me he was stressed and preoccupied. He'd always been so clean shaven before. It was a new look for him, and it suited him better, gave him a more rustic, harder look. The hair that I used to love running my fingers through was growing back. Although he kept it very short on the sides the top was longer and brushed back off his face.

There was a different-named person sitting across

from me, but every time he spoke and every time my eyes were drawn to his, he was the Simon that I fell in love with, the Simon that I kept coming back to. With almost a month between us, I still had a soft spot for him. I still sometimes wanted it all to be a dream. The back and forth between Spencer and Simon, the media, the fact that my life was upside down and from the outside didn't resemble who I was at all. I wasn't a socialite. I wasn't a supermodel.

But the fact was it did happen. Simon wasn't Simon. Spencer did love me, and the media was everywhere, whether I liked it or not. I was done being mad and sorry for myself. The best way that I knew to start anew, was to become a person I could be proud of. I had to hold my head up, accept my fate, and forgive those who had hurt me.

I glanced up at and saw Nick, not Simon. Simon was gone, but Nick was here on his behalf. "I accept your apology."

His eyes sparkled as he smiled across the table at me. "Thank you, Elizabeth, you have no clue what that means to me."

"You do understand that I'm with Spencer now, right?" I asked.

"Elizabeth, I don't think—"

"Nick, I'm with Spencer," I said as sternly as I could.

"He's not—you need to stay away from him." The sternness in his voice reminded me of how Teddy talked to me when he was trying to keep me away from Spencer, or anything bad, for that matter.

"Why?" I snapped back. I was so tired of people telling me who to be with and what to do. "If you want me to stay away from him so badly, please enlighten me."

"*Why*? I want you to stay away from him because I don't want to see you get hurt!" Nick spat back.

"Not good enough. You hurt me. Should I stay away from you too? Should I be screaming at the top of my lungs right now and running for a nunnery?"

I was dead serious. I was a few choice words and actions away from giving up on everyone and running for a freaking hilltop nunnery. No boy trouble there, if I'm not allowed to sleep with any!

"He almost beat a man to death!" Nick shot back in a whisper across the table.

The words took a moment to sink in. *Beat a man to death?* I searched Nick's face for any signs of joking, but there were none. I knew Spencer had a temper, I'd seen it firsthand, but his record was clean. Teddy couldn't find anything on him.

"This is really sad, Nick. I'm not going to sit here and listen to lies."

I stood from the table, grabbing my jacket that lay over the back of the booth. I slipped my arms through the sleeves and, as I was about to zip it up, Nick stood.

His hand wrapped around my wrist, stopping me from zipping my jacked up all the way. I should have snatched it away, but, as always, his touch had a calming effect on me. His eyes urged me to sit back down and, as if by telekinetic powers, I slumped back down in the booth.

"You know I'm not lying, that's why you haven't left."

"I don't believe you," I hissed back.

"Would you believe me if I told you I saw him in his hometown, trying to frighten a poor girl into keeping her mouth shut?"

"When?" I demanded. I wanted him to say the wrong date, but he didn't.

"Three weeks ago," he said, knowing that I knew he wasn't lying. "I've been trying to call you. I've been doing my damnedest to get you alone, and I swore to myself that when I did, I'd tell you everything, and that includes what I found out about Spencer."

"So he got into a fight, big deal," I said, trying to brush it off.

But as much as I tried to tell my head otherwise, my mind was racing back and forth, fighting with itself. I knew he went to his hometown to deal with something from his past, something that could hurt him, me, us. I just didn't want to believe it.

"I was sent there to—"

I held my hand up. "Wait a fucking minute! You were sent there? You're still working for Fame?" I was shocked. After all, the shit that had happened, he was still working for the enemy.

"No—listen, I'm just trying to prove that Salvatore is a fake, abusive man who shouldn't be trusted. You shouldn't trust him!" Nick went on raving about how bad Spencer was, but all I heard was that he was still working for Fame.

"Seems like I can't trust anyone these days." I stood from the table, disgusted by everything. "Goodbye, Nick."

I grabbed my bag and headed for the door. I stood on the side walk drinking in the warmth of the sun through the brisk cool air. Hearing the door behind me close, I turned to see Nick standing behind me, his hands by his side, his eyes begged for me to stay and not run.

"I'm not lying, Elizabeth. Ask him yourself. See what he tells you, then you can make your own judgment. It's going to come to light. The world will know what he's done. Do you want to be by his side when they do?" he threatened me.

I took an aggressive step toward him, getting up in his face. I was tired of being pushed around and taken advantage of.

"What would you have me do, Nick, run from his arms and into yours?"

"I didn't say that. I know you like your privacy, and you're never going to get it if you're with him. Just remember that I warned you. I promised you that I'd be there for you when he fucks it all up. You need me, you find me," he said, holding out a piece of paper between our bodies.

I looked down at it in disgust.

Click.

Click. Flashes of light went off at the corner of my eye. I turned to them, and that's when Nick moved closer, whispering in my ear.

"Take it, don't take it. I love you, Elizabeth, and I won't stop. I'll be there for you when you need me, because you will need me."

His warm breath circled my ear, taking the cold February chill and turning it into a warm tropical heat around my face. I moved toward it and found myself face to face with him. The warm caring brown eyes I'd come to rely on were fixed on me.

"I'll see you around," he said softly before kissing my cheek and turning to leave.

Just like that, the cold February air chilled me to the bone as flashes of light went off in every direction. I came out of it and saw the swarm of people with cameras. I pushed past them, and jumped into a cab that had been waiting by the curb.

"Drive," I lashed at the cabbie.

I must have taken him off guard. He put the car in drive and zoomed away from the curb. "Where am I going?" he asked.

"Salvatore's," I said through a clenched jaw.

Chapter 13

Nickolas

I had said my peace. I'd told her everything, and it was up to her whether she wanted to believe me or not. The moment my lips got to touch that soft skin upon her cheek, I wanted them to linger there. I wanted to move an inch over and feel her lips against mine. Instead, I walked away from her. I left her standing there, cameras and eager men only looking for their next big photo break. I handed it to them on silver platter. I should have just left her, but I would have always regretted it if I'd walked away and never, at the very least, kissed her cheek. I strode off down the sidewalk. Pulling my phone out, I made one final call. Comfortably sitting in the back of the car that had been waiting for me, I let the driver know to take me to the airport.

"Nickolas my love!" Natasha sing-songed from the other end.

"It's done. You can do whatever you want with the information," I said flatly.

"Oh dear, I guess it didn't go as you planned did it?" Natasha asked.

"I expect to see my money in my account in the next hour." I was done playing around, and I was definitely done being Natasha's errand boy.

"I still think you're a fool for leaving me."

"Maybe I am, but at least I'll be able to sleep at night. What about you, still having nightmares?"

Natasha had let it slip long before all the Salvatore/Beth stuff happened that she had a disturbing upbringing. I never asked, she never told me more than that. But I could tell when things got to her, when her past crept back into her present, and it seemed it all started with Salvatore. I had no clue what tied the two of them together, but I sure as hell knew you didn't want to mess with Natasha.

"Don't push your luck, Nickolas, I made you and I sure as hell can destroy you," she threatened.

"Calm down, don't get your panties in a twist."

"Oh, you'd like that, wouldn't you?" Natasha had a way of switching from bitch, to normal, to psycho in seconds. Another thing to add to the list of shit I wasn't going to miss about working for Natasha.

"I'm not even going there with you. Do you want anything else, Natasha, my soul, my first born, a kidney maybe?"

"Your money is being transferred as we speak, so don't worry your sweet little ass off. Where are you headed anyway, Nicky? Somewhere far away from our wicked, two-timing, little vixen I'm sure. Oh, maybe I shouldn't say little. I still don't get the draw to her. She's plane Jane and what, a plus-sized-want-to-be model now? Oh, I'm sorry, she's a boring librarian, right?"

I took a deep breath before I spoke. I wanted to tell Natasha to fuck off, but I didn't trust her. I needed the money that was supposedly in route to my account. Without it, I wasn't going to be able to get my gallery up and running as fast as I would have liked. Rent wasn't cheap in New York, and that check was going to supply me with enough money to solely work on my craft for as long as I wanted to. I might not have been a billionaire bachelor like Salvatore, but I was set up to live comfortably from there on out.

"You'll never know, Natasha, because you promised to stay away from her, remember? Did you ever think that people like her because she's real and not fake, like most of the celebrities out there?"

"Oh you're so funny, Nickolas," she cackled from the other end. It sent shivers down my spine and a loud thump against my chest. "You honestly think I'm just going to walk away from the whole situation? Darling, she's quite possibly the biggest news story out there, in more ways than one."

"You promised!" I yelled into the phone. "You promised me you'd leave her out of it if I did you this one last thing to bring Salvatore down."

"I lied," she said, as if it was clear all along and I should have known from the beginning.

"Natasha, what is your deal with Salvatore? You've turned into an even nastier, heartless, bitch than usual. What the hell did he ever do to you?"

"Nicky baby, if I told you, I'd ruin the big finale, now wouldn't I?" she said with an eerie tone to her voice.

She was officially off her meds. "Tell me what's going on." I waited but only heard silence on the other end. "Natasha! Tell me what you're going to do!" I insisted again.

"Oh, I'm sorry. You don't work for me anymore so it looks like you're just going to have to wait, like the rest of the world." There was silence followed by her cackling laugh. "Okay, fine, I'll give you a bit of a sneak peek. You see, after I let it be known that he's got quite a temper, and that his daddy covered a lot of things up, I plan on going after the one thing he cares the most about—you guessed it, your precious, plus-sized vixen. Which, by the way, I have you to thank for. I wouldn't have even had the idea to go after her, if it weren't for you—"

"You stay away from her, Natasha!"

"Sorry, I can't. She's just everywhere, like on my screen right now. Oh, and look, you're on there too! Kissing her cheek? Oh, the jealous, violent boyfriend is going to love seeing that."

She was wicked. There wasn't a better word than wicked to describe her.

"I swear to god—"

"What, Nickolas? What are *you* going to do stop me? You can't. You can't do a damn thing, and you'd be smart to remember that," she hissed.

"Don't do this."

"Too late." I heard a click of keys coming from the computer I knew was in front of her. "It's out in that glorious cyber world, and there ain't a damn thing you can do about it. Goodbye, Nickolas, it really was a pleasure doing business with you."

Click."

"Natasha—Natasha!" I yelled into the phone.

It was dead on the other end and, if I knew Natasha, she'd already had the number changed. I had no way of getting in contact with her unless I went all the way to LA and stormed into her office, but I even had a feeling that she might have moved that too. I had one number to call her on and that was her home number. She didn't know that I had it, and I didn't want to give that one piece of information to her just yet. She was known for her secrecy. No one knew who ran Fame, and no one dared to betray Natasha. And that included me.

I didn't like it but there was nothing I could do to stop

her. I told Elizabeth everything that I knew, I warned her about Spencer, I came clean to everything and she still walked away and back to his side. Did I hope that he'd get upset about seeing a photo of her with me? Hell yes! But on the flip side to that, I was worried about Salvatore's temper and Natasha's unyielding need to make Salvatore pay for some act that I had no clue about.

Chapter 14

Elizabeth

I slammed the door to the cab after tossing some money in the front. I stormed into 21, knowing Spencer was there. I strode past the bar where one of the head bartenders was training someone.

"Hey, Beth," Taylor called as I walked by.

I changed my course and headed for the bar, instead. Clutching the counter, I glanced around. "Salvatore here?" I asked.

"Yeah, he's been up in the office all day. You want me to call him and tell him you're here?" Taylor asked.

"Nope, but I will take a shot of whatever you're making there," I said, pointing to the many bottles on bar.

"Sure, no problem."

He had the new guy test out his skills on me. The amount of alcohol that the new guy used made more than one shot, so I took all three of them.

"Thank you for the courage," I said, before tipping my invisible hat and heading toward the stairs that would lead me to Spencer's office.

The three drinks had warmed my insides and given me

the added courage for what I was about to do next. I grabbed the handle of the door and threw it open. It crashed the wall behind it, the noise echoing throughout the office.

Spencer's chair hit the back wall as he stood abruptly. "Jesus Christ, Elizabeth! What the hell's going on?" he asked, placing his hands on his hips.

He was in a white button down shirt, the sleeves rolled up to his elbows. A black and gray tie was loosed around his neck and the top button that should have rested perfectly against his Adams-apple was undone. His dark gray dress pants hugged his thick hips, and the black leather belt shimmered from the light bouncing off it.

I lingered in the door way a moment more, drinking in his good looks, because I had a feeling that after the chat that I was going to have with him, we weren't going to be on the best of terms. I wanted to remember him just like this, sexy, a cocky smile, and all mine.

"Elizabeth," he called again, taking me from a delicious fantasy that involved me bent over the desk, screaming his name in delight.

"You need to tell me everything that happened—now," I demanded.

"What are you talking about? Tell you what?" he asked, standing there all sexy and oblivious.

"I just had a conversation with—" I stopped there, catching myself from saying Simon—Nick—whatever his name was that particular day. "You need to tell me what happened when you were in Vegas 'taking care of things.'" I air quoted while stepping into the room. The door closed behind me with a bang. I waited and watched as his demeanor changed. The smile on his face fell and his body stiffened up.

"Who did you talk to?" he asked, fixing his sleeves.

"Doesn't matter. What happened in Vegas, Spencer?

What were you trying to cover up?" I demanded again.

"I told you—" He paused as the phone on his desk rang. He looked up at me from the phone. His sea blue eyes were clear but unreadable. "Hello," he answered, never taking his eyes off of me. "I got it," he said, glancing down at his computer screen for a split second. He hung up the phone then rubbed his temples with his fingertips. His eyes closed and he exhaled a sigh.

He then turned his lap top around, and there on the screen was an image of me and Nick, leaving the café. Nicks lips barely touched the corner of mine. I stared at the picture and, as I did, I felt the warmth of Nick's lips on me, as if I was still standing in the cold, February air. The only problem was it wasn't the warm breath of the deceiver Nick. It was embarrassment and nervousness that kept my cheek flush.

"You were with him," Spencer roared, slamming his lap top closed so harshly it bounced on the table.

I jumped at the noise. "Don't turn this around on me," I shouted back.

It was official—our honeymoon period was over. Gone were the looks of desire and sweet-nothing talk. We were back to fighting, yelling, arguing.

He shoved his hands through his hair. "What did he tell you?"

"He told me to talk to you—so start talking, Salvatore."

"You realize he's a parasite. He's using you like he's been doing since the beginning."

"And what are you doing? Are you using me? Don't think I haven't noticed the amount of attention we're getting. It's kind of hard not to. I'm sure it's not hurting any of your businesses. Are you just stringing me along to keep up appearances? What would the public think if they knew you threatened someone to keep one of your

hundreds of secrets? You sure as hell don't tell me anything." I threw my hands in air, all dramatically. "What,
do you not trust me? Or am I right in thinking I'm just a
publicity stunt? I mean let's be totally honest here.
Someone like you would never be caught dead with
someone like me unless they benefitted financially from
it."

I was beyond pissed. I was ranting and raving about
everything that had ever crossed my mind about why
Spencer was interested in me. It would hurt like a bitch to
know it was all a lie.

But I got over Nick, and I was sure I'd be able to get
over Spencer, if that was the case.

"You don't tell me anything!" I yelled in frustration.
"We've been together for over a month now and I still
don't know anything new about you? Why are you keeping so many secrets from me?"

He just stood there, his hands shoved into his pockets.
I wanted to run over to him and slap him. I wanted to
shake him. I wanted him to tell me I was wrong, that I
was over reacting, but he didn't. He just stood there.

"I'm not going to let you use me," I said quietly.

"I'm not using you, Elizabeth. I've never used you to
benefit my businesses. My personal life, yes, I've used
you. I used you to clear my head, to reward myself, even
though I don't deserve you."

"Then tell me what happened in Vegas," I begged,
walking over to the desk he was standing behind.

He shook his head and clenched his jaw tightly. "I
don't want to tell you, because I don't want to lose you,"
he said, sitting back down in his chair.

"You're going to lose me if you don't start talking,
Spencer. You promised me no secrets, no lies."

"Fine!" he growled from the desk. "I'll tell you about
Vegas."

I stood behind one of the large chairs in front of his desk waiting to hear the worst.

"I wasn't patient then," he began.

I rolled my eyes at that. He wasn't patient now either—jumping to conclusions and freaking out over small stuff.

"I've learned to control things. I've learned how to handle my temper."

Again I rolled my eyes.

"Elizabeth, stop rolling your eyes. I know that you and I have had our differences and our share of arguments, but it was only because I've worked every day at controlling myself."

I immediately thought back to what Teddy use to say when he tried to get me away from Spencer. If he was worse in the past and learned to control his temper, I'd have hated to be the one on the other side of Spencer Salvatore in the past.

"When I was a teenager, I fell in love." He began to walk around the desk as he continued to speak.

I'd never felt threatened by Spencer and that included this conversation. He could be intimidating, with his dark hair, sea-blue eyes, and large stature, but I was never afraid.

"I loved her with all my heart, and maybe that was my problem. I was young and thought the world revolved around her. You remember when I told you I gave my family a run for their money when I was younger?" he asked.

I thought back to our brief conversation about his past outside of my building, months and months ago. It was one of the few things I knew about Spencer, other than him telling me he was born in New York. Besides those two facts, all that I knew about him was also public knowledge. That wasn't totally true. I mean I did *know* him. I knew how he liked his coffee and I knew what kind of music he liked to listen to while working out in the mornings and relaxing in the evenings. I knew the small stuff, like what kind of deodorant he used and what brand of toilet paper he preferred to wipe that fine ass of his with.

But I wanted more. I wanted to know what he was like as a child, where he came from, what made Spencer, Spencer.

I nodded for him to go on. "I'm listening."

"I was a hot head, got into fights easily. My girlfriend wasn't as in love with me as I was in love with her. I caught her in bed with someone else at a party for our high school graduation."

It felt weird hearing him tell me about a past love. But I listened and felt the pain right along with him. I'd been cheated on, lead on, used. It wasn't a good feeling back then and having been on the other side of it as an adult, it sucked even more.

"What did you do?" I asked, expecting to hear the worst.

"I pulled him off of her and almost killed him. I lost my temper with the girl I was in love with. I was betrayed, hurt, and angry. I shoved her and hurt her," he said with a straight face.

I felt my mouth go slack. I'd expected him to beat the guy, but to hear that he almost beat him to within inches of his life, and that he hurt a girl—I didn't know how to react.

"Nick, as he likes to be called now, is trying to sell the information to Fame. I went to Vegas to stop him," Spencer said, leaning against this desk in front of me. He sat there as if it was common to cover such things up.

"So no one knows about this?" I asked. "What happened to the guy and the girl?"

He shrugged. "My father paid for their silence, and now I am as well."

At first I wanted to punch him for paying someone off. Then I felt bad for him—this supposed love broke him to the point he pushed people away, he pushed me away. My next thought was one of panic. Nick had succeeded in finding everything out. It was only a matter of days, hours, until Fame was going to report on it. And there was no amount of money to pay Nick off. He had nothing to lose.

"They know," I said, staring up at him.

"What do you mean?" he asked.

"Nick, he knows everything. He told me Fame's going to put it out there. He warned me to stay away from you, that shit was going to go from zero to sixty." I covered my mouth and for once thought about myself and the media storm that seemed to follow me around. I checked my phone for the first time since I'd left the café—one new voice mail.

I was supposed to be back at work. It was three-thirty and I was supposed to work till three. *This isn't happening. This can't be happening. I've worked too hard to lose everything now.* I stood abruptly. Spencer stood with me, watching me freak out.

"I have to go, I have to leave," I rambled. Grabbing my jacket, I pulled it on along with my bag. I turned from Spencer, not giving him a second glance.

"Where are you going?" he asked, reaching for my arm and successfully grabbing it so I was forced to stop and turn around.

"Let me go, Spencer, I'm late. I need to get back to work." I ripped my arm from his hand and went to the door.

"Elizabeth," he roared from behind me. I turned to him, giving in to his booming voice, and raised my eye brows, indicating for him to go on. "I'll see you at my place, five o'clock," he asked—demanded.

I stood there a moment, letting him sweat it out, then finally nodded and threw a "Yeah" back at him before I walked out of the room and down the hall.

Chapter 15

It was six by the time I finally made it to Spencer's. I ran in the back door, avoiding the media storm out front.

"You're late," Spencer said from the kitchen.

He was cooking, and something smelled amazing. The garlic hit me even more as I came around the corner. Italian food. I should have guessed. His adopted family was Italian. They looked just like him with their tan olive skin, dark jet black hair, and light eyes. I'd only ever seen a picture of them, but it was hard to tell he wasn't one of them if you didn't know.

The heritage ran deep in his veins, and I was the only one that benefited. His cooking was amazing. Although I'd never let him know that, didn't want that head of his getting any larger. I also benefitted in the fact that I was the only person that got to see him cooking in nothing but a pair of sweat pants that hung perfectly on his hips. Goddamn he was sexy—*No, Beth! You're mad at him, you are mad at him...*

"Why are you so late?" he asked, turning from the stove to find me standing on the other side of the large island.

"I had stuff to do," I responded with an attitude, because I had a right to have one. I ran from 21, jumped in the first cab I could, then made the poor cab driver run through a red light, and almost knocked over a lady to get back to my internship as fast as I could. It was pointless though. Carmen was standing in my path to the back door.

"Don't bother," were the only two words she said before, "your stuff is all here." She pointed to the bag at her feet. "Don't come back tomorrow. We've already contacted your school, so you might want to touch bases with them. Have a nice life. I hope he was worth it all," she said, holding her hand out.

She was waiting for me to place my badge in her hand, and it killed me. It was like ripping my own heart out and handing it to her.

I grabbed my bag after she went back into the building. The thick metal door slammed shut behind her, making me jump. I had lost everything I had worked for my whole college career. Without my internship, I had nothing. My future plans to work there had been pulled out from under me. My degree was likely not going to happen, because I'd refused to intern anywhere else.

All of this happened because I wasn't focused. I had always been so focused before. All it took was one night at a club that I should never have gone to in the first place. There wouldn't have been notes and flowers, lies, or paparazzi. *My god!* My life would have been so different, if I hadn't gone to that damn club. Everything I had worked for was ruined.

So as I stood across the room from a disappointed Spencer, it was taking everything in me not to pick up the apples in the bowl in front of me and chuck them at him for ruining everything I had worked for. I didn't want fame, or to be recognized. I wanted a quiet life. I wanted to work at the Library of Congress. I wanted to go home to a cute house and spend my time reading and hanging out with friends. I didn't know what I was going to do, but I was going to start by yelling at the main culprit!

"Like what?" he asked, licking the wooden spoon that was covered with gravy, or for everyone who isn't Italian, sauce.

"Oh—do you want to know what I did before or after I had to go and withdraw from school."

"What? Why would you withdraw from school?" he asked, as if he somehow forgot I wasn't already on probation and was late getting back to my internship today because of him. I rolled my eyes and slapped my hands on the granite counter top in a huff.

"Use that beautiful head of yours to think about that again, Spencer. Why would I have to withdraw from school?" I asked him.

I narrowed my eyes on his. I had to ignore the sexy body that now rested against the counter top. His arms crossed over his chest, making his muscles bulge. I didn't want to, but I watched as the size of him widened even more as he took in a deep breath. *Focus, Beth! That sexy, mound of muscles just lost you your dream job!*

"You're blaming this on me?" he asked, pointing the wooden spoon at himself.

"You're damn right I'm blaming this on you!"

"Would you like me to call them?" he asked.

Is he kidding me right now? Call them? Like I'm a little kid, and he's calling to tell them I deserve to be excused for my absence?

"Wrong thing to say, Salvatore."

"Why is it wrong? I'll talk to them, and you'll have your internship back and be re-enrolled in school within the hour."

He grabbed for his phone that was sitting on the island

in front of me. I reached across the island, or more appropriately belly flopped on it, and snatched his phone before he could take it.

"What makes you think you can fix any of this? You can't just wave your hand and have everything go back to normal—there is no normal with you," I ranted as I slid back off the counter and waved his phone in the air. I regretted it the minute it left my lips. I watched as my words hit him like a slap to the face. "You know what I mean," I said, trying to recover from my major flub.

He didn't say anything, just nodded and turned back to the stove to stir his gravy.

I found myself apologizing and trying anything I could to get him to turn around and speak to me—until I realized that I came here pissed off at him and he should have been the one apologizing to me, not the other way around.

Why did *I* feel bad? He was the one who screwed my career up!

"You done?" he asked when I had shut up. He was facing me again.

I rolled my eyes, crossed my arms, and popped my hip out. I didn't have to say anything. My stance did all the talking.

"Move to New York with me?" He'd done it again, that ask/demand way that he always spoke to me.

I felt my mouth hang open as my face scrunched up. "What?"

"You don't have anything to do here, you'll be alone—I don't want you alone, I want you by my side. I can't stay here any longer. I need to get back to New York. It's the hub of all my businesses, and I need to be there overseeing things. I was going to tell you tonight over dinner but now that you're free to leave, you're coming with me."

"You want me to move to New York with you?" I asked, using his phone to point to myself.

"Yes, tomorrow if possible."

My mouth fell a little bit wider. Soon it was going to be resting on the counter top, and I was going to need a spatula to peel it off.

"What would I do there? Where would I live—"

"With me. You'd live with me of course, you practically do now. I can find you a job—"

"No! You're not going to find me a job. I can find a job on my own." Sure, it would have been easy to take a job from him but this was me we were talking about—stubborn, feisty me. I was not going to take a hand out from anyone, especially my super-hot, super-rich, super-everything boyfriend.

"If that's what you want, fine but know I can pull a few strings and get you something at the library in New York, all you have to do is ask."

I was too pigheaded and stuck in my ways to accept any help, even if I needed it. I nodded anyway. "I'll be fine, thanks."

I fake-smiled at him and was shocked when he smiled back. Usually, a smart ass remark like that had me walking on eggshells with him, but he just smiled and shook his head.

"Now that that's all settled, I've been holding dinner over an hour, are you ready to eat?" he asked, talking over his shoulder as he added pasta to a pot of boiling water.

"I think I'm just going to have a salad."

His shoulders fell, and he turned back to me slowly. I assumed he was staring at me, but I wouldn't know because I was picking at the counter top.

"What's the matter now?" he asked.

I gave in and glanced up. Was I hungry? Yes. Did pasta sound amazing? Yes. But I had, in not so many words, just agreed to move to New York with him. The media was going to go haywire, not only from that but I knew that Nick had given all of his findings about Spencer to Fame, and it was only a matter of time before that got out as well.

I was going to be living under an even bigger microscope. People were going to be judging me on everything, and I didn't want my size or weight to give them any more ammunition than they already had. So how did I tell that to him? The man who always made me feel the right size, the perfect weight. There was no way that he was ever going to understand that.

"Nothing, I just want a salad."

"To start with?" he asked, confused by my request.

In the time that we had been together, I didn't change who I was, not in my stubbornness, my ramblings, or in my day to day, which included the way I ate. I loved food, but I never changed because I was with him and suddenly afraid of what he might say if I had dessert at the end of dinner or ate two rolls instead of just one. He made me feel comfortable, so it was a change for him to hear me just ask for a salad.

"No, just a salad for dinner," I answered.

"Are you sick?" he asked in all seriousness.

"No, I'm not sick. I just want to cut back on the carbs that's all."

There was a shield going up between us. The more I lied, the higher it went. But he lied and kept things from me all the time, about more serious things than my eating habits.

"Since when do you care about carbs?"

Is he kidding me right now?

"Are you trying to say something?" I only said that to make him feel bad and back off.

That backfired, of course. He placed his spoon down on a paper towel and walked away from the counter. He strode over to me, all Greek God like, just like he always did. His muscles flexed in his chest and arms as he stood in front of me. He smelled amazing, he looked amazing. He jumped up on the island counter and leaned over, resting his elbows on his thighs. He folded his hands but left his index fingers out. He placed them over his lips. A few strands of hair fell out of place as he studied me.

"What?" I asked.

"Get over here."

I took a hesitant step forward. He moved his elbows off his thighs as he reached for me. His hands gripped my waist and pulled me so I was standing between his legs.

"I know it's hard for you to believe this, but I don't care what your dress size is. What I do care about, is that you're happy. I understand you don't like the media. We've had many lengthy conversations about it, but it's part of my job, part of my life."

"That's not why—"

He cut me off by placing a singer finger over my lips. "It *is* why. I thought we weren't lying to each other anymore?"

Damn—

"You don't know what it's like—" I began to say, but he put his finger back over my lips.

"Yes, I do. Remember, they've been following me long before they even knew who you were. Why do you think I look like this?" he asked, gesturing down to his perfectly tanned muscles.

"Because you're trying to impress me?" I said, shrugging my shoulders.

He cracked a smile and shook his head. "I do this to make my business look good. I look good, the clubs look good, I get paid."

"You mean you don't get up at five in the morning to work out for me?" I said jokingly.

"Not a chance, baby. But I don't want you to have to worry about it. I want you to be happy. And I know what makes my woman happy." He winked.

"Oh and what's that?" I asked, leaning back from him.

"A plate full of my amazing spaghetti, which I slaved over all afternoon, that's what."

"This has been one hell of day. I get fired, drop out of school, I'm apparently moving to New York—tomorrow—and I get to end it with your 'amazing spaghetti.'"

"No. You get to end the day with dessert."

"What's for desert? You?" I said it as a joke but the sexy stare I was getting was anything but a joke. "Can we skip the spaghetti and just have desert. I have a feeling it's going to be less carbs."

He reached around me, grabbing my ass, and pulled me till I was flush against him and the counter. Kissing me, he lifted his hand from my ass and held onto my neck. "You can have whatever you want."

Chapter 16

I had my dessert first that night. It was delicious and, as I suspected, no carbs. The next few days were a whirlwind of packing, getting depressed, getting excited, and getting depressed again. I had to tell my brothers I was moving in with Spencer, which of course went over like a fart in church. It brought on more arguments and another bought of depression, but they got over it. They couldn't change my mind and, after about two hours of them trying to talk me out of it, they finally gave up.

Gia was excited I was moving to New York, not so excited I was moving in with Spencer. She still blamed him for the whole Teddy fiasco. Overall, it was an emotional rollercoaster getting from DC to New York. But I made it, all size twelve of me.

I wasn't even fully unpacked before I was informed that I had to get dressed up for some restaurant opening that Spencer and I were to attend. Gone were the days I could just sit around in my PJs on a Friday night. I was expected to be seen with him in all public settings, but if I was being honest, I didn't mind it, as long as we were together. Plus, if I wasn't there, the media would have jump on my absence and come up with some wild story about why I wasn't with him.

I knew that moving with him—hell, being with him—was going to change my life. I wasn't use to having people bring me dresses and fix my hair and make-up. Actually, I didn't think anyone was, unless they were a movie star, and I was far from a movie star. Spencer had hired a whole team to make me camera ready, because he knew I hated it. It took the stress off of me, and I was grateful for that.

Since moving to New York with Spencer, things had been good. I didn't know how he did it but the information that was leaked about his past barely made a blip on the social media radar. The story broke on a Monday, and by Wednesday it was old news, thanks to the complete mental breakdown of some movie star.

Most of our evenings were spent between attending openings for night time hot spots, restaurant, and charity events. Now that the world knew Spencer had gone to my family's charity event, he was expected to attend every single one that he could.

He blamed this on me, of course.

"Why don't we just stay home? We don't have to go," I moaned from under the covers.

It was rainy and cold out, and I refused to get out of bed that day. It wasn't like I had to. I still didn't have a job or…well, *anything* going on. At that point in my life, I was strictly an accessory on Spencer's arm, which wasn't too bad, except on rainy, cold days when I didn't want to get out of bed.

"You got us into this, so you have to go," he said, drying his hair with a crisp white towel.

"How did I get us into this?" I asked, outraged that he would blame this on me. He was the celebrity, not me.

"If you wouldn't have been so damn cute in that elevator at your brothers office, I wouldn't have come to your little charity event—"

"Little? That hurts, Salvatore. That charity event is the talk of the town, I'll have you know!"

"Okay, I'll give you that. It was the talk of your little town."

I tossed a pillow at his head, but he caught it, totally defeating the purpose of me throwing it in the first place.

"Anyway…you were the sexiest, most intriguing woman I'd ever met, and that elevator ride gave me the push I needed to take the steps necessary to see you again. And for the record, no woman has ever mentioned a boyfriend in front of me to intentionally get me jealous."

I winked. "Well, there's a first time for everything."

I was beaming on the inside. This man had become my everything. It scared me to be so wrapped up in him, but I was having the time of my life. A different life—not the one I imagined a year ago, but equally wonderful. I'd navigated far away from the path that I always thought I was going to be on. I used to think that I'd be alone and become consumed in my job, friends, and probably the fifteen cats I was going to purchase, because I didn't want to be alone. Plus, what went better with being a librarian than cats?

The life I was living now was the dream. The if-I-could-choose-my-own-path-this-is-what-it-would-be life. It would be lying in bed with the man I loved on Sundays and going out and feeling like I was the prize to be won. I was getting so use to going out with him to all these different events. It didn't bother me anymore because, as long as he was by my side, I didn't have anything to worry about.

I was learning the ropes and, for the most part, I loved going to the charity events. I found myself going to luncheons and helping out special causes that were dear to my heart. I was using what little fame followed me to do good. I stepped up to be the role model I was afraid to be in the beginning. I was silly for ever thinking I wasn't capable of doing it. All I had to do was be me, and I could definitely do that.

"You didn't have to come," I said, sitting up on my elbows in bed.

"But I did. And now I can't say no to the..." He picked up the invitation that was on the dresser next to him and read. "The Association for solving homelessness for all animals of New York." He chuckled as he placed the pamphlet back down on the dresser.

All right, so maybe it was on me. If he gave to one charity and not another, he would get bad publicity and social media would have a field day. Every charity known to man had come out of the woodwork, begging for him to donate to their cause. Thankfully, he drew the line at the association of naked clowns. I wasn't sure I'd be able to attend that one, even if he donated to it. Better yet, I thought, I'd have to have a serious talk with him if he did.

He was mysterious, but I didn't think I could handle naked-clown Spencer.

"God forbid, we don't support the Teenage Mutant Ninja Turtles that live in the sewers of New York," I mocked.

Spencer's face lit up with a smile. "I think it's more for abandoned pets roaming the streets. But I'm not going to lie, I'd definitely support the TMNT if they had a charity event. I'd love to meet Raphael. He was always my favorite."

"He would be. Must be the whole temper control thing, right?"

"Um, no, it's because he has cool sias. They're the

best weapon. Are you trying to say something about my temper?"

I busted out laughing and fell back onto my pillow. "You're funny." *He's kidding, right? I hope he's kidding.* I felt his presence over top of me and, when I opened my eyes to see his non-smiling face, I thought, *Oh, shit, I just stepped on a landmine.* I readied myself for an argument.

"You think I have a temper?" he asked from above me.

"Umm…" I didn't know what to say. One, because I didn't know if he was being serious and two, because I didn't want to make things worse with my sarcasm.

His tongue darted out, wetting his lips before they curled up in a sexy smile. "I thought you liked my temper?"

I laughed. "It depends?"

"Hump." He sat back and tossed the covers off of me. Grabbing my legs, he spun me to the edge of the bed. I gripped the sheets beneath me as he traced his hand between my legs. The boy-short underwear I had on was removed.

I sucked in, lifted my hips, stretched my body, and prayed to the heavens above that I looked as good as I was imagining I did.

Mid-stretch I received a full on palm-to-ass smack on my right ass cheek. "Ouch!" I shifted away from his hand. "What the hell?"

I tried to sit up, but thought better of it because it was daylight, and I was naked under a freak of nature that only had a towel around his hips. I made the wrong choice of glancing down at his perfect twelve pack abs and swore to myself, in that moment, that I was going to exercise later.

"This is what you do to my temper," he said as the towel loosened from his hips and fell to the floor. He took himself in his hand and grazed against the inside of my thigh.

"You didn't have to smack me," I shouted.

He grabbed my hips and tugged me closer. "I did and you know why."

My legs wrapped around him, and he pounded into me. I sucked in as he hovered over top of me. Again, he smacked my ass. I gave an excited squeal. A bad habit I was still trying to break had me arching my back and, although he didn't stop moving over me, he smacked my ass again a little harder than before. This time, I lifted my head to look at him. He had this smug expression as he kept at it. I couldn't take the sexy smug look any longer or I might have exploded right there. My head fell back. I reached above me and grabbed the sheets. He smacked the side of my thigh as I sucked in again.

Then he just stopped, and I was reduced to begging when he pulled out. "All right! Okay, I'll stop!"

"See, I knew you liked my temper."

The confident bastard new me too well, another reason I was falling for him.

"What about all the homeless animals? We're going to be late if you keep smacking my ass like you've been doing," I asked, grinning up at him.

"Screw 'em! I'd rather screw you." He gripped my legs and continued on. We missed the event and ended up paying for it the next day. The media had a field day. He was ridiculed for not caring about animals. They even went as far as to say that he was for the killing of all strays.

Needless to say he spent the next week cleaning up the mess that we both made. From that event on, we didn't miss one.

ഗ്രരഗ

"I can't sit in here one more day," I huffed from the bed as Spencer got dressed.

"Are you ready for me to make a call?" he asked as he buttoned his shirt.

"No!"

He reached in his huge closet and grabbed a tie. "Then stop complaining. You've been here two whole months. That's plenty of time to get adjusted."

I fell back in bed, pulling the covers with me. "I'm not that desperate," I called from under the covers. I heard footsteps getting closer and the covers flew off of me. "Hey—"

"If you'd stop being so stubborn, you would be getting ready for work this morning too." Spencer kissed my forehead then tossed the covers back over my face. I sat up and threw a pillow at him.

I hate it when he's right.

I'd been staying in, reading a few books—*okay I read thirty-four books in one month.* I had a lot of time on my hands. I did go to visit Gia. We'd go to dinner once a week, but that was about it. She was swamped with her new life, and I didn't want to get in the way of it. There was a moment about two weeks in to my self-lock-up, that I thought about giving in and asking Spencer to get me a job. But the stubborn, pigheaded side of me won out again.

I found myself taking everything out on him. I'd complain about not being able to finish school, then I'd yell at him till I was in tears because I'd lost my dream job. But every time, he'd sit with me and take it. He'd take it all in silence—the ill wishes, the threats. And then he'd hold me till I calmed down.

We'd grown so much closer since we'd moved to New York—or maybe I had. I'd opened up to Spencer about any and everything. *Stop lying.* Okay I hadn't told him about my parents, not in depth at least. All he knew was that they died in a car accident when I was little. He didn't know any other details. That was all about to change, though.

It was their wedding anniversary the night that I decided to tell him everything. I was lonely and missing my family. Teddy was in LA, Gran was at the beach, and Charles was always jet-setting around.

Spencer and I were sitting on the couch. My feet were resting on his thighs. He was reading some papers for work as I watched my guilty pleasure TV.

I sat up, moving my feet from his lap, and turned the TV off. "Can we talk?"

He put his papers back in their manila folder and turned to face me. "Of course. But if you're going to start yelling at me at least let me get a drink first."

I hit his shoulder. "Not funny. I'm serious. I want to tell you a story of sorts."

"A story?"

"Yeah, I want to tell you about my parents."

He sat up a little straighter. I couldn't tell if he was eager to hear about my parents, or maybe he was expecting that I'd want to know about his family, his real family, in return.

"You've never talked about your parents before. What's bringing this on?" he asked in a business-like fashion.

"I just want to tell you about them. I miss them and I'm pissed off that they never got the chance to meet you or me. You know they died when I was only two—"

"I know. But why now?" His voice changed, his demeanor changed. He was on edge. The veins in his neck began to throb. If I had been a vampire, I could have easily gone for the jugular.

I sat on the edge of the couch and stared at him. "I told

you I miss them. I want to talk about them, remember them."

He raked his hand through his hair before holding his hand out between us and resting it on my knee. "I'm sorry. Tell me about them."

I took his hand in mine and studied him a moment. Just when I thought I had him figured out, he always surprised me.

"The earliest memory I have of them is watching them walk out the front door. It's one of those fuzzy memories where you can see outlines but not sharp details. I remember the color green. My mother was wearing a long green dress. I remember her turning back to me at the door and blowing me a kiss..." I drifted away into the memory, like I always did. It was the only thing I remembered about them.

"I remember my father was tall. Or maybe he just seemed tall because I was so young. Anyway, when he'd toss me in the air, I remember feeling like I was able to touch the sky. I'm sure you have a memory like that, too," I said, shrugging my shoulders.

In the months that I'd been with Spencer, I learned that his face couldn't lie to me and the night I asked him if he had a memory like the one I had of my father, his smile was a lie. It wasn't genuine. It was forced and uncomfortable.

"That's a beautiful memory, Elizabeth," he said, ignoring my rhetorical question.

I didn't mean to pry or to have him tell me anything about his past. It kind of just happened.

"Anyway," I said. "They were on their way to a charity event when it happened. Halloween was a few days away, so it was a costume party. Someone came across the median in traffic and ran into them head on. They never made it to the party."

I felt Spencer stiffen next to me.

"You said you were two correct?" he asked in a rush.

"Yeah, I was two, I'm sure what I'm remembering is from a picture or something. I know it's really crazy to think a two-year-old could remember anything, why do you ask?"

"Where were they going?" he asked—demanded.

"To some party. They were always going out, or so my brothers told me."

"Think, Elizabeth, where were they going, what direction?

"I—I don't know. I was two, Spencer. I didn't really have the four-one-one on them."

"Well, you need to think harder."

"Where is this coming from? I don't get it? Why is it so important to kn—"

"Just try to think, please. Where were they going? Into the city? Somewhere in the suburbs?"

He was acting crazy, like a crazy person had taken over his body and made him paranoid. I sat back and searched through all my memories of that night. I glanced at Spencer and watched as his eyes went wide. He must have thought I came up with something but honestly I couldn't come up with any other facts about that night.

"I'm sorry. I don't know." I said, shrugging my shoulders, nervous that this might make him fly off the rails.

"What about your brothers? They were older. They might know, right? Was it in the papers or covered in the news?"

"I guess…well, now that I think about it, I've never seen a newspaper clipping or anything like that."

Spencer was reaching for my phone that was sitting on the coffee table in front of us before I even finished talking. He shoved it into my hands and urged me to call one of my brothers.

"Why is this so important? Does it have something to do with—" Again, I was cut off.

"I need to know. I want to know all the details. It's important to you, so now it's important to me."

"That doesn't make any sense, Spencer." I dropped my shoulders and let my hands fall into my lap with the phone still in them. "I just wanted to tell you about who they were. It's not important to know every horrible detail about that night, that's not why I was telling you."

He leaned in and took my hands harshly in his. That crazed look was still in his eyes. "I understand that, but maybe I can help you get some closure. Maybe we can find the person responsible."

"That's pointless."

"Why—why is it pointless?"

"Because the person who hit them is dead. It was some crazy lady who was drunk or something. I don't know her story, but there's no point in blaming anyone if the sole person who caused the accident is dead, the same as my parents."

Spencer dropped my hand and sat back against the couch. He stared straight ahead and went into zombie mode. All I'd wanted to do was to tell him about how awesome they were. I didn't, in a million years, expect him to act like this.

He turned his head so fast I thought he was going to have whip lash. "Was there anyone else in the car with her?"

With my heart racing at his sudden movement and my eyes wide with shock, I knew for sure there was something else entirely going on. I sat there studying him, shaking my head to answer his question.

"Are you sure?"

"Spencer, you're really starting to scare me now. What is going on?"

"Nothing. Is there anything else you wanted to talk about? I have a ton of work I need to get through."

He reached for his manila folder and stood from the couch. I pulled my legs up and crossed them underneath me. I shook my head then grabbed the pillow next to me and placed it on my lap. Leaning over, he kissed the top of my head before turning tail and heading into his office.

I knew about his adoptive family and the problems that he had with his temper, but he still had yet to open up fully. We had come so far in such a short time. If we did argue, it was over petty things, things that, in the long run, didn't really matter. Maybe it had to do with me accepting who I was now that I was with him, or maybe it was him finally letting his wall down.

Since we had been living together, he was telling me stories about growing up with three younger sisters. He'd tell me about each of them and how, one day, he'd like me come and meet them. He told me how having them in his life helped him to move on. He was protective over them, and I wouldn't expect anything less. We would talk for hours about our childhoods, but he only talked about life after he was adopted, never before. I knew everything there was to know about Spencer Salvatore age eight to now. Well, I thought I did.

I guess I couldn't blame him. Where he refused to talk about a past he wished to forget, I'd kept mum about my parents because I thought that if I ever brought them up, he'd pull back from me, like he just did. Our parents weren't something either of us talked about. He referred to his adoptive parents as Ellen and James, never Mom and Dad. And I only spoke of Gran and my brothers.

I figured he was insecure about it. I had this image that maybe he was impoverished, possibly even lived on the streets.

The thought of Spencer as a small boy, cuddled in a

blanket, sitting outside of an abandoned building, shivering, was one of the many images I had of him.

I went to bed that night alone. On my way, I stopped by his office to see if he was coming to bed. He was on the phone when I walked in and, instead, of the usual smile that appeared on his face when I walked into a room, he averted his eyes and continued talking and writing something down.

I strode in and stood at his desk. He immediately turned a few papers over and closed a folder.

When he hung up the phone, he looked up at me. "Do you need something?" he asked.

It wasn't harsh or mean, but it was cold, and it made me feel unwanted.

"I'm just heading to bed. I wanted to say goodnight." I picked at his desk while I waited for a response. When the seconds turned into a minute, I cleared my throat. "Are we okay?"

He rubbed the scruff along his jaw line and suddenly came back from Crazy-Ville. He shook his head and looked up at me for the first time since I entered the room. The lips I loved kissing turned up and that megawatt smile lit me up like it always did.

"Of course, we're okay."

"You were acting a little weird. I just...I don't know what I thought."

"You don't have to think. I'm in this, you're in this. I just have a lot of work to get through. I'm sorry if I came across a little harsh." He was talking at me, like I was a business opportunity that he didn't want to lose.

"Does this have anything to do with earlier, my parents, maybe your past? I know that, that's crazy. You were...what?...eight, not like you knew them or anything. I just don't want to pressure you. I can be kind of a pressure cooker when I want to. Maybe I should look into being a reporter, I am pretty good at getting information out of people…well, everyone but you—"

"Elizabeth, you're rambling," Spencer said, cutting me off with a clip to his voice.

"Oh, right, I'm sorry if me talking about my parents brings up stuff about your own." I said it all sorts of sarcastically, because that's what I did when I went on the defense.

"It doesn't," he said ruthlessly.

"Okay, calm down. I won't talk about it anymore. Clearly, it's a sore subject." I turned from his desk and started walking to the door.

"Elizabeth, stop."

"Whatever, Spencer, I'm going to bed."

With that I left the room and slammed his office door behind me. Ooo, he could still make me so mad sometimes! I stormed down the hall toward the bedroom. I was two steps from entering when I heard his office door open and slam shut again. I was struck with the sight of him rushing toward me.

The closer he got, the more I backed away. I backed up until my back hit the wall behind me. I wasn't scared of him, just intimidated by his size and the energy he was putting off.

"Look what you do to me?" he said, when he got toe to toe with me.

His hands hit the wall beside my face. I didn't cower, I didn't flinch, I stood there and gave it right back to him.

"And what am I doing to you? Because I'm pretty sure I was only telling you about my parents, and I didn't expect it, but I thought maybe, just maybe, you would open up and give me just a sliver of information about yours."

"That's never going to fucking happen!"

"Why? What is so bad that you can't open up and tell me anything about your past? Look what it's doing to us.

Your past is tearing us apart. It's—never mind. I'm not going to fight with you about this," I said, holding my hands up in retreat.

"Good, because I don't want to fight with you either. My past is in the past, and that's where it's going to stay. Do you understand?"

"Yeah, I got it. Mr. Secret Mysterious Playboy is back."

"No, not a playboy. Your mystery man, maybe, but I'm far from a boy," he said, pushing up against me. His hard body was flush against my own cushiony one.

"I don't know. Sometime you act like a little boy not getting his way," I said matter-of-factly. I refused to look up at him, glanced sideways, and acted annoyed.

He hummed a deep throated response that just happened to tingle down my spine. I shivered as it made its way to the depths of me. The hand that was next to my face left the wall and snaked its way down between us before moving up the inside of my shirt. His thumb grazed my harden nipple, and I had to try with all my might to keep an agitated look on my face.

"Would a boy do this?" he said, grabbing hold and molding my breast to his hand.

I had to lick my lips to keep them from drying out, but I didn't lose my cool. I stared right into those sea blue eyes of his and shrugged. "It's happened before."

"I see, and what about this—" His hand moved from my breast down to the waistband of my sweat pants. Slipping his hand between the fabric and my skin, he cupped my bare core. *Shit, shit, shit, I can't do it.* I was always rendered useless when his hand was there.

"I think I'm the only one who can do this, and I know, for damn sure, no little boy has ever made it this slick."

I gulped, trying to wet my mouth so I could spit out a smart ass remark but, apparently, all my wetness was concentrated in one particular location, and it sure as hell wasn't in my mouth.

"Don't flatter yourself," I snipped back.

Two…hell, maybe it was three…fingers entered me. I gripped his shoulder for dear life and damned my hips for moving closer to his.

"I think I just did," he whispered in my ear.

Chapter 17

Nickolas

I have to move on. That was the one thought that I kept making myself say over and over again. I was living in New York with only days until my big gallery opening. I knew that Elizabeth was sometimes only a street away, but I made sure to keep my distance. I followed her in the media. It was easy because they hadn't eased up on her at all. If anything, it was worse than ever.

Every other day there would be a new story about them breaking up or him cheating on her for some model or pop star. Deep down, I prayed that it was true but I, of all people, knew how the media manipulated things to their advantage.

It was a random Thursday night. I was in the gallery, working on a few last minute things for the opening the next day. I was in the dark room messing around with a few different negatives when I heard the door at the front of the gallery slam shut. *I thought I locked it.* I put the negatives that were in my dish on the drying rack and headed out of the dark room.

I grabbed a towel on my way to wipe my hands of the

chemicals. As I came around the corner I saw a man looming near one of my pictures. It was a picture of Elizabeth. I'd blown it up, made it black and white. It was on a thick canvas hanging on the wall as soon as you walked in. It was my favorite picture of her. It was a little more than a head shot. She had her hand draped over her opposite shoulder covering her chest, her long hair was falling all around her, and her eyes were beckoning you to come closer.

I'd taken that picture on Christmas, in her closet. She was beautiful then and always would be. Her skin was soft and, even though she would hate that I thought this, I loved the way I could melt into her. She wasn't hard or breakable. She was like coming home to your comfy bed after sleeping on a rigid floor for years. I missed resting my head on her stomach and just lying there, feeling her breathe and hearing her heart beat within her chest. I couldn't let myself think like that anymore. I'd moved on, I'd even dated a little. I was going in the right direction with my life, and I couldn't keep looking back.

"Can I help you?" I asked the stranger standing in my closed gallery.

This guy really had some nerve. The figure turned to me, exposing his true identity. *Oh, shit*! It was Salvatore, and he looked pissed. Never in a million years did I expect it to be him. I gripped the towel at either end and pulled it tight, assuming I might have to use it as a weapon if he charged me.

"What are you doing here?" I asked, griping the towel a little tighter.

He stood for a moment then turned back to the picture of Elizabeth before glancing around at the other ones. He expensive shoes clicked and echoed in the large open room as he went from picture to picture of Elizabeth. Most of my gallery was of her, there were only a few with her face, the rest were close ups of different parts of her body. It could have been anyone if you'd never seen the curve of her back or the u shape of her side.

"You still love her?" he asked, turning back to me.

"I'm not falling for that, Salvatore. I also don't want another broken nose, so why don't you just leave? If you're here about the pictures, she already gave me permission, so I'm not taking them down." I stood my ground across from him.

"Do you still love her?" he asked again.

"I don't understand what you're asking. Do you want me to say no, because I hate to break it to you, I can't say that. I'm just trying to move on—What—what do you want from me?" I asked, pointing to myself.

If he wasn't here to bust my balls for having naked pictures of his girl up on my wall for the world to see, then I had no clue what he could possibly want with me.

"She really cared about you—I bet she could again," he said over his shoulder before turning to look at me. I was so lost. I narrowed my eyes on him and attempted to read him. He stood there like a statue, solid and well-dressed in his suit.

"As I'm sure you know in your line of work—" he started.

"Ex-line of work. I'm done with anything having to do with Fame. I paid my dues, and I'm free of them now."

"Like I was saying, I'm sure you know what demons can hide behind a handsome face and lots of money. You also know that if those demons get out, they can hurt the people you love—in my case, the only person I love."

"I don't know what you're asking me, but I'm not going back to Fame to cover your shit up."

"They're getting close to my secret, if not already on it," he said in an even, eerie tone.

"I'm sure the media will be on your side, just like they

were when they found out you almost beat a man to death. Even Elizabeth got over that. I still don't see what the world sees in you. All I see is a man trying his damnedest to keep the monster caged up. I can see it in your eyes. The need to yell and hurt people, must run in your blood." I said it only because he was pissing me off the longer he stood in my gallery.

"I need the name of your boss."

"I don't work there anymore. I told you that."

"Fine, you don't work there anymore. I still need their name."

"Can't do that."

"I think you can," he challenged.

"If I could, I just might, but I don't want to end up in a shallow ditch. Besides, once I left they changed everything. I have no way of contacting them and, even if I did, what makes you thi—"

"You can have her."

"What did you just say?" I took a step toward him and shook my head in disbelief because I was pretty sure I just heard him say, I could have her. "She's not a fucking toy you can pass back and forth when you're tired of her," I yelled at him.

He stormed toward me faster than I thought possible for someone of his size. I held my ground and, when he got in my face, I saw the monster behind his eyes rattling the cage. He turned red and the veins in his neck pulsated with anger. "Don't you think I fucking know that? I'm doing this for her, not you—not me, but for her."

"You've lost your fucking mind, dude. Back the hell up," I said, pushing right back.

I stood there eye to eye with him before he finally took a step back, shoved a hand in his hair, and turned away from me.

At first, I was confused then everything started making sense in my head. He had a past. I knew that. But there was one thing Natasha had told me, that at first I didn't believe but now—now that he was standing in front of me, telling me he had the worst kind of demons in his past, I believed her a little more.

I blurted it out the minute it crossed my mind. "You killed someone."

Salvatore spun around on his heels, one hand covering his mouth, the other firmly planted on his hip. His eyes widened. He dropped his hand from his face and pointed at me. "What did you say?"

I was torn between running for the door, punching him, or calling nine-one-one. To think Natasha was right was as bad as it got. He didn't officially say that he killed someone but the look on his face gave him away.

"Nothing," I replied. I wanted to know more, but I didn't want to end up on his hit list. Even if he hadn't killed someone, he'd done something horrible. I had to find out what it was and warn Elizabeth before something happened to her. "So what do you want from me? I can't give you what you're asking for, and Elizabeth won't talk to me, so I don't know what you're expecting me to do."

"After tonight, she'll talk to you. All I'm asking you to do is what you promised her, that you'd be there for her when I fucked up. She'll be at your gallery opening."

With that, he turned and walked out the door, not a glance or another word out of him.

What the hell is he going to do that's going to make her talk to me again? I didn't know and, right then, I didn't care because the more I saw of him, the more I realized that she was better off without him. Salvatore was a ticking time bomb, and the last thing I wanted was Elizabeth to be near him when he went off.

Chapter 18

Elizabeth

We'd had a run-of-the-mill fight. A misunderstanding. A hotheaded argument. It ended the way all our arguments ended, with me on my back and him over top of me, apologizing for acting like an ass, because he knew he was. Or me saying I was sorry for being stubborn and jumping to conclusions.

Unfortunately, this particular misunderstanding started a divide between us that I didn't think was possible. With every day that passed after I told him about my parents, he became more distant. Slowly at first. He'd stay in his office. The day trips for work were turning into two-and-three day trips, and, as the weeks went on, he just wasn't the same. He wasn't my Spencer.

I had no one to confide in. Gia was a car ride or phone call away, but I just couldn't let her know that maybe she was right. I was certainly not giving her that satisfaction. I'd never hear the end of it. I couldn't tell my brothers either—one, because they were both so busy with expanding their businesses, but two, because, I didn't want them to worry. I was an adult. I could handle this on my own. I didn't need my brothers coming to my rescue. So—I'd sit in Spencer's huge condo and sulk instead. I knew it wasn't very mature of me, but I couldn't seem to help it.

When Spencer was here, he was attentive to my "needs." He'd lay with me in bed at night, but when I woke up, he'd always be gone. I'd find him on the couch or sometimes in his office asleep at his desk. It had been three weeks since I'd seen his genuine megawatt smile. He was distant and pulling away from me.

As those weeks went on, he still gave no indication of why. So my mind went to that dark place. We were still attending our fair share of events but, unlike in the past, I let my mind wander and be suspicious of every single action he made. A friendly gesture, a kiss on the cheek, a gaze a moment too long in someone else's eyes, I was seeing things I never noticed before. My mind was playing tricks on me.

And I could only take so much paranoia before I completely lost my shit. The media didn't help either. Every other magazine and gossip site was reporting that he was cheating on me or that he was seen with another woman. Things were getting bad, really bad, but I held my head up and acted like nothing was wrong.

When I'd go to talk to him about it, he'd conveniently have to take a call or leave to oversee something. Other times, he'd stroke my ego, telling me I was being paranoid and that nothing was going to come between us.

This wasn't the Spencer I fell for. He was passive and not passionate about anything anymore. He stopped cooking, he stopped arguing with me, and he let me win battles I had no right winning. I'd been pushing him to argue back because I knew that we both got off on it, but he'd simply let me win. He'd comply and agree with me.

Something was bothering him, making him pull away

from me. He'd promised me he wouldn't leave me, wouldn't hurt me, yet he was whether he wanted to believe it or not. He was turning into someone I didn't even know. I missed the demanding hot head. The sexy beast who could get my blood boiling in more ways that just one.

Spencer was going to be gone almost a whole week, so I took that as an opportunity to spend time with Gran. Spencer had insisted on dropping me off and meeting Gran officially. He'd told me that he'd talked with her briefly at that infamous first charity event. He'd told her how impressed he was with her grandchildren.

Gran opened the front door as Spencer and I approached it.

"Hell has frozen over. My little muffin has come to visit me," Gran said, holding her arms out to embrace me in a hug.

I pulled back from her and turned to introduce Spencer. "Gran this is—"

"I know who he is," she said, eyeing him up and down.

Spencer and I exchanged looks.

"He's the man who has captured my little muffin's heart. Come on inside, it's freezing out here." She and I turned to walk back in the house.

"I'm sorry but I need to catch a flight. I just wanted to make sure Elizabeth got here safely," Spencer said, making Gran stop in her tracks.

"Oh, I didn't realize you were in a hurry."

"I'm sorry, Mrs. Monroe, maybe another time we can sit and have a nice chat," Spencer said acting dapper as ever.

I frowned at him. He was putting on an act, and it was painfully obvious, to me at least.

Spencer turned to me and took my hands in his. He

kissed the back of them. "I'll see you back in New York at the end of the week."

"Yeah."

"I love you," he said, pulling me in and kissing me softly.

"I love you too."

Gran and I watched as he walked back to the waiting car. That night I told Gran everything.

"I don't know, Gran. I don't know how to get him back. You saw him tonight. That was not the Spencer Salvatore I know."

We were sitting by the fire, under a quilt on the couch.

She shrugged. "It seems like he's having a rough time dealing with what ever happened in his early childhood. And I thought he was a gentleman tonight."

"I know, but he's acting like nothing is wrong, when clearly there is something going on. I've been racking my brain, trying to figure out what could have possible traumatized him so much that he's pulling away from me. He's acting like a robot."

It was true. My poor mind had come up with every disgusting, sad, and horrible thing that could happened to a young boy to make him protect his past to the point of ruining a relationship.

Gran pulled me in a little closer and rubbed my back. "It sounds like he just needs time. Maybe, just like you, a memory has crept back to the forefront of his mind, and he's having a hard time dealing with it."

My week with her reset me. It gave me hope that maybe this was just another obstacle that we had to get through.

Spencer called every day and, although short and sweet, he'd tell me he loved me and tell me about new gossip he'd heard about the TV shows he knew I liked. He was meeting with producers out in LA that were interested in teaming up for a new restaurant opening.

I came back to New York with a renewed, calm out-look on things. I was able to keep that calmness as I attended a few luncheons and charity events, and even spoke to a few reporters about said charity events. But with every day that he got delayed, the more anxious I became.

It was a Thursday night. I knew he was back in town, and he was refusing to answer my calls. I was sitting on the couch in silence. He'd texted me, telling me that he was on his way home. So there I sat, fueling the flames that were sure to erupt once he walked through the door.

I was going to tell him off. I was going to yell and make sure my point was understood. This whole non-sense about his past was tearing us apart, and I didn't want that to happen. I wanted my hot headed Spencer back. I was so done with the robot version. I would do anything to keep him, because I loved him, because I still got butterflies every time he walked into the room, be-cause I still felt the electricity when his fingers touched mine. I didn't want to lose that. It was too precious to me, too important.

The door opened—slow at first, then all at once. I watched as he walked in, closing the door behind him. His head was hung as he leaned his broad shoulders against the door. I stood from the couch and walked to-ward the entry way. He must have heard me coming be-cause he stood up straight and fixed the hair that had fall-en from its slicked back spot.

I planted my feet beneath me, thinking that maybe if I did this it would make me stronger, more confident. I held my head up as I'd done many times before. I was well versed in standing up for myself. I had a take-no-shit attitude, and I thanked god that I was that girl who had to be strong for myself, because it made me who I was today. Not even the Greek God, Spencer Salvatore, was going to walk all over me.

"Where were you?" I asked, getting right to it.

"Working. I told you it was going to be a long week." He was quick with the comeback—a little too quick.

"So when you got done 'working,' you what, went for a walk?"

"I'm not doing this with you," he said, shaking his head and unbuttoning his suit jacket to take it off. There was the robot, speaking for him again.

"Just tell me where you were," I pressed. I knew he wasn't working. I called his office and Tara his reception-ist said that he left for the day and not to disturb him. *That was at three o'clock—it's now almost nine. So where the hell was he?*

"I was working."

"Stop, just stop lying."

I watched as he shrugged the rest of his jacket off and placed it on the table to his left. He undid the cuffs of his sleeves and rolled them both up. He didn't say anything. He just stood in front of the door.

"All right, fine! Who are you sleeping with? Just tell me now. I want to hear it from you and not some trashy tabloid." I waited—he said nothing. "What do you want me to do, roll over and let you walk all over me? You want me to just be okay with you sneaking around and doing god knows what with god knows who?" I yelled from across the room.

"No," he roared back. "I never want you to do that. I wasn't with anyone. I'm not sneaking around with any-one. I would never do that to you, ever. And don't you dare ever let anyone walk all over you, including me. You hear me?" Finally, he was back. The robot was un-plugged and Spencer was in charge.

"Well, that's good," I said, rolling my eyes and tossing

my hands in the air. "And just for the record, I'm not going to let you walk all over me. You don't scare me, Spencer Salvatore." *Lies, all lies.* I was terrified to push back too much. I knew what it was like to not have him in my life and I never wanted to go back to that—ever. I was weak.

He'd made me so weak, weak in the knees, weak in the heart, weak in the mind. I'd never been so fragile.

"I should scare you. You should run away and stay away from me. It's in my blood. I've been screwed up since the day I took my first breath. I never stood a chance and, no matter how much I love you, I'm still fucking petrified that I'm going to ruin you and turn into him. I'm scared as fuck that I'll be just like him and hurt the one and only thing that I love!"

He was yelling so ruthlessly that his face was red with anger. His body shook as he yelled at me. He hit his chest with his own fist then shoved his hand back through his hair to get it off his face. I'd never heard him yell like that before.

All the weeks of keeping everything in must have spilled over.

"What are you talking about, Spencer? You can't hurt me unless you leave me! And you're not leaving me. I won't let it happen. And who is this 'him' you keep referring to?"

I knew in that moment, and all the moments before, that there wasn't another woman. This was all coming from his past. He'd kept quiet about it for too long. Now the dam was overflowing, and he couldn't control it anymore. I knew that was what scared him the most, losing control.

Someone must know his secret.

"It doesn't matter. We shouldn't have done this. I shouldn't have done this with you. It's why I haven't—

We shouldn't have done this," he said, shaking his head and repeating himself over and over again.

"What are you saying, Spencer?" I asked, taking a step closer to him. I stopped after that one step because it all clicked into place. Who was I trying to kid? I knew what he was saying. He was saying he regretted this, me, us, all of it. He was going to leave me just like he left me the night of the charity event. He was going to leave me, standing there more confused and heartbroken than I'd ever been because he was scared.

"You should pack your things and go stay with Chuck. This—I'm no good for you, for anyone," he said, hanging his head and shoving his hands down his tailored-clad thighs.

"You don't mean that!" I let the words hang in the air for a moment. When he didn't reply, I flipped. I was pissed and I wasn't going to just cower up to my room like I did all those months ago. "I came up here to be with you! I left everything, lost everything, for you! You can't kick me out, I live here," I shouted at him like I never had before.

"I can, and I am. I'm going out of town for two days. When I get back, please don't be here." He wouldn't look me in the eye. Instead, he turned from me and headed back to the door, he'd just came in through.

"Spencer," I screamed from where I stood. He stopped but didn't turn back to me. "I don't know what the hell you're so afraid of but I know that you love me, I know because I love you just as much. Look what we've already been through. We can get past whatever this is. You have to talk to me. You have to let me in," I begged.

He turned from the door to face me. His eyes were on the floor at my feet. They drifted slowly up my body until they met my own. There was sadness in them. This was killing him.

I couldn't understand why he was doing this to himself.

"I'm trying to protect you. If you stay with me, I'm going to hurt you. I already have." His eyes were pleading with me to just give in, to just let us go.

"No shit, Salvatore, you're hurting me now!" Again, I waited for him to say something, anything. "Just tell me why, why are you leaving? What changed? What did you figure out on your trip? What is so bad that it's making you do this to us?" I asked, taking another step, hoping but realizing that he probably wouldn't come clean about anything.

"Hopefully, you'll never know. Hopefully, you can go about your life and never know the horrible things I've done."

What the hell kind of cryptic bullshit is that? It was official. I was lost, like a mouse in a maze with no sent of cheese anywhere. I didn't know what was going on anymore. I stood across from him, only a few feet away instead of the whole room.

"If you leave, I'll hate you forever," I spat at him, hoping it would make a difference. "If you leave right now, I'm not giving into you again. This is it, Spencer. I'm done if you leave me this time."

It was an idle threat, of course. *I'd let him have a second...or was it a third?...chance by now.* Things had been so good between us. I would take these bumps between us, knowing that when it was good, it was so damn good. I could handle bumps, what I couldn't handle was the end. I wasn't going to be able to handle the end of us.

What would I do? Go back to just being Beth? I'd probably eat myself silly, gain twenty pounds, and lock myself away from everyone and everything.

I could already hear the tabloids. "Dumped and growing fatter by the hour." Or "We knew it was all a publicity stunt." Maybe "He never cared for the chubby no-body."

"I hope you do," he said, pulling me out of my own head and the horrible things I was sure the media was going to say once they got a hold of what was happening between us. "I hope you hate me, you should."

I ran at him and shoved him so hard in the chest he had to take a step back to keep his balance. I hit him, I yelled at him to stop, to stop saying things that he didn't believe. I kept hitting him until he grabbed my wrists. He pulled them together between the two of us.

I was so mad at him, angry tears rolled down my face. The more I struggled the more the tears stained my cheeks.

He held my wrists together, tighter than before. The act made me move closer until I was flush against his large frame. It was always the same with us. The closer we were, the more we needed to touch one another. I stared up into his eyes, his sea blue eyes that were becoming more vacant with every lie he was telling me. He didn't want this either. It was written all over his face.

He let go of my hands and laced them around the back of my neck. His thumb ran across my cheek, wiping the tears that fell from my eyes.

"It's going to be okay. Breathe," he said, wiping my tears away.

"No. Not without you it won't. I won't be okay," I blurted out between shallow breaths. I didn't want to fight with him, I wanted him to take me in his arms and just let me in, all the way in. No more secrets no more trips to cover things up.

"Please don't cry," he pleaded, clearing my cheek of fresh tears.

"Then stop making me."

I placed my hands on his hips as he gripped my neck a

little more. His forehead fell to mine, and I closed my eyes, relieved that maybe he was changing his mind, maybe this was just another bump that we were almost over.

Chapter 19

It happened so fast—one moment I was hitting him, angry and crying, the next he spun me around, pushing me back against the door. The moment was intense, both of our emotions were on high, and the electricity radiating off of us was something I had been craving for weeks. His lips slammed down on mine, and it was like coming home. He lifted me up and shoved me up against the door. I gripped his shoulders and wrapped my legs around him.

He'd wiped the tears as they fell from my reddened eyes and told me it was going to be fine, that everything was going to be fine. He carried me to bed, the bed that we had shared for months. I tried to forget everything that had happened but, something had shifted. It had shifted so much so that when Spencer laid me down, he wouldn't look into my eyes. Up until that night, he always looked into my eyes. His beautiful blue eyes refused to land on mine. He spent the time above me in the crook of my neck or kissing me. He'd close his eyes and appear to be lost in the moment, but I knew better. I knew that he only got lost in me. How could he do that if he wouldn't even look at me?

"Spencer," I called to him. I was trying to get his attention but he continued on, thrusting in me and kissing my neck. I pushed on the broad, thick shoulders that covered me and called his name again. "Spencer."

Still nothing. He kept at it, only harder. His harsh grunts echoed in my ear as he pushed on.

"Please," I whispered as I drove my hands through his hair. I thought that this might get him to move his head from my neck so I could see him. *No such luck.* His hand ran down my body and hitched behind my knee, lifting it to curl around his body. Still, he wouldn't look at me. I called him again, "Spencer."

His head shot up from my neck, his face was over mine, red and fierce looking. "What?" he clipped.

His lips trembled and, as my eyes drifted up to his, I caught a shimmer in the corners of his beautiful eyes. I tried to hold his face with my hands, but he snatched it away, crashing both our hands on the pillow to the side of us.

"Do you not want this?" he asked.

There were so many thoughts going through my head, but when he asked if I didn't want him, I thought maybe I had fallen into some wormhole where up was down and yes was no.

He blinked harshly, making any trace of shimmer I thought I saw in his eyes vanish. I lay there beneath him, still feeling the way I always felt when I was around him, out of control and needing more.

The warmth of his body covering mine made me feel safe beneath him, and for a moment, I thought maybe I was imaging it all.

Here he was, the man on every woman's radar on top of me, loving me, taking care of me.

"Elizabeth." He called me back. I watched as his genuine smile curled his lips. It was the smile I lived for, the one that set butterflies off in my stomach. "Can we finish?" he asked.

"Do you love me?" I asked, or rather blurted out.

For some reason, the need to hear him say it to me in this intimate setting was what I needed to put my wandering mind at ease. He'd apologized but I needed to hear this last part to put the night to rest.

He hovered over me before dropping to his elbows at either side of my head. He combed his fingers through my hair before his thumb ran over my cheek. His eyes studied me like they never had before.

"I've never loved anything as much as I love you. I've never felt as alive as I do when I'm with you," he said, smiling down at me. "If I died right now, I'd die the happiest man, because I've known what it felt like to be in love with you. There's nothing I wouldn't do to protect you, I love you that much."

"Really?" I asked.

He nodded, smiled, then kissed the tip of my nose.

"Do me a favor for the rest of the night?" he asked. "Forget about any disagreements we've had. Forget about the paparazzi, the media, your brothers, your friends. I want us to forget about everything but the way it feels to be with each other. Close your eyes and just feel me." He was smoldering to the point I thought he was going to catch the room on fire.

I nodded, gulped, and grabbed onto him with the intentions of never letting go. "Say it again," I said on a shaky breath next to his ear. "Say you love me."

"I love you," he whispered and held me as tightly as I was holding him.

இஇஇ

I opened my heavy eyes as the sun began to show

through the huge floor-to-ceiling windows. They spanned the whole wall opposite Spencer's bed. The morning light told me it was going to be a beautiful day. I curled into the plush white down comforter, adjusted my head on the fluffy pillow, and tried to close my eyes and fall back to sleep. I splayed my legs out, expecting to hit Spencer's, but the sheets were cool. I reached a little farther behind me, thinking maybe I had pushed him to the edge of the bed. I liked to spread out when I sleep.

The coolness only increased until, finally, my foot curled around the edge of the mattress. I sat up like a bold of lightning and flipped around. He was gone. The bed was empty and, from the feel of it, it had been empty for a while. I glanced at the bathroom, and saw the light on from under the crack of the door. I scooted to his side of the bed. My feet touched the floor and as they did I happened to notice his nightstand was clear. The picture of his mother, his real mother was gone. *Weird—don't panic. Maybe he's getting a new frame for it?*

I stood from the bed and made my way to the bathroom. My fingers reached out to the knob, and it was then that I realized they were shaking. I grabbed the handle and pushed through the nerves and the door. It was empty, and not just because there was no one in there. The bottle of cologne that drove me wild was missing, the comb that rested on the counter was missing, toothbrush—gone, razor—gone. I quickly turned to the shower. My insides did a flip when I saw nothing but my shampoo, my soap, and my razor.

I ran out the bathroom and into the closet. His suit case was not there. Half of his things were gone. Almost every suit jacket, crisp, white shirt, and all his favorite shoes had vanished. *Poof, he'd done the ultimate disappearing act, and I fucking slept through the whole god damn thing.*

I stumbled out of the closet and into the bedroom. I stood at the foot of the bed, honestly not knowing what I should do next. I stared ahead blankly until something caught my eye. There sitting perfectly against the lamp on my nightstand was a white envelope with my name on it.

I took a deep breath and grabbed it. I sat on the edge of the bed and held it between my fingers. *Maybe he had to go on a business trip? Maybe he had to go home to his family? Maybe you're just a stupid girl trying to come up with a logical explanation, when you know the real reason he's gone all Houdini on your ass.*

I was so mad that I gripped the envelope tighter, scrunching it up as if I was going to rip it into a million little pieces. I wouldn't have done that, though. I might have thought about it, but I couldn't do it. I loosened my grip and flattened out the envelope on my lap.

I stared up at the ceiling and actually started laughing. I laughed because I was crazy. I was crazy thinking we could make it work. I was crazy for ever believing that he loved me as much as he told me he did. I was crazy for moving in with him so fast, for giving into his charm, his good looks.

I'd been played again. I was the fool who thought Spencer Salvatore loved me. *The man should win a fucking Emmy! And I should win the biggest fool award.* I should have left it at that. I should have packed my shit up, left, and never looked back. I should have left that envelope right where he left it and went the hell on with my life. But I wasn't smart, I liked to twist the knife a little deeper, shove the hot iron in a little more. *I think I need to start seeing a therapist.*

I slipped my finger along the sealed flap, reached inside, and pulled out the piece of paper. Unfolding it I took a steadying breath before I looked down. I didn't know what I expected to see, maybe an apology, a reason for his absence. *I should have known.* Mr. Salvatore was a jerk, a confusing note-dropping jerk from the very beginning, I didn't know why I thought things would ever be different.

13421 S. 22nd St.
New York City, New York
@730
It's all for you
~S

An address—he left me a fucking address! Immediately, I opened my laptop and googled the address. It was a nice building in the fashion district, but beyond that I had no idea what this message meant. *Did it have something to do with Gia? Oh-my-god! Was he sleeping with Gia! Is that why she always refused to hang out with us? I thought it was because she still had a grudge about the whole Fame incident with Teddy and Chuck. Jesus, could she be secretly in love with him. Damn that's a hell of a cover story if she was—and now I'm rambling in my own head.*

The old Beth would have called Gia, crying and upset, but this was the new and improved Beth. The Beth who had had her world rocked, flipped, and shaken to the point of maximum destruction. I'd dated two men, dealt with my best friend hooking up with both of my brothers, and battled the media, all at the same time, and I came out fine on the other side.

That address could have had something to do with his past, maybe it was his way of including me. *Hell, maybe he was moving and going to surprise me.* The fact of the matter was, I didn't know. Like always, I didn't know anything.

The only way to find out was to show up at seven-thirty and see what happened.

Chapter 20

Nickolas

I reached into my pocket after the door slammed closed behind Salvatore and dialed a number I'd sworn I'd never call.

I cracked my neck as I waited for the line to pick up. "Well, well, I've missed you, Nickolas," Natasha said from the other end of the phone.

"Well, unfortunately, for you, I haven't."

"Don't be mean. You must be in a pickle if you're calling me on this number, which I didn't know you had. Seems you're sneakier than I once imagined."

"What the hell are you doing?" I demanded.

"Well, I'm sitting in my Jacuzzi bathtub, with the most spectacular glass of wine I've ever had. I have an array of scented candles going—Oh, and I have some calming music on in the background, but I'm sure that's not what you were getting at. Am I wrong?"

"You broke him. You realize you broke a man, right?" I said, pacing the gallery.

"I haven't even started."

I could head the sloshing of water on the other end of

the phone as she adjusted herself. Her chipper, smart ass voice turned into the deceptive, cruel one I knew all too well.

"You need to stop this."

"The hell I do! You have no idea the amount of sinister, heart-wrenching, evil that that man has inflicted on other people. I will not stop until he's paid for everything he's done. I will not stop until he reaches the same fate as the ones he's destroyed."

"Natasha, listen to yourself. You're taking this too far. I'm all about getting revenge but he's going off the deep end. He came to me tonight, asking if I'd take Elizabeth back. He's letting her go." I was shouting by the end, I needed her to hear the seriousness in all this.

"So what the hell are you complaining about? My plan's working. He's losing everything he's ever had. You're getting the girl. I don't understand the problem here."

"What the hell did he do, Natasha? He told me he was sending Elizabeth to me. He's scared shitless, and you told me once that he murdered someone. Is that true? Is that the dirt you have on him? Or have you been bluffing all along?"

"Keep your nose out of my business, Nickolas. You're getting your girl, your precious Belle, back, aren't you? Stay out of it."

Click.

I squeezed my phone so tightly I thought I was going to crack the screen. I wanted to toss it across the room and punch something, I was so mad. I had no way of contacting Spencer and, at this point, I figured Elizabeth wouldn't give me the time of day, even if I tried to call her. I was stuck. I didn't have a clue to go on or direction to head in. All I knew was the bullshit Natasha kept threatening with. I didn't know if it had any merit, but after everything I had experience tonight, parts of her threats had to be true. Why else would Spencer give up?

Even though I wanted to figure it all out, I had a gallery opening in less than twelve hours and, for once, I had to put everything else aside—the drama, the questions, everything—and focus on myself.

Chapter 21

Elizabeth

I wasn't a total fool. I called Spencer on every single number that I had. He never answered, though. I called his office, all four of them, even the international one. Go figure. All four of them told me the exact same thing.

"I'm sorry, Ms. Monroe, he's unavailable at the moment, and we're not sure when he's going to be able to get back to you. We'll give him the message."

They were like robots on the other end. Knowing Spencer, he probably gave them a huge incentive to lie for him. He didn't seem to have a problem getting other people to do his bidding.

After calling every number I had, I sat on the bed and contemplated who to call next. Gia? *No way.* Chuck? *Like he cares that Spencer is MIA.* Teddy? *No, he'd blow up and most likely fly home from LA.* I didn't want to do that to him.

I was basically stuck in Spencer's condo. The only thing that I had going for me was the address in the envelope. It was all I had to go on, and I was praying it was going to lead me to him and not on some wild goose chase.

After spending the morning on the phone getting robotic answers, I spent the rest of the day vegging out on the couch and sulking. That is until the doorbell rang. I dropped the bag of sour cream and onion potato chips and immediately panicked. *Oh, shit, what if it's him? Of course, it's not him. It's still his house, he'd walk in. What if it's security really kicking me out? Oh, God, what if it's the media?* I sniffed my breath, *Whoa, not good.* I ran fast to my black hole of a bag grabbed a piece of gum, and shoved it in my mouth.

The rap on the door got louder. I chewed as fast as I could to help with the onion breath. I opened the door just as the person was going to knock again. It was one of the managers of the building.

"Ms. Monroe, I was asked to give this to you," the manager said.

"Who—"

"Mr. Salvatore asked me to bring it up to you at six tonight, I'm just doing as he asked."

The man held a box in his hand. It was wrapped with a red ribbon and had a perfect bow on top of it. My heart fluttered in my chest at the chance that this was all a scheme to impress me, woo me, or even apologize to me. I thought he did enough apologizing last night, but I'd take a fancy box and mystery note to a special location any day.

I took the box from him, thanked him, then closed the door. I kicked the bag of chips on the floor and sat down on the couch. Placing the box where the chips had been, I got all giddy. I ripped into the box, expecting to see a note—because this was Spencer, after all. I was shocked to see nothing but tissue paper.

I tore through it like a kid at Christmas. Tissue paper

went flying in every direction until I hit fabric—red, soft, expensive fabric. I reached in with both hands and held up the red Ann Robin dress I wore the first night I met Spencer. It was exactly the same as I remembered it. I studied it a little more closely. *No, this can't be? How could he?* There on the bottom of the dress was a small stain, the same stain that I had on the original dress. I had spilled some red wine on it back when I was getting ready to go out with Gia and my brothers the night we went to Blue. That night suddenly felt like forever ago now.

It was also the night Spencer ripped the dress off my body. He'd fixed it for me. I hugged the dress and then swiftly panicked again. I was supposed to meet Spencer in this dress in less than forty-five minutes, and there wasn't a stylist team in sight to get me ready this time. I was on my own, and I was petrified.

So I did the unspeakable, I called Gia.

"I'm only doing this because…I don't know why I'm doing this, but I don't trust him, Beth," Gia said as she tugged a comb through my hair.

I was playing a game on her phone when she went in for another big tug, which made my head jerk to one side. "Calm down. Everything's going to be fine. He's just making things adventurous, and watch it with that comb. I'm not going to have any hair left if you keep that up." I watched Gia roll her eyes in the mirror as she continued combing my hair with a little more force than necessary. "So how's Charles?" I asked, taking her totally off guard.

"What? Why—why would I know how he is?" she stammered, trying to play it off.

"Well, first off, you smell like him—"

"I do not!"

"Second, you got here way too fast if you were coming from your place."

"There was no traffic. And would you believe I hit every green light."

"Hump—well, he's calling you—you sure you don't know how he is?" I said, holding her phone up over my head so she could see the caller ID.

"Damn him, I told him to—shit. Okay—fine I've been hanging out with him."

Who was she trying to kid?

I snickered up at her. "It's fine. I'm not going to get into fate's way. I'll keep my opinions to myself."

"Turn around and let me finish your hair. I can take a hint," she said, shooing me to turn back around on the chair.

I hadn't meant to—*ah hell, I guess I did.* If I could keep my mouth shut and support her—I expected her to do the same for me.

"So do you know anything about this place?" I asked, holding the note that was left on top of my mended dress.

"No. I do know that the building is refurbished and there's a lot of up and coming buzz around that area. I think there are some designers renting space in the building, and I also heard that the pent houses are huge, like movie star huge."

That was all I needed to hear. The sheer thought that maybe he had bought us our own place and was surprising me tonight put my mind at ease. *I mean, come one, what else could it possibly be?*

⌘⌘

The driver pulled up to the building and placed the car in park. "This is it," he said, glancing at me from the rear view mirror.

"All right then."

I waited and stared out the window at the huge building. I noticed that, inside, there seemed to be a party going on in one of the main floor rooms. *Wedding*? I sat back in my seat a moment.

The driver cleared his throat and raised his brows at me. I smiled up at the rear view mirror. The older man smiled back as he waited for me to get my ass out of the car.

"I guess I should get out," I said, not only to him but to myself.

I had to talk myself up again. It was like I was back at the first night I wore this dress, only I knew Spencer was waiting for me somewhere inside this gorgeous building and Nick—Nick was out of my life, and the chances of me seeing him again were slim to none.

"Well, miss, you don't have to, but if I were you I'd get in there and find whoever you're looking for."

With that, I clutched my small bag and exited the car. I walked up the front stairs and into the building. I expected to see a large lobby. Instead, it was a huge white room with tons of people milling about.

People in crisp white shirts and slick black pants walked around with trays of champagne and hors d'oevures. I stood at the entrance of the large room and, as I scanned the faces, I realized that this wasn't a wedding nor was it a lobby with a concierge waiting to help me. It was my worst nightmare.

The first flash of light came from my left, the second from my right, and so on, all around me cameras went off. Not only was it large paparazzi cameras, but cell phones and tablets soon followed suit. All around me were huge canvas photos of what I knew without a doubt were the curve of my back, the soft bend of my leg, the length of my neck. If those images held any doubt it was me, the one with a strap of a bra laying next to a dark freckle that I knew was on the edge of my collar bone told me it was definitely me or my doppelganger. As I spun around, taking in all the pictures, the last picture I saw was of the delicate diamond necklace in the shape of an S staring straight back at me. I'd walked into the bear's den, and Spencer Salvatore was nowhere to be found.

Chapter 22

Nickolas

The night was going great. I had a huge turnout. People from the art society, magazines, I even talked to a woman from the *New York Times*. I'd been promoting to all the right people for the last three months, and I pulled every single string I could to get that room filled with every important person available. I'd recently been told that four pieces had sold for a combination of over a million dollars. I was walking on air, living the life I always dreamed of. Everything was going great. That was, until I heard the commotion coming from of the front of the gallery.

Honestly, I hadn't thought about what happened the night before. I had a feeling Spencer Salvatore was full of shit and Natasha was so off-her-rocker crazy, I didn't want to feed into her threats anymore. The simple fact was—there was no way that Spencer Salvatore would leave Elizabeth Monroe.

I was talking with a well-known art gallery manager when I noticed the flashes of light and crowd forming toward the front of the gallery.

"So, as you know the market is wide open, and I know that we have room to—"

"I'm sorry," I interrupted, clutching his shoulder. "I— I have to check on something."

I left him standing there and walked to where the crowd of people were huddling. With every step I took, I felt my heart drop a little farther into my gut. There were rows of people and, as I pushed my way through, it was obvious the crowd was getting rougher and the flashes were going off more frequently. I hadn't invited these types of people. There was no reason for it. I wanted a small opening with people that cared about art and photography.

I'd been in crowds like that in my previous profession, and I knew that grown-ass men and women only acted like this when there was money to be made off a picture. I pushed my way between them and, as I broke through, I found myself standing face to face with a ghost of a woman I once knew. These people had been brought here, given a tip. They must have been waiting in the wings unseen by myself or the other prestigious people I had invited.

She looked up at me with as much confusion on her face as I'm sure I had on mine. Her golden brown eyes shimmered as tears began to well up in them. She looked panicked, taken off guard. She clearly wasn't expecting this, or me. The noise around us quieted as we stared at one another.

I was gazing at my Belle, the woman I ruined, the woman I let slip through my fingers. I didn't know what to do. Of course, I wanted to grab her, hold her, feel her skin against mine again, but I couldn't. I couldn't touch her, she wasn't mine—she was his.

The flashes erupted again, people yelled at her, said awful things to get a reaction. Her eyes left mine as she scanned the sea of faces behind me. I knew she was looking for him. She was looking for him to rescue her. She wasn't going to find him here. I took in her appearance, she was in the same red dress, the same shoes, and her hair was even done the same. It was as if he sent her here for a do over.

He knew there was going to be media people here, maybe not to this extent because clearly someone else was responsible for most of them, but he still sent her. He sent her without any warning of what she was going to be walking into. She went to take a step to the right but the people around her closed off any chance of escape she might have thought she could make.

Her eyes were begging me to help her because she was stuck, trapped. She couldn't run out the front. They'd just follow her. She couldn't stand there and let them shout at her. I knew her temper, and if she did stay, someone was going to end up with a black eye, and a hefty lawsuit was most likely going to follow.

I took the remaining steps toward her. Her eyes grew as I leaned closer. I whispered in her ear, "Do you trust me?"

She took a moment but nodded back.

"Hold onto my hand and don't let go."

She glanced down at my hand that was between our bodies before placing hers in mine. I gripped it tightly. It was as I remembered it, soft and warm.

I took a steady breath with her before I pushed past her and the people that had closed her in. She clutched at my hand as we rushed past everyone and fled out the front door. More paparazzi were out front of the building. I stopped in my tracks. My plan was to beeline across the street. My studio apartment was a quick walk across the street in a secure building. I gripped her hand tighter and pushed on.

My arm was out stretched behind me as we darted across the street. When I glanced behind me, she had covered her face with her bag. More flashes erupted when we made it to the other side of the street. The people around us multiplied. I was a step from grabbing the door handle when she tugged on my arm. I reached for the door anyway and held it open. As Beth hurried in under my arm I saw the devil herself standing in the middle of the crowd.

Natasha stood amongst the raucous of people in a posh black dress. Her arms were crossed under her chest and, as we locked eyes, her lips curled. Her jet black hair was swept off her face and her clear blue eyes were as cold as her personality. All she needed was some dark smoke around her and maybe a henchman by her side. She was the epitome of the word villain.

And just like all villains, she disappeared into the crowd of people. I wish I could have said, to never be seen again, but I knew that woman too well. She was just getting started and seeing the destruction she had created was only going to fuel her passion for destroying more lives.

As the door closed behind me, the sound of the grown men and woman yelling outside was muffled and soon gone. I didn't say anything as I led Elizabeth to the elevators. We rode up in silence. I sure as hell didn't know what to say and, by the look on her face, she was more confused and hurt than I'd ever seen her. I imagine she was racking her brain, trying to figure out what went wrong, what would make someone who said they loved you turn on you and leave you for the…who knew how many times it was now?

I'd been there the first time he left her and, once again, I was the one standing here, picking up the pieces and trying to put them back together again. She followed me down the hall to my door. I pulled my keys out and un-locked it. I pushed the door open and held it for her to walk through. She slipped by me, keeping her distance as she did. I followed her in and closed the door behind me. I locked it, took a steadying breath, then reached for the light switch next to the door.

I didn't know what to expect when I turned around to face her. Sure, I had saved her from the crowd of walking zombies with cameras tonight, but I was the one who put her on that path. I was the first one to snap a picture of her, and I was the one to blame for turning her life into a media storm.

Did I still care about her? *Of course I do. I always will.* I fell for her hard and the mere threat of someone taking her from me made me do unthinkable things in the past. But that wasn't the case now. No one was black-mailing me. She knew who I was, and I prayed to every god, deity, and savior I could, I prayed that she'd be able to look past what I had done and just look at where I was and what I was doing now.

She had her hands covering her face, when I gained the courage to turn around. I went to say something to her, but I didn't know what the hell to say. I pushed the sleeves of my already rolled up shirt up a little more and waited. She was as beautiful as the first night I'd seen her. I'd never admit it back then, but she took my breath away. I could remember standing in the crowd, waiting for Spencer to make an appearance at Mood. When Eliz-abeth stepped out of the limo after Gia, who had pranced around on the tiny red carpet like a pro, I felt bad for Elizabeth. I didn't know who she was then, and I knew a lot of people.

The guy next to me faked gagged. I remember she had a blanket or something wrapped around her. It wasn't re-ally what people like me wanted to photograph. As she scanned the crowd with a deer-in-the-headlights look, she locked eyes with me. And I remembered in that moment thinking, *Wow, she's got a beautifully proportioned face.* Just as that thought crossed my mind some ass yelled, "She's a nobody."

I didn't think the deer-in-the-headlights look could get any more dramatic, but Elizabeth Monroe's eyes grew ten times bigger. I had to look away. I couldn't watch. I was messing with my camera when the guy next to me hit my arm. "Holy shit, dude, she's a fucking bombshell." I glanced back up out of curiosity. I didn't expect this wide-eyed, covered-up, scared—*all right, I'll admit it, I thought she was bigger girl*—to turn into a glamazon.

So when my eye's landed on the red dress that hugged every curve of her body as if it was made for her, I nearly choked on my own spit from shock. Beyond that, I didn't think anything of it. She'd had an ugly-duckling-turned-into-a-swan moment. A lot of celebrities did that. She was okay looking from where I stood. I'd had better, and I'd had worse, but most importantly, I had a job to do that night, and I didn't have time for anything else. Honestly, I never had time for women. I was constantly working, betraying people, gaining their trust, and turning around and using it against them. I was in no way, shape, or form interested in bringing someone into that world with me.

From a corner in Mood, I watched as people ignored her. I wasn't watching her, but I found myself keeping an eye on her. I'd scan the room for my mark and, every time, my eyes would land back on her. I didn't think any-thing of it back then. Suddenly something caught her eye. I followed her gaze and finally saw my mark. Spencer Salvatore had entered the club, and it was my job to be-friend him, get him to trust me, and then turn on him.

I watched from my perch as he entered and parted the crowd in front of him. He had his sights set on something—someone. When I put it together I noticed he was walking toward the girl in the red dress. From what I knew, he didn't go after women, women came to him. So I pulled my phone out and snapped as many photos as I could as he touched her ankle and talked to her. It was a one sided conversation. The poor girl was frozen.

Suddenly, a brilliant idea popped into my head. I called Natasha and told her my plan. Natasha agreed and, soon after that, I was cozying up behind the vixen in the red dress on the dance floor. I held her close and didn't hate it. She smelled amazing, moved good. What was there to complain about? I inflated her with compliments, which were half true, half a ruse.

Everything was going great, until she saw through it. She called me out, and I was scrambling to keep her interested. I knew then I liked her spunk, her take-no-shit attitude, but I needed *her* to get to *him*. I could remember exact minute I knew I was going to be fucked. It was the moment her cheeks filled with that rosy blush. It was endearing, and she looked beautiful, and as her brother barged into our moment, I snapped back to reality. I shook the feeling off and left when I saw Spencer walking our way. I made myself scarce and snapped more pictures of them. I had to laugh to myself. She was falling for Salvatore's good looks and charm. Here I thought she was going to be different with her little attitude and sarcastic tendencies.

I thought it was going to be a cake walk, but the more time I spent with her, the more I liked her. It got to the point I was begging Natasha to drop this stupid crusade. I felt responsible, hell, I was responsible for dragging her into this. I was stuck playing the part, if only to protect her then. If Natasha would have sent in someone else, it would have gotten worse. When she realized I was falling in love with her, Natasha used it as a weapon against me.

She was able to keep me in line with one simple threat. She would tell Elizabeth exactly who I was.

"Thank you." A delicate voice danced around in my ears, brining me back to the present.

"I—I'm glad—No problem." *Stuttering? Get your shit together, Nick!*

Her smile lit her face up and the tension dissipated from both of us.

"Are you—nervous?" she asked.

I tried to laugh it off but fear was, without doubt, written all over my face. "No, why would I be nervous? Are you okay? Those people were pretty nasty out there." Again, I tried to play my nervousness off. I wanted her to confide in me, let me take care of her, but I knew firsthand how stubborn and hard headed she could be.

"Something's not right," she stated.

I waited for her to elaborate. "You mean, aside from the walking dead outside of my building, trying to take your picture." She nodded. I sighed. "You were looking for him, weren't you?"

Chapter 23

Elizabeth

I placed my bag on the table behind me and took a moment to scan the room I was in. It was a studio apartment, large and grand. It was lacking that feminine touch but wasn't as cold as I might have imagined it to be. Glancing around Nick's home, I learned a lot in five seconds. One, he was single. Two, he wasn't a struggling photographer. Three, he might be turning into a hermit. There were boxes lining the walls, mail stacked on the table that looked months old, and take-out bags covered almost all the counters.

I never expected to be standing in his place. I expected to be standing in my brand new condo with the man I was in love with. *Is it really over between us?* It didn't feel over. It felt like he was running, hiding.

Turning back to Nick, I asked, "Was he there at all?"

I was praying he'd say yes. I prayed that he was going to tell me, "Yeah, he came and bought all your naked pictures." That would have been the best case scenario. Unfortunately, the look on Nick's face told me a different story.

I wanted to curl into a ball and melt into the floor. Then again, I wanted to find Spencer and beat him upside the head. I was mad, I was sad, I was confused. Last night was rough, but we made up. *Didn't we make up?* I was fine, but he—he must have been saying goodbye—*No, no way! He doesn't get to do this to me again!*

"Did you know about this?" I snapped at Nick.

I had a feeling he was behind this with Spencer. My hand glided over the fabric covering my stomach and I realized that he had to be. This was some sick way of rec-reating the night we met.

"No, I didn't know—" Nick took a step toward me, holding his hands up in surrender.

I fisted my hands ready to punch the closest thing to me. "Don't lie to me, Nick. I'm so tired of people lying to me!"

"I'm not the bad guy here. I had no idea he would ac-tually go through with—" Nick abruptly stopped, scrunching his face and slapping his hand over his mouth, because he knew he'd let something slip.

"Spit it out, Nick," I urged. "If you know what's going on, you need to tell me."

"Elizabeth, all I know is that he came in here last night, asking me if I still loved you. He told me you were going to be here, and he told me it was in your best inter-ests. He looked scared. He said that someone was close to his secret, close to destroying everything he has. That's it. He didn't say what it was or—"

"Fuck!" I did punch something, the air in front of me. I knew I had to get to the bottom of this. I wasn't letting him walk over me and decide what he thought was best for me. I knew what was best for me, and that was him. I'd never felt so alive as when I was with him, and I'd do anything to get that feeling back.

I kicked my heels off and pulled my hair back off my

face. With my hands on my hips, I decided then and there I was going to figure his secret out. If he wasn't going to tell me, then I was going to figure it out myself and prove to him that it didn't matter what it was, that I'd still love him, dirty past and all.

Just as I exhaled, nodded, and accepted the deal that I had just made in my own head, I realized Nick was looking curiously at me. I went to open my mouth but— surprise, surprise—his phone began to ring from his pocket. I tossed a half smile and urged him to take the call.

He pulled the phone out of his pocket and answered it, not bothering to look at the number calling. "Hello," he answered.

I could hear the voice. It was a woman. *Maybe he does have a girlfriend.* The more I listened, the more familiar the voice became. It was raspy and at first could be mistaken for a man's voice, but the feminine giggle gave it away. It was the same voice I'd heard every time the phone would ring when we were together. I never thought anything of it back then. Funny, my jealous side never spoke up, never planted thoughts in my mind like it did with Spencer. I soon realized the person on the other end was the same person who'd blackmailed Nick, the same person who'd had a hand in turning my world upside down.

"...I don't know what you want—" Nick had been talking to her this whole time while I put everything together in my head.

I interrupted him. "Let me talk to her." I wasn't asking, I was demanding. I shot my hand out toward him and waited from him to place the phone in my hand.

He moved the phone from his ear, shook his head, and kept the phone just out of my grasp. "I don't think that's a good idea."

"Give. Me. The. Phone. Nick."

He shook his head but placed the phone in my hand anyway and let his hands fold over his broad chest. He had a this-is-a-bad-idea look on his face but I ignored it. The woman on the other end of the phone was toast—crispy, burnt toast that I was about to toss in the trash.

I put the phone to my ear and skipped the pleasantries. "Why the hell are you so determined to make my life a living nightmare?"

"My, my, it is nice to meet you too."

I didn't know her name, and I didn't care to know her name. All I wanted to know was why, why was she so eager to hurt me? What had I ever done to her? Before that night at Mood, I'd kept to myself and stayed out of the limelight that followed my brothers. I kept my head down, studied, kept to myself. I didn't get it.

"I'm going to ask you one more time. Why are you doing this?" I waited for a response but all I could hear on the other end was cackling—yes, cackling, evil, hyena cackling.

She took a moment to calm herself on the other end. I could hear her draw in a few breaths before she spoke. "Why don't I introduce myself first? I'm Natasha, and let me just tell you, it is a pleasure to finally speak with you. Of course, I've heard so much about you via Nick. Oh, right, you might know him better by the name Simon. You know, I thought you'd be a bit sweeter. They say big girls should have a pleasant disposition to help cover up the pounds, makes them more likeable."

It was my turn to take the deep breaths. My temper was already at the max, and this woman was only making it worse. "What did I ever do to you?" I spat into the receiver.

"Oh, darling, you didn't do anything. You know who I'm really after. Unfortunately, in wars, there are sometimes civilian casualties. I didn't mean to drag you into this but, man, has it paid off. Did you know that a single picture of you eating is worth over a hundred thousand dollars?"

I felt myself suck in air. *Is she serious, or is this just another way for her to get under my skin?*

"I know, it's rather barbaric, but sadly the world wants to see you fall short. They want to see you crumble under the microscope. Did you know that for every overweight, naive woman who looks up to you, there are five who want to see you fail?"

"Stop!" I shouted. I wasn't going to let her manipulate me, or make me feel bad. Because even if five people wanted to see me fail, that one woman who I helped gain some self-confidence was worth it. I might have been scared and unwilling to be the role model some thought I was in the beginning, but not anymore. I was strong, and I was standing up to people like Natasha who only wanted to hurt and crush people beneath her. "You don't scare me. They don't scare me, not anymore."

"Your picture tonight says otherwise, my love."

"What do you want from him?" I got back on track. If she wasn't after me, then she was after Spencer, and if he wasn't going to do anything about it, I was.

"Oh, back to the sexy billionaire. To be honest—" She paused for a dramatic effect.

I rolled my eyes.

"—I'm really enjoying watching him self-destruct. For example, I just found out that he's drunk in public, in Vegas, with women hanging all over him. Now, we all know he never does that. His uptight façade is wearing down and the bad boy that I know is buried beneath all the suits and hair gel is dying to come out. It's only a matter of time, and I'll be sure to post everything along the way so you don't miss a beat. If I were you, I'd stick with Nicky boy. He's still in love with you, poor thing, and even though it kills me to say it, you should give him a chance. It was him, after all, who always saved you from that mysterious Salvatore. You don't deserve him, but he's like an S—don't screw with him, or you'll be next."

I started to rip her a new one but Nick had yanked the phone from my hand and hit the end button.

"Why the hell did you do that?" I grabbed the phone and tried to bring up the number she had called from. I waited as it dialed.

"I'm sorry the number you have called doesn't exist." It was maybe thirty seconds, forty max from Nick taking the phone from me and me calling Natasha back. *How could it not exist? I was just talking to her.*

"It was a burn phone. You're not going to be able to call her back," Nick said.

I huffed in frustration. I shoved the phone back at him then rubbed my temples to help ease the pain in my head. "I can't believe this is happening." I said it to myself but soon realized I'd said it out loud.

"Neither can I. Come on, let's sit down. I need a drink, you?"

"Please."

I followed Nick and sat on his couch. I watched as he rummaged through his messy kitchen to find two glasses that weren't dirty. It was obvious that he was nervous. He fumbled with a few things in the kitchen, and I couldn't help but smile. I wish I would have gotten to know this part of Nick when I met Simon. It was cute and completely different from the confident man I first met at Mood. It was refreshing.

"All right two Coke and rums. Sorry, it's all I have, unless you want to do shots of tequila."

I reached out and took one. "This is fine, thank you." I

took a sip. The crisp soda hit my lips first then the warm rum as it slid down my throat.

We both took another sip. With our glasses up to our mouths, we locked eyes, and I wasn't sure why, but both of us cracked a smile. Maybe it was the rum, maybe it was the fact that we never expected to be in this situation. All I knew was I felt safe. The last time I'd seen Nick, I didn't feel that way. I was still convinced he was working for the enemy, still trying to make a buck off of me. But I knew he'd moved on, I saw it firsthand. *Oh shit, his gallery opening!*

I pulled the glass from my lips and choked on the liquid still in my mouth. "Oh my God, Nick. Your photos—your gallery opening. You need to get back there." I put the glass down on the table and went to stand.

"It's fine, please sit back down. Trust me. No one's going to miss me."

"Are you kidding? It's your big night, you've been dreaming about this." He shrugged his shoulders as if it wasn't a big deal. "Nick, there are naked pictures of me in your gallery, beautiful artistic, elegant photos of me that you took. You need to get your ass back over there and make sure everyone knows who you are."

He sat back and smiled a warm genuine smile. His brown eyes seemed to twinkle. "You know, I thought I might have to take them down."

"Why's, that? I did give you permission," I joked.

"Well, to be honest, I thought Salvatore was going to have me sued or beat the shit out of me for having naked pictures of you hanging on a wall for the world to see. When he came in here last night, I seriously thought he was going to punch me in the face again."

I sat back on the couch and drifted off to the previous night.

The fight with Spencer, his rambling about me moving

out and us going our separate ways because he was scared he'd hurt me.

"I—Elizabeth, I didn't mean to bring him up," Nick said, probably noticing my reaction to hearing Spencer's name.

"No, it's fine. Listen, Nick—" Just then a thought crossed my mind. If Nick was able to trace down what happened in Vegas when Spencer was a teen, maybe he would be able to help me uncover whatever it was that Spencer thought I couldn't handle. Even if he didn't work for Fame anymore, he had to have some connections that I was never going to be able to make.

"What?" he asked.

"Would you help me? Would you help me find out what Spencer is hiding? Maybe if I can figure it out and show him that it doesn't matter, maybe he can get past this paranoia that he's going to hurt me."

It was a long shot, asking Nick. I just hoped that we could be friends, and that he could help me out, *I mean, come on, he does have naked pictures of me that I'm sure are selling like hot cakes.*

"I—I umm, I guess—"

"Excellent!" I snuck that in before he could say no. "I think I'll take that tequila, if you don't mind."

"You're trouble," Nick said, moving from the couch and heading toward the kitchen to grab the bottle of tequila.

"I like to think that I'm adventurous, maybe a little crazy."

Nick poured the light amber liquid into my empty glass and then poured some into his own. He sat next to me on the couch. Holding his glass up, I let mine clink with his.

"To finding the truth," he said.

"To starting over," I added.

"To starting over," he repeated, before clinking his glass to mine.

His face lit up in a dashing smile before he took the shot. A part of me knew that deep down in the depths of my heart it was wrong. It was wrong to ask him to help me, but I was desperate. I had to make sure to keep my emotions in check. I couldn't go falling for Nick again. I didn't want to be that person anymore, and he deserved better than someone who could only give half their heart.

Chapter 24

Nickolas

I didn't know why I agreed to help her. I left her in my apartment and headed back to the gallery. I told her I'd only be an hour or so. As I made my way to the front of my building, the swarms of people were still there, waiting for her to come back out. No one budged as I opened the door and headed back across the street. There was, however, one flash of light as I made my way down the front steps. I caught a glimpse of the man who'd taken the picture and immediately knew he was one of Natasha's henchmen.

Not long ago that was me. I was the one doing her bidding. I was the face of betrayal so she could hide behind her desk. She was the master, controlling her puppets. The sad part was we did it without even thinking. All I needed was one call, one name. I knew what was expected of me, and I delivered because Natasha was scary as shit. I'd heard she had ties to the mob, and I believed it. People would disappear, never to be heard of again. You didn't want to get on her bad side, but when you were on her good side, you were taken care of, given every luxury—vacations, cars, houses, money. So I stayed on her good side. It was only when I met Elizabeth that I crossed over.

The time had slipped away from me, and I was glad it had. It made me forget about the beautiful woman in my house who was totally off limits. I'd watched Spencer and Elizabeth from the very beginning. I watched from the sidelines as the powerful, controlled man the world knew as Spencer Salvatore lost himself to a woman. I saw him fighting against his instincts to keep to himself in the beginning. Now when I saw them together he'd look at her with wonder and admiration. If he wasn't smiling for the camera, he was smiling at her.

On the flip side, I watched as Elizabeth blossomed into a stronger, more confidant woman. With every appearance and every camera that clicked with him by her side, she transformed into the one thing she told me she didn't want to be, a role model for women everywhere. I liked to think that I had a little to do with that, but I knew the bond that those two had was something that wasn't so easily broken.

I didn't know how we were going to figure Spencer's secret out, but I felt this was the best way I could apologize for everything that I'd had a hand in doing. It was my way of washing my hands of it all. It was going to be hard as fuck to be with her and keep the feelings I still held on to submerged, but I'd do it for her. She might not have been the other half to my soul that I thought she was, but I was at peace with helping her find hers.

I turned the lights off after the room was empty, locked the door behind me, and made my way across the barren street. The zombies were gone, called to find some other poor soul to ruin. In the elevator ride up, I loosed my tie and undid a few of the top buttons on my dress shirt.

I slung my jacket over my shoulder and waited till the doors opened.

I figured Elizabeth would be sleeping on the couch or watching TV when I walked in. I knew she loved her TV almost as much as I loved taking pictures of her. When I arrived at my door, I could hear the TV blaring. I laughed to myself. *Some things never change.* I swung the door open and had a witty one liner ready to go. Unfortunately, I never got to use it because my jaw had hit the floor.

I wasn't the cleanest person. I had a tendency to stack things. I guessed if I let it get too bad, I might be called a hoarder. It wasn't that I didn't want to throw anything away. It was the fact that I really didn't care because I spent most of my time in my studio. What I saw when I walked in had me so confused, I honestly thought I was in the wrong place. I even check the number on my door to make sure.

It was spotless. Every dish was clean, every surface was wiped clear of dust. My stacks of mail were organized, my boxes were unpacked, there were pictures hanging on my walls, and my dining room table was set perfectly for four. *I didn't even know I had table settings.*

I had one area in my condo that had nothing in it. No furniture, no nothing. It was usually where I hung all my pictures when I was deciding which to use and which to toss. That area wasn't bare anymore. It looked like a police station complete with pictures, facts, maps, and red, blue and green string connecting things this way and that. I felt like I had walked into a sound stage for CSI. Elizabeth sat in the middle of the floor with papers spread out all around her. My laptop was on her lap, and she was wearing a pair of my sweat pants and a T-shirt from my closet. Her hair was pulled up in a mess on top of her head with pens sticking out in every direction.

I let the door close behind me. The sound must have

gotten her attention because she looked up from my laptop. She scrunched her face up. "Sorry."

I stood just inside and did a once over of my home again. "You've been busy."

She put the laptop down and stood in the middle of the sea of scattered papers. "I didn't mean to..." She was fumbling, as if trying to find the words and chewing on the inside of her cheek. Suddenly, she crossed her arms and popped her hip out. "Nick, it was a mess in here, I don't know how you lived like that."

I nodded in agreement. "I don't know either to be honest with you. What's all this?" I asked pointing and walking toward the detective crime board. Elizabeth's face lit up as she bounced on her toes. She was clearly proud of all the work she had done in the few hours I was out.

"What do you think?" she asked with a smile plastered on her face. "Is this how you guys do it? I didn't know if I was executing it correctly."

I had to laugh at that. *What did she think I did when I worked for Fame?* She was going to be very disappointed when I told her I didn't have a clue how to go about finding out Spencer's secret.

"I think you're going in the right direction," I said, laying my jacket on the back of the couch. "Do you mind?" I asked, walking toward the makeshift board to get a better look.

"No. Please take a look," she answered, moving out of the way.

She'd printed off pictures of herself, her brothers, Gia, Spencer, me, and an image of Fames logo. She'd made a time line of everything. A long red string ran the length of the wall. From the string were events in time. I soon put it together. It was Spencer's life line so to speak. I went backward in time as I read each note she had made. She'd gotten it all on here—his first night club opening to her telling him about her parents and him becoming distant and eventually leaving her.

Something I didn't know. He was born in New York. I didn't even know that, and I was curious how she found this out. I pointed to it on the makeshift timeline. "How do you know this is true?"

"He told me."

"He told you he was born in New York. I didn't even know that."

"You might not have known, but I have a feeling Natasha does." Elizabeth took a step to the wall. Standing next to me she pointed to the huge gap between birth and when he popped up in Las Vegas. "I think she knows what happened here too."

"So you have no idea what happened to him before he popped up in Las Vegas with his adoptive family?" She shook her head. I shrugged. "I guess that's a good place to start then."

"That's what I was thinking too." She took a deep breath. "All right, Nick, bring out your secret weapons, your spy kit, your huge data base, or whatever it is that you used when you worked for Fame." She had this eager, naive look on her face.

I chuckled a few times, glanced around at the scattered papers that had whatever information she could find on Spencer. "Elizabeth" I said through a chuckle. "I don't have anything like that."

Her face fell. Her smile went from eagerness to disappointment. "What?"

I shook my head. "I don't know what it is that you thought I did when I worked at Fame but intel wasn't it."

Her arms slumped to her sides. "So what does that mean? You can't help me? Ugh!" She tossed her hands in the air, yelling up at the ceiling. "Why are you so against me? One step forward, a thousand back. I don't get it. Do you want me to be miserable and alone? Because I'm really thinking you do."

Poor thing was ranting. She did this when we dated, talking to the heavens above. It was cute but I could tell she was getting more and more upset.

She was facing away from me as she scolded my ceiling. I reached out and placed a hand on her shoulder. My hand rested there a moment. A sliver of skin that wasn't covered by my shit made contact with my fingers. She was warm and soft like I remembered. She turned with my hand still on her shoulder. I let it slide down her arm. I wanted to, but I knew I couldn't go down that path again, even if every fiber in my body was telling me to grab her, hold her, kiss her, make love to her.

We were both silent, standing closer than we had been in months. I'd swear I heard her heart pounding against her chest, and I knew she could hear mine. It felt like it was only moments away from bursting out of me. I wondered in the moment if I would ever be able to feel this way for another woman. I was watching my hand drift down her arm, when out of the corner of my eye I saw her watching as well.

"Simon…"

I instantly looked up to see her staring at me.

Her eyes locked with mine. They shifted back and forth before she held them closed. "I'm sorry, Nick. I didn't mean to—"

"It's fine." I tried to bring her back but she had taken a step away from me and placed her hands on her hips as she stared down at the scattered papers around us.

"Okay, so you're not James Bond, and we're going to have to do this the hard way. Where do you think we should start?" Her cheeks were flushed as she attempted to get back to the task at hand.

"Are you sure you even want to do this? I mean I'm

not a physiatrist or anything but maybe he's—maybe he's pushing away for a reason."

"Of course I'm sure. The only reason he left was because he's afraid that once I find out his secret, I'm going to—to—I don't know what he thinks, but I know in my heart that nothing he could have done is ever going to change the way I feel about him. He's scared and, quite frankly, being a bit of a moody teenager. I think he's used to getting his way and having this barrier up that no one can penetrate. I know that I can, I know I can get over it, I just need him to see that, no matter what's on the other side, I'm not going to leave him or stop loving him."

"You shouldn't have to get over anything. He should trust in you that you would stay by his side. I know you trust him and you let him into your world. He should have done the same."

"What are you trying to say, Nick?" she snapped.

"I'm saying—I"

"Spit it out, tell me what you really think?"

"Elizabeth, I think—"

"What, Nick? What do you think?"

"I'm tired of seeing you get hurt," I finally yelled back. "Aren't you tired of getting hurt yet?"

Chapter 25

Elizabeth

I knew he meant well. I knew that he only said those things to help me, to get me to see it from another side, but it wasn't helping. Yes, I had been hurt way too many times and, yes, I was tired of it. But I didn't want to walk away because I knew that I'd be more miserable without Spencer.

When I had something in my head, a means to an end, I was determined to get to it. I'd been that way my whole life. If someone told me no, I thought yes. If someone said go right, I'd ask, why can't I go left? If someone told me it was for my own good, I needed to know for myself, and if someone walked away from me, I wanted to know the real reason why, not some stupid excuse about protecting me.

This wasn't the 1800s. I wasn't waiting around for a man to come save me, and I wasn't a frail girl on the verge of shattering, not anymore.

"Of course, I'm tired of getting hurt," I blurted. "I just can't let it end like this. I can't let him decide what's best for me. Only I can do that, and the only way I *can* do that is to figure his secret out, confront him, and see what happens."

Nick was shaking his head in disapproval. I didn't need his approval, but I did need his help. He might not be James Bond, but I had to assume he had some connections, or at the very least ways to get around the system and the people who controlled it.

"Listen, if you don't want to help me, I get it. I just need to know." I stood there waiting for an answer. He seemed to be having an internal battle, much like the ones he had when we first started hanging out. "Nick, I don't expect you to help me, if that's what you're thinking. I don't want to pressure you into it if you don't want to. I can do this on my own." I knelt down when he kept silent and began gathering the papers I had fanned out on the floor.

"Get up," he called from above me. "Put the papers down. I'm going to help you. I just wanted to make sure it's really what you want."

"It is," I said, standing before him.

"All right, I trust you. I trust your instinct. Lord knows you had me pegged from the beginning. If you say Spencer's the one, then I believe you," he said, cracking a cheeky smile.

"He is," I said, needing *him* to hear that as much as myself.

When Nick had placed that comforting hand on my shoulder earlier, and when I took the chance to look into his warm caring eyes, I had this flash of him and me, but it was an image I had put into my head when I was with Simon, when I thought we were right for each other. I'd loved this man. I'd been invested in him once, but the feeling that something was missing between us always rang clear in my mind.

Although I knew our relationship was built on lies, it

was hard when I looked into his gentle brown, eyes. I knew he cared for me, and I could have easily given him another chance, given us another chance. I was sure it would have been fine. We would have been okay, but I didn't want just okay. I wanted amazing, I wanted butterflies in my stomach, fireworks behind my eyes. I even wanted that overwhelming sadness when we were apart.

It wasn't fair to Nick, and it wasn't fair to me. I needed to keep that at the forefront of my mind as we worked together to solve the mystery. It would be hard, because I was a sucker for handsome face, and Nick sported one proudly. *I should help him get back out there.* I knew plenty of girls, looking for a nice, handsome, established guy. Loads of charity events and making rounds with Spencer had widened my acquaintance list to well over what I ever thought it could be.

"I think we need to go to Vegas. I think it's time to meet your boyfriend's family," Nick said through a wicked grin.

I jumped out of my thoughts and back into the present. "Are you serious? Meet his family? I was technically dumped. What makes you think his family is going to want to meet me? What am I going to do, knock on the door and say, 'Hey, Spencer's family, I'm your son's kind-of girlfriend, can you tell me all about his past?' You're insane," I said, tossing my hands in the air. I knelt down and grabbed the laptop before turning from him to the board I had created. I was thinking that maybe, if I stared at it long enough, something would pop out. It didn't.

"I think that's a great place to start. His adoptive parents will most likely know where they got him from. Plus, you can test his statement about being from New York. I can book us tickets now and have us there by tomorrow afternoon."

"Chill out, Bond," I said over my shoulder.

"Here give me the laptop. I'll find a flight."

I swatted at his hand when he reached around me to take the laptop out of my arms. "I can't just leave and go to Vegas," I said in all seriousness.

With a furrowed brow, Nick stared at me.

"I can't," I said again, getting nervous under his watchful eye.

"Stop lying to yourself. You can go to Vegas. You don't have anything holding you here."

I went to challenge that statement but quickly closed my mouth and cursed myself for never getting off my ass and getting a real job while I sat around and waited for Spencer to get home from his.

"Fine!" I shoved the computer at him. "Book away. What the hell do I have to loose in meeting his family?"

Was it going to be a huge mistake showing up at his family's home, claiming to be his girlfriend? I had no idea, but if it got me close to figuring things out and eventually closer to him, I was going to do it.

Nick made us reservations to leave the next afternoon. I still had to pack and let my brothers and Gia know what was going on. Nick also had a few things he had to handle the next morning with his gallery. We spent a few more hours, going over what we knew about Spencer. I felt like I was doing all the talking. I was telling Nick everything I knew about him, hoping that maybe one small fact would lead us to another, and then another and then, hopefully, something useful. That didn't happen, though.

I remembered lying on one side of the couch with Nick at the other end. He must have pulled a cover over me when I fell asleep, because I woke up the next morning all warm and toasty under a wonderfully soft blanket. I sat up a little to see if Nick had left and he had. I sat all the way up and did a once over. He wasn't anywhere to be seen. *Must have gone to his bed.*

I checked his room but found that it was empty. I checked the bathroom. Saw a raccoon staring back at me in the mirror and decided then that I needed to tame the beast.

Fresh faced and rodent free, I sat back down on the couch. It was then I noticed the folded piece of paper on the coffee table with my name on it. I quickly grabbed it and huddled in my soft cocoon of covers. I turned it over and read.

> *Don't freak out. I just went to get some coffee and something for us to eat. You might have cleaned like Cinderella last night, but you forgot to hit up the grocery store and fill the fridge.*
> *I'll be back in a few.*
> *Nick*

My face hurt as I smiled down at the witty note. *At least he signed it with more than an S this time.* I grabbed the remote and turned on the TV. When the TV was warmed up, the first thing that I saw was Spencer's face. I'd left it on an entertainment channel the previous night because I just had to watch my trashy TV shows. It had been a long while since I cringed when I saw my name attached to Spencer's. Since we'd gone public, most of the publicity had been good, now it was like I was sent back in time.

In the first photo I was hit with, Spencer was lounging in some club with women sitting all around him. His eyes seemed glazed over, and he looked like shit. I mean he was still freakishly handsome, but he looked worse for wear. He was in California, or so the entertainment anchor told me.

We are sad to say the short whirl-wind romance of Spencer Salvatore and reserved sister to the Monroe brothers, Elizabeth Monroe, is over. Last night both were spotted out on different sides of the continent. It seems as though Elizabeth has dumped Salvatore for acclaimed up and coming photographer Nick Holsen. The vixen who stole America's heart seems happy and in love as the two raced away from paparazzi last night.

"I can't believe this," I shouted at the TV. I grabbed the remote next to me and turned it off. I prayed then that Spencer's family didn't follow entertainment media, because if they did, I was going to have a hard time explaining this one. Just as I buried myself under the covers and was milliseconds from dozing off again, the door opened.

"Ah, dammit," I heard Nick yell from the other side of the couch as he got inside.

I tossed the covers off my head and sat up. He was juggling bags and a tray full of coffee cups.

"What's with the look?" he asked as he placed the bags on the floor and steadied the tray of coffee.

"Your boss is—"

"Ex-boss."

"Your ex-boss is fucking things up again."

"What did she do now?" he asked as he handed me one of the coffees.

"Everything. Thanks." I said, taking the drink from him. I took a sip and expected to taste coffee but was pleasantly surprised to find it was tea—perfectly made tea with two sugars and a splash of milk. I sighed as it slid down my throat.

He winked at me. "You thought it was coffee. Such little faith in me. I know how you love your tea. I did date you, and I didn't forget anything."

I couldn't help my smile as I took another delicious sip of the hot tea. "My faith has been restored with this single cup of tea."

"So what did Natasha do?" he asked, picking the bags up and taking them to the kitchen.

"She's saying I dumped Spencer for you."

"Don't give into her. She's just trying to stir the pot. She's trying to make Spencer jealous, and we both know the one thing that's going to get under his skin is him seeing you with me."

He had a point. It wasn't the truth, I knew that, he knew that, and even though I wanted to set the record straight with the world, I had to keep my head down.

Nick grabbed two bagels from one of the bags and joined me on the couch. I took the warm bagel from him and got comfortable on the couch again. We sat there, eating our breakfast and discussing how we were going to go about gaining the information we needed.

"Is that your phone ringing?" Nick asked.

We had been going through every possibility that could have happened when we knocked on Spencer's family'sdoor, when my phone rang from the coffee table. I reached for it, seeing Charles name light up on the screen.

"Hello?" I answered.

"Would you like to tell me why all your shit is sitting outside my front door?"

"Are you serious?" I jumped from the couch and started pacing. *That fucker actually tossed me and my crap out of his place?*

"I'm currently staring at boxes of crap with your name written all over them. So, yes, I am very serious. Why the hell is your shit at my door step and not in Spencer's million-dollar penthouse?"

He was mad. Charles didn't get mad. Scratch that. He

did get mad when people would gang up on me or say something about his family.

I sighed into the phone. "It's a long story."

"Do I need to call Teddy—"

"No! Don't call him."

"You better start talking, baby girl. Did he do something? Did he hurt you?"

My mind was racing by this point. Charles kept on yelling from his end of the phone then, in-between his rants, I could clearly hear a female voice yelling as well.

"Is Gia with you?" I asked, cutting off one of his rants about Spencer being a no-good sickly twisted freak.

"What? Why would she—"

"Cut the crap, Charles. I know that's her in the back ground. Put her on the phone."

I waited while he handed her the phone. I glanced at Nick, who was watching me from the couch.

He mouthed, "Is everything okay?"

I rolled my eyes and shrugged my shoulders because that was how I felt. Everything was crumbling and, once again, I was dragging everyone into my problems.

"I told you that—"

"Drop it, Gia," I said, cutting her off abruptly. "I've got everything under control. This is all a big misunderstanding. Spencer and I are fine."

"Define fine because your definition and mine must be worlds apart. I'm looking at a picture of him with women all over him." I could hear her clicking so she must have been on Fame's website. "Oh-My-God! Elizabeth Monroe, where the hell are you right now?" she demanded.

Perfect, she's looking at the pictures of me and Nick.

"I'm at Nick's."

"Nick?"

"Simon," I clarified.

⌒◞⌒◟

I waited with Nick as we rode the elevator up to Charles's place. When the doors opened and I stepped out, I ran right into one of the boxes with my name on it.

"He couldn't take them inside? What a jerk," I said, kicking my own box again. I didn't bother knocking, I just barged in. I did a quick scan and caught the tail end of Gia jumping off my brother's lap.

"Jesus, Beth! Ever heard of knocking?" Charles yelled from the couch as he stood.

"I don't have time for knocking. Thanks for bringing all my stuff in."

"Oh, no problem, I love cleaning up your messes. Been doing it since you were born. Why stop now?"

"Chuck!" Gia called, hitting his shoulder.

I didn't need her to reprimand him for me, but I was grateful—one less thing I had to do.

"I'm leaving this afternoon, so my stuff's going into the spare bedroom until I get back," I said with a curt nod before returning to the hallway to grab my boxes.

"Whoa, whoa, whoa. You can't move in here."

"Why the hell not?" I demanded.

He didn't have a good reason. He was a man, thinking with his smaller head, because he didn't want me messing up whatever arrangement he and Gia had going on.

"Ugh—fine, whatever. Take your shit in there," Charles said, pointing to the spare room like I didn't already know where it was.

"I will, thanks."

Nick was standing behind me silent as a mime the whole time. When I turned to grab the first box, I caught him nod at Charles.

"What's that for?" I asked Nick before whipping around to question Charles.

"Nothing," Charles answered for both of them.

Chapter 26

Nickolas

I listened as Elizabeth tried to explain herself to her brother and best friend. They didn't give her any leeway. I sat back when they told her that this was for the best, that Spencer was wrong for her.

Stubborn, Elizabeth was hearing none of it. She defended Spencer at every turn. With every bad thing Chuck and Gia said, she had ten good things to say about him.

I didn't want it to be true, but the longer I heard her talk about him, the stronger my respect for her bond with him grew.

Spencer was a jackass for leaving her, for not trusting in her love, for giving up on her. He was a coward, and I wanted to swoop in and take her back, but there was no going back. There was only forward, and I'd promised that I was going to help her, so I sat back and let her argue with her brother and friend.

When Chuck nodded my way, I tried to nod back discreetly but Elizabeth saw me. She called us out, and, thankfully, Chuck was on it. Now the girls were in the spare room, going through the boxes that Spencer had packed up for Elizabeth. She was packing a bag so we could leave for Vegas and, while she did, I stood in the kitchen with Chuck.

"You didn't tell her, did you?" Chuck asked.

"Tell her what?" I questioned him.

"About me helping you find dirt on Salvatore."

"No, of course, I didn't say anything to her."

"So why did he leave her? And why the hell is she with you?" he demanded.

He tried to hide the big protective brother vibe, but the man loved his sister and, even though they fought almost every time I saw them together, both of them always had the other's back.

"I heard her explain all this to you over the phone. What don't you get?"

"I don't get why you're helping her. You and I both know Salvatore's a dick. Did you plan all this? Have you been behind it all?" He was digging but wasn't going to get anywhere.

"I swallowed my pride a long time ago. I'm just trying to help your sister, it's the least I can do. And for the record, I had nothing to do with this."

Elizabeth's voice came from around the corner. "All right I got everything I need." She was pulling a small overnight bag behind her.

"Great," I said, moving away from the kitchen and Chuck and heading for the door.

"I swear to god, Beth, if you—if he does anything, I mean anything to hurt you—"

"Charles, I'm fine. Spencer and I are fine," Elizabeth said, trying to sooth her brother's mind. Behind him Gia was rolling her eyes and shaking her head.

"Gia—" Elizabeth called to her friend. "I love him. I'm going to figure this out, find him, and put all of this nonsense behind us. I was wrong about you and Charles. Maybe you're wrong about Spencer."

"I hope I am," Gia said, before hugging her friend.

They were a dysfunctional family, but they were a family. I didn't have that and being around them made me want it. It made me want friends who, even though they didn't agree with me, still supported me, and a family that had my back, no matter what.

The flight was a full one, and Elizabeth got mobbed at every turn. She held her head up, smiled, and moved forward. We had a car waiting for us outside the airport. I gave the driver the address and off we went.

"So you're sure this is the only way to get more information?" Elizabeth asked from beside me.

She was nervous. It was about the millionth time she asked me that question, or some form of it. She kept messing with the seat belt and chewing on the inside of her lip.

I nodded. "I think this is our only chance. He has everything else so locked down, it appears he got beamed down by aliens. There's nothing, Elizabeth. You saw the records or lack thereof. Just take a deep breath."

"Ha! That's easy for you to say. You don't have to meet you boyfriend's family alone and bombard them with private, personal questions."

I nudged her shoulder with my own and smiled at her. "Bright side—they love you and show you humiliating home movies of him with head gear, thick glasses, and zits."

She gave me a smile back and some of the stress seemed to melt away.

"This is it," I said, looking out the window at the huge iron gate that lead to the Salvatore family home.

"We're here already? That was too fast. Are you sure this is the place?"

I pointed to the huge S on the gate. "Looks like it."

Our plan to get past the gate was simple. We were posing as stylist for the oldest Salvatore girl. I did still have some connections, and I found out that she was awaiting a style team for an event she had that night.

Once through the gate, the drive down the driveway seemed longer than necessary. The house came into view and, honestly, I didn't expect anything less from a world renowned surgeon. It was huge and opulent.

"You're sure about this? Because once I do this, there's no going back. I'll have met his family and be labeled as the crazy girlfriend."

"Or you meet his family, and they understand and love you, because they know Spencer and his issues."

"All right. I like that scenario better. Let's go with that." She nodded as she stared out the window at the huge house.

I sat in the car and watched as Elizabeth got out. She stood against the door a moment before whipping back around and tugging the door open. She stuck her head back inside with a panic-stricken face. "What the hell are you waiting for? Get out here. I need you," she pleaded.

I expected to wait in the car until she got done. I didn't think she'd want me by her side to do this, especially with all the history. When I got out of the car and stood next to her, she glanced up at me a moment and didn't say a word, but still said so much. She told me she was thankful, scared. Her eyes told me, "I know this is hard but I wouldn't want anyone else by my side."

So I stood there and helped hold her up because I loved her and because maybe she could be the family that I'd needed. After all of the lies and scandal, she was still by my side and I by hers.

Chapter 27

Elizabeth

Spencer had told me about his sisters. They were younger than he was, and all of them still lived in their family home. The oldest, Camilla, or Cami as he called her, was following in her parent's footsteps and becoming a doctor. Lucy was nineteen and attending LVU. And then there was the youngest Stella who was still in high school.

Spencer kept it vague when it came to his family, even this new one that he had. They were private and liked to keep it that way. There were no pictures of them on the internet attending wild parties or being too risqué. They all seemed like good girls, staying on the straight and narrow. I was sure having Spencer for an older brother helped in keeping them in line and out of the lime light.

I didn't know what to expect, or who to expect, when the door opened, but I was thanking the stars above it was a youthful round face and beautiful blue eyes that greeted me. It was Stella, the youngest of the Salvatore sisters. The one photo Spencer had shown me of his family didn't do Stella any justice. It must have been an older picture because the young woman who stood in front of me now was nothing like the young girl in the picture.

I knew they weren't Spencer's eyes, but they could have been. They were clear as the clearest ocean blue. Her hair was long and jet black, like his, curled and pulled half back in a high pony tail atop her head.

She stared at me for a moment, shorter than I was. Her eyes drifted up to my face and widened as everything must have clicked in her head.

"Hi," I blurted.

"Are you really standing here right now?" she asked with a bit of a valley girl accent.

Oh, god, this is going to be bad. Can I still run to the car? I really don't want to get chewed out by a seventeen year old. I didn't run, of course, I nodded like a scared mute.

"What are you doing here? Is Spencer with you?" She looked around me and found Nick instead of her brother. "I knew you didn't dump him. He's so in love with you, it's all he ever talks about when he calls. So where is he?"

"Well—" I cleared my throat. "He's not here, but I was wondering if I could talk to your family."

"It's just me and my sisters here this weekend. Mom and Dad are at some surgical conference in Chicago, I think. I'm so glad Spencer sent you over here. I've been dying to meet you, and you know him—he kept on putting it off. Come on inside," she said, all chipper.

Her hair bounced as I followed her into the large kitchen. Nick followed close behind me.

A voice came from the stair behind us. "Stella, who was at the door?"

"Get down here and see for yourself," Stella yelled happily.

Clunky boots hit the stairs as Lucy the middle sister

came barreling down them. She stopped half way when she saw me. Where Stella was young and delicate, Lucky was not. Her hair was cut short to her chin. It was the same dark color at the roots but lighter as it got to the ends. She was in a tank top and her arms were covered in tattoos. Her green eyes bore into mine as she studied me.

"What the fuck is she doing here?" she asked, crossing her arms and giving me the evil eye.

I gulped down the huge lump in my throat and prepared for a fight.

"Stella, why are you letting a cheating, whoreing, woman into our house?"

"Calm down, Lu."

"Calm down? This girl broke our brother's heart, more than once, and shows up here with the other guy—" She pointed to Nick, who shifted next to me. "—I think it's time for you to leave," Lucy said, addressing me now.

"I didn't do anything to your brother. He left me."

"Right and we're supposed to believe you, the girl he never let us meet because he was afraid of you breaking his heart. You're pathetic."

"Listen, Lu—" I said, moving from beside Stella and Nick. I began advancing on the female version of Spencer Salvatore himself. She clearly had picked up on his attitude, and I knew how his attitude brought mine out. "—I get that you're upset. I even get that you think I'm a whore. The media's a twisted lying bitch like that. I came out here because I need your help."

"Why the hell would we help you?" Lucy asked, taking a final stand across from me. With her arms propped on her hips, she squared her shoulders to mine. She was just a hair shorter than me, but every bit intimidating as her brother.

"Your brother is hiding something from me, something about his past. He thinks it's for my own good, but it drove him away from me. Do you see how that doesn't work for me?"

"How do we know your friend back there isn't going to go run and tell the world? He's done it before. We know it was him who leaked what happened with Spence when he was in high school."

"He doesn't work for Fame anymore," I clarified.

"I don't give a shit. Stella, you better keep your mouth shut and kick these home wreckers out of our house."

"Lucy, listen to her. She's not here to cause problems. She loves him," Stella said, confronting her sister.

"Don't be a silly wide eyed teen right now. This isn't one of your stupid books, Stella. They're not going to live happily ever after," Lucy yelled.

"How do you know? You won't even talk to her! God, you're just like him!"

"Maybe that's a good thing! There are too many softies in this family. Someone needs to stand up and take charge."

"Who's taking charge of what?" A mature, calm voice from the stairs made its way down to the kitchen.

Everyone turned to see the last of the Salvatore sisters gliding down the stairs. Camilla Salvatore was regal and graceful beyond her years. She was stunning, tall, dark haired, and light eyed like her sisters.

She moved toward her fighting siblings and, when she did, I glanced next to me at Nick who was staring at Camilla.

"You might want to pick your jaw up from the floor before she comes over here," I joked, hitting his shoulder.

"You jealous?" he asked through a sly grin.

"Maybe," I nudged back.

"Then I'll leave my jaw on the floor."

What a smart ass.

"Elizabeth Monroe."

I turned when I heard my name. Camilla watched me as I straightened up.

"It's nice to meet you." She held her hand out. I reached out and took her hand in mine, shaking it lightly. "Why don't we go and take a seat?" she said, pointing toward a sitting room off to the left.

I nodded and followed behind her.

"This is a bad idea, Cami. If Spencer finds out—"

"What is he going to do? He's our brother, Lu, not our father."

I could sense a little hostility in that statement. Seemed I was not the only one Spencer had been trying to "protect" for their own good.

We all took a seat around the room. Nick and I sat in a love seat, Camilla in a chair, and Lucy and Stella sat on the couch across from Nick and me. The room was decorated in an affluent way. Everything was lush and rich. I almost didn't want to sit.

"Do you know where Spencer is?" Camilla asked.

"No, not exactly. I know he was last in LA."

"Tell me what happened, from the beginning."

I sat there and told his sisters my story. I told them everything, from the first night we met to the night I told him about my parents, and finally what had happened only yesterday when I awoke to find another note from him. Every once in a while, I'd glance at Nick, who would urge me on through the hardest parts of my rollercoaster romance with Spencer. I was so glad he was with me.

When I finished, the sisters sat back in their seats and exchanged looks. Their eyes flashed back and forth between the three of them.

"Does the story sound at all familiar?" Camilla asked her sisters.

I was confused and, quite frankly, a little lost until Camilla filled us in.

"Spencer is a control freak. You know that firsthand, and so do we. There have been plenty of times he's done things to keep us safe or protect our fragile hearts. But he has no right to do that. What do you need to know?" Camilla asked.

I was speechless. I honestly didn't think it would be this easy. That they would just tell me anything that I asked. I was expecting a little groveling, maybe some begging.

The one thing I had going for me was the fact that they knew their brother well, and they also knew I deserved the truth and an opportunity to make my up own mind about him.

"Thank you so much," I said to all of them.

"Elizabeth—" Camilla said, reaching over and placing a hand on my knee. "We know he loves you. When I've talked to him, he was always raving about you. I don't know what could have made him leave you, but it must be bad. I want to help, but I also don't want my brother to get hurt."

"I understand that. That's the last thing I want too. The person who owns Fame is after him. I don't know why, but I think she's figured out his secret."

"Then we have to call him and warn him," Lucy said.

"I've tried calling every number I know. He's not answering my calls, maybe he'll answer yours," I suggested.

Lucy took her phone out of her pocket and dialed Spencer's number. We waited on the edge of our seats to see if he would pick up.

Lucy shook her head. "It went to voicemail," she said, dropping her phone in her lap. Stella and Camilla tried next with no such luck.

"He always answers when I call," Stella said, slumping back in the couch.

"How do we stop this bitch Natasha?" Lucy asked more to Nick then to me.

"Nothing can stop her," Nick confirmed.

"If she knows what he's done, it's only a matter of time before she goes public with it. I need to find out now before that happens. That's why I'm here. If I can figure this out and prove to Spencer that it's not going to change what we are, then Natasha will have nothing. She thinks destroying him and tearing us apart is the ultimate win."

"We don't know anything," Camilla said, confirming my worst fear.

"But Mom and Dad have to," Stella suggested. "They did adopt him. Why don't we ask them?"

"That won't work. They're not going to tell us anything. If they did something to protect Spencer in the past, there's no way they are going to reveal it," Lucy said.

"Dad's office," Camilla said, standing from the chair. "If there's something, it's going to be in there."

We all followed her into the office of Dr. James Salvatore. We looked through everything. For at least an hour, we searched that room and came up with nothing. It was as if Spencer magically appeared in this family with not one trace of evidence.

We had nothing. We came all this way and weren't even a step closer to solving the mystery of Spencer Salvatore. The only thing that I'd managed to do was put my problems on his sisters. Now they were pulled in. They were worried about Spencer as much as I was.

From the corner of my eye, I saw Stella pull her phone out of her pocket. Her face lit up. "It's Spencer!" she shouted. She ran to the desk and put the phone down. Answering it, she put it on speaker so we could all hear.

"Hello," she said eagerly.

"Stella, is everything all right?" Spencer's voice came

through the receiver, and I had to clutch onto the desk with relief, plus I had to stop myself from grabbing the phone so I could cuss him out for doing what he did to me.

"Yes and no," she said looking up at me.

"What is that supposed to mean?" he asked.

"Elizabeth's here."

Silence came from the other end of the phone. I'd never heard such silence.

"Tell her to leave," Spencer finally said.

"Why? You love her. You told me you did. I don't—"

"Stella!" he growled.

Stella pulled back from the desk and looked like she was going to cry. I sure as hell wasn't going to let that fly. I snatched the phone from the desk. "Don't yell at your sister like that!" I couldn't help myself. "She doesn't deserve to be barked at."

"Why are you at my family's house?"

"Because—because you left me! You left me without any explanation. You left me thinking everything was fine when it wasn't. Spencer, you think you're trying to protect me but you're not. Please just tell me what happened in your past, tell me why you keep pulling away from me."

"Don't do this to yourself, Elizabeth. I gave you Nick. Please just go be with him. Go be happy and forget all about me.

"No! I don't want to forget you. I love you, and I know you love me."

There was silence again. It was silent because he knew I was right.

"Spencer, stop being so ridiculous and just tell her," Lucy demanded. "She's still going to care about you. We all are."

"Jesus is everyone there?" he asked.

"Yes, we're all here," Camilla answered.

"Cami, you have to know I'm only doing this—"

"To protect us," she finished for him. "We don't need you to protect us. We need you to tell us the truth."

"No one can know what I've done, and no one will," he said, matter-of-factly.

"Fame knows and, for some reason, she wants you to go down," I told him.

"She?" he asked.

"Yes, I've talked to her."

"How did you talk to her? Did she hurt you, did she do something to you—"

He was saying things in such a rush, I couldn't answer fast enough.

"Yes, no—Spencer, she's out to get you. Let me help. If I know, then I can help you keep it hidden. Nick said she's crazy and having talked to her—"

"So you're with Nick?"

"Stop changing the subject, Spencer. You know I'm with him. I know you're watching my every move—"

"Is he there now? Is he in my house?"

I turned to Nick

"I'm here," he answered.

"Keep her away from my family. Keep her safe and stop digging for things you have no business digging for." Silence. "I can't love you anymore, please stop calling me, and leave my family alone." *Click.*

We all stared at the phone.

When the dial tone came on, Stella picked it up and turned it off. "He's lying," she said through gritted teeth.

"Why does he do this? He always pushes people away," Lucy said, shaking her head.

I didn't believe him either. I didn't believe that a few days ago he was in love with me and now he said he couldn't love me anymore. Unless he was a freaking robot, he couldn't turn it off like that.

"He's only said those things to push you away," Camilla said. "When we were little, and I used to try to play with him, he'd tell me to stay away from him because he was a bad boy, and he didn't want to hurt me. I remember trying to sit on his lap, and he had an ugly scar that ran down the center of his chest—wait a minute, there was a picture of him in a hospital bed just before I was born. Our mom and dad were at his bedside. I found it when I was little. I think it said Spencer age eight on the back. I don't know if that helps, but it's one of the earliest memories I have of him, and the only picture I've seen of him before I was born."

"You can't give up," Stella said from beside me.

I wrapped my arm her shoulder. "I don't plan on it."

Chapter 28

Nick and I left the Salvatore home with only more questions. They hadn't shown me home movies, but they did tell me about a photo of Spencer, a photo that could very well be the key to figuring everything out.

I pictured Spencer, small and fragile in a hospital bed with a huge wound going down the middle of his chest. A helpless child hurt and needing his parents, but they were not there. Instead, an up and coming doctor and his wife sat by his bedside, trying to comfort a pain I had yet to figure out.

We were staying in one of the many hotels on the Vegas strip—in the penthouse—for the night, The room was spectacular and the view was one for the books. I tossed my bags down next to the couch and coffee table full of complimentary fruits and chocolates.

"I got to get out of my own head for a while. I'm going to go for a walk around the hotel. I'll be back," I said, reaching for my bag. I slung it around my body and fixed the hood on my sweat shirt.

"Let me go to the bathroom, and I'll go with you," Nick said, dropping his bag as well.

"No, no, no it's fine. Stay here and relax. I kind of want to go alone."

"All right" he said, sticking his hands in his pants pockets. "Call me if you need anything. I don't think anyone knows we're here, but you never know when it comes to Natasha."

"I will. Thanks, Nick."

"Be careful," Nick said before walking in the bedroom to find the bathroom.

With the door closed behind me, I made my way through the winding hallways and to the elevator. I spent the next hour walking aimlessly through the hotel. I walked by the pool, the shops, the hundreds of restaurants, the casino. No one noticed me in my jeans and sweat shirt. They were all too busy, gambling and shopping, to see anything else. It was nice to be invisible again.

I took the time, walking the hotel, to remember why I was putting myself through all this. Why I was fighting so hard to keep Spencer. I sat on a bench near an abandoned hall way.

Traffic was rushing past this way and that only a few feet away but it was peaceful where I was.

I lowered my head into my hands and tried to remember what it was like to have Spencer's hands caress my face. It had only been two days, but to me it felt like a lifetime apart from him. I was spoiled. I'd woken up and gone to sleep with him next to me for months. Now, I fought to remember what it was like to see him walk into a room and lock eyes with me, and only me.

When I looked back up, I caught a figure to my left lurking in the shadows. I waited a moment and, when it didn't move, I did. I rushed toward it. The large figure tried to get away, but we were in a dead end hallway and, unless it was a ghost that could go through walls or had a secret passageway, there was nowhere for him to go. It was a him, by the way, a very large him.

"Hey," I yelled.

The figure stopped when he realized he was trapped with nowhere to go but past me. He didn't answer me. He put his head down and walked in my direction. Fight or flight took over and, as the adrenaline ran through my veins, I reached out and grabbed his arm when he tried to walk past me.

I was tired of people walking over me, walking past me. His arms were thick with muscles and when I heard him grunt in protest I let go quickly. *Are you trying to get murdered? This guy is huge and could easily take you down, tie you up and cut you into a million little pieces and no one would be the wiser.*

I pushed my own dark thoughts down "What are you doing lurking in the shadows?" I stuck my hand in my bag. "I got my hand on my phone ready to dial nine-one-one, so don't even think about doing anything to me, or the cops will be here any minute."

He shook his head. I heard him chuckle under his heavy breathing.

"I am the cops," he said, finally looking up at me.

His voice. *I know that voice.* The man before me was tall, like Spencer. Built like him too. He even kind of re-sembled him, like he could have been a long lost relative.

"You're—I know you," I said, still trying to put all the pieces together.

"No, you don't."

"Yes, yes, I do. Your voice, it's—I've heard it. You're T." I took a step back and covered my mouth because I knew who it was. I'd heard his voice muffled on the other end of Spencer's phone more times than I could count. "Why are you following me?" He didn't confirm who he was, but he also didn't deny it. "T," I growled, "why are you following me?" Still he kept quiet. "Spencer sent you, didn't he?" I demanded.

The man I knew only as T nodded. "He wants to make sure you're okay, that's all." T hung his head because he knew this was wrong. He knew Spencer was going off the deep end, trying to keep everyone in line and everyone safe from his secret.

"He wants to know if *I'm* okay," I repeated. This time I laughed. I laughed until tears came to my eyes. "Tell him I'm not okay. Tell him I'm miserable. Tell him I'm hurt. You tell him he's a real ass hat for doing what he did."

T nodded in agreement. "What about his sisters? Were they good when you left? Was Cami okay?"

*Cami, why would he single her out—unless...*I thought back to Camilla and how she said Spencer had also decided what was best for her.

"They're fine. Worried about their big brother, but I think they'll survive."

He placed his hand over his chest and at first I thought it was a sign of relief but then he snuck it inside his jacket pocket. He pulled out his phone.

"I'm guessing that's him," I said, wiping the few stray tears that managed to well up in my eyes.

He nodded again. T hit a button and shoved his phone back into his jacket pocket.

"What are you, his little puppet?" It was a nasty remark, but by that point, I didn't care if I insulted him. He was a part of this whole cover up too.

"It's not like that," he said. He was stern but calm. "There are things that we both need to keep locked away. Spencer's my best friend. I'd do anything he asks, and he'd do the same for me. We have each other's back. His secret is also my secret. Drop this crusade because you're only going to get hurt in the end. I know that for a fact."

"What about Camilla?"

"What about her? She's his little sister."

"Yeah." I nodded. "Just his little sister that you're in love with." I took him off guard. His face gave him away.

He stumbled with what to say next. "No, that's not what's going on—She and I aren't in love—We can't—"

"Why are you letting him decide what is best for you too?"

"God, you don't quit, do you? I see what he likes in you so much—Like Spencer, I know I can't have everything I want. I won't cross that line again with him. He's right in letting you go. It's easier this way."

"Easier for whom? Him? I bet it is easy to walk away when you have people following the one person you care about to make sure they're okay. This whole I'm-with-you-but-not-with-you is for the birds!"

"I don't know what else to tell you, Elizabeth. Best to part ways and—" He sighed as if he knew exactly what I was going through.

Maybe he did. Maybe he and Camilla were in love, and he had to push down those feelings because of his past. Or maybe he was just scared of losing, not only his best friend, but someone he loved.

"Stick with Nick. He'll keep you safe, and I'm sure he can make you happy."

I shook my head. It was disgusting that this secret past of theirs had destroyed more than just me and Spencer.

"Just tell me what happened. What is making both of you act like it's life or death whether you love a girl and let her in."

"I can't tell you. But know that Spencer did what he had to do to survive. I have to go." He shoved past me, leaving me standing there in the vacant hallway.

"Fuck!" I yelled at the top of my lungs.

Chapter 29

Nickolas

I thought about going after her. It had been over an hour since she left, and I was still sitting on the couch staring at the walls. I had an overload of information. I'd never told Elizabeth that Spencer might have killed someone. I tried to forget about it. I tried to pretend like that conversation I had with Natasha was a dream. I left out the part in my story when I blurted out to Spencer that I thought he had killed someone.

Every time I went back to that night I couldn't get the shaken look on Spencer's face out of my mind. I'd never seen a man look so scared. The more I worked with Elizabeth on this "case," the more I was getting a really bad feeling about it. She wasn't giving up, though. I could see it in her eyes. She was determined to figure it out and, so far, nothing had deterred her.

The ringing of my phone cut through the silence in the room like a knife through soft butter. An unknown number appeared on the screen, and I knew even before I answered it, that it was Natasha.

"Why are you calling me?" I said into the receiver.

"Nicky my love, you use to be so much happier when I called you."

"I use to be a lot of things, Natasha. Now, what do want?"

"I wanted to give you a heads up. I just got my hands on the one thing that can put everything into place." Her cackling laugh on the other end was starting to give me a headache.

"What did you do now? I think you're bluffing. I don't think you have anything unless you have Spencer tied up, spilling his guts. He's not a bad man. You're just—"

"That man is a monster," she roared. "I'm not bluffing."

"Then pray-tell what did he do?"

"All in good time, Nicky."

"You don't have shit. If you did, you'd have already blown up social media." I didn't believe her, but this was Natasha. So I pulled my laptop out of my bag and checked Fame's website just to make sure. I wasn't surprised when it came on that there was a picture of Elizabeth front and center. She was sitting on a bench in what looked like one of the many hallways in the hotel. The caption read:

Mistake of a life time. Elizabeth Monroe in deep depression over break-up. Angry and bitter Elizabeth on the verge of mental break down.

"What the hell is all this shit on Fame about?" I asked.

"That's what I was calling to warn you about, Nicky boy. I have to use her for one more ploy, and then I promise you can have her back."

"This is a lie. No one's going to believe this."

"I don't need everyone to believe it, just one person. Oh wait, did I tell you I have a really good sound bite of her saying so? Why don't you scroll down a bit and click on it for me." I did as she asked because I didn't think that it was real.

"I'm not okay. I'm miserable. I'm hurt."

It was her voice, but it was choppy. The bite had been tampered with. Parts were taken out and rearranged. The average person wouldn't have noticed but because I'd made a few in my life, I knew what to listen for. The fluency was off. Her breathing was choppy and not natural. Natasha had strung it together perfectly to make it sound like Elizabeth was giving up and spiraling down into a deep depression, which was far from the truth that I knew.

"What are you trying to do with this? If you're trying to get the public to betray her, this isn't going to work. You're just making her look better. You're making her look real, and we both know the public loves real."

"That's not what I'm trying to do at all. Like I said before, I don't care what everyone thinks. All I need is for one person, one man, one despicable, horrible, ruthless man to believe it. It's the last piece to a very complicated puzzle I plan on finishing very soon." Click.

I stared at my phone after being left on the edge of my seat again. The time frame to figure things out just jumped by a million percent. We needed to leave and get back to New York. Everything started in New York and now that we knew he met the Salvatore's in New York while he was in the hospital that was the place we needed to go to. Hospital records were going to be the best chance of us figuring everything out.

The door to the room opened and slammed shut as Elizabeth came storming in. When I looked up from my phone, she was tossing her bag down and throwing herself on the couch. She looked tired and stressed, but we didn't have time to lie down and mope.

"Grab your bags. We have to get out of here," I said, before reaching for my own. She moved her arm from over her eyes and scrunched her brows at me. "Come on, grab your shit, and let's go." I nudged her with my knee to prove I was serious about leaving.

"What's going on? I thought we were going to stay here and see if we can find anything else before we leave." She sat up as she spoke, never taking her eyes off me.

"Plans changed. We need to get back to New York and get our hands on his medical records."

"How the hell are we going to do that? We can't just walk in and ask for files."

She was right, but I had a plan.

"I know someone. They owe me. We won't have a problem getting in or getting the files."

"You know someone?" she asked.

"Yes. Now, come on," I said, urging her to get up.

"Does this someone work for Natasha?"

"No."

"Does this someone know your real name is Nick?"

"Not exactly. She's a—"

"She?" Elizabeth's left brow rose higher in skepticism. "You used this girl the same way you used me, didn't you?"

"That really doesn't matter right now. I have a way to get our hands on the files. Do you want to figure this out, or do you want me to sit here and confess to you all the people I had to screw over to get a pay check?"

Elizabeth stood from the couch, grabbed her bag harshly from the ground, and slung it over her shoulder. "We definitely don't have enough time for you to do that." The starkness in her words shredded my already wounded conscious a little more. "By all means, let's go so you can manipulate this poor girl again."

I stuck my arm out to stop her from walking past me. I held my hand over her chest as I took a step toward her. She was under my nose. Her eyes were hard and vacant. I wanted to say fuck it. Fuck it all. What did I care if she figured this out or not? I shook my head down at her. *What am I doing? Why am I even doing this?*

"I'm giving you everything. I've given you all of me. But that's not going to change anything, is it? You still think I'm the same guy who was only using you to get to something else." I took a step back from her and stared at the woman I thought had accepted me, flaws and all. She wouldn't look at me. Her eyes kept searching for something to occupy them.

"That's not what I think," she said, finally coming back to me.

"It's not? Are you sure about that?" I asked skeptically.

"Yes, I'm sure. This isn't just hard for you, you know!"

"Don't," I said, holding my hand up to her so she'd stop with the lies. "You used me just as much as I used you. And as far as this being hard for you, I don't believe it. You never cared about me. I was just an excuse for you to stay away from Salvatore."

All the emotions I had been bottling up began to spill over. I couldn't just sit next to her and be the happy, fun guy anymore. I had feelings, feelings for her, and she could give two shits about me as long as she got Salvatore at the end of all this.

"That's not true," she said in her defense.

"I really wish I could believe that."

She pointed at herself and shouted at me. "I loved you! Don't tell me I didn't. The feelings I had for you were there, and they were strong. Why do you think it hurt so much when I found out you were lying to me?"

I'd had enough for one night. "I think you were thankful that I lied to you the whole time. It made it easy for you to run into his arms. Don't act like it didn't."

"What's going on with you? Where is all this coming from?" she asked.

I shook my head at her because I was at the end of my rope. It was slipping from my hands, and I wasn't sure if I wanted to keep a hold on it anymore. "I feel like I'm always standing here, watching him destroy you, hurt you. What does he have that I don't? What keeps making you, choose him? I'm standing here, Elizabeth, right in front of you. Where is he?" I challenged her.

"I'm not doing this with you," she said, holding her hands up in surrender and backing away from me.

"Why not? You fight with him all the time."

"No, I'm not doing it." She pointed at me and shook her head. She always tried to hide the tears that welled up in her eyes when she got scared, and this was no exception.

"Why?" I pushed her. With every move she took away from me, I gained the ground back.

"What do you want me to say, Nick? I fell in love with Simon, then he broke my heart. Then I met you, I met Nick. I like Nick a lot. He's been in my corner this whole time, but he looks just like the man I fell in love with and, sometimes, I see him smile and I think, 'God, I miss Simon. I miss how easy it was to be with him. I miss how he could make me laugh.' So, no, this isn't easy for me. There will always be a place in my heart for you—it's just, Spencer's is bigger."

So there it was. She did love me but would forever love him more. I staggered, the back of my legs hitting the couch. I let the furniture win as I fell back, landing on the plush fabric. I felt like I had been punched, stunned by a laser beam, slapped in the face. You name it, I felt it. I didn't know what I was thinking. Maybe deep down I thought I could win her back after all this. I was stupid, a stupid man, trying to live out a dream that should have never been there in the first place.

I felt hands clasp my knees tightly. I was staring up at the ceiling and had no intention of moving from that position.

"Nick"

I heard my name being called. I lifted my head from the back cushion. There, kneeling on the floor between my legs, was the most beautiful woman I'd ever loved. She chewed on the inside of her cheek. A nervous habit of hers that I picked up on when I was the man she fell in love with.

"I know this isn't ideal or even remotely normal, but I need you. I can't do this without you."

"I don't know if I can. You might have moved on, but I haven't. I lied when I said just friends. I want more, I need more. I deserve more, if not from you, then from someone who's going to love me for me, and I can't find that when I'm near you."

It hurt like hell to say, but it needed to be said. If I wanted what she and Spencer had, I needed to get away from her, get away from everything that was connected to Simon and Colin and every other fake name I'd had over the years.

"You're right. You do deserve good things and, if you feel like you can't have those things unless you're away from me, then I'll understand, but I need you this one last time. I need to be selfish this one last time and ask you to wait a few more days."

She was giving me the puppy dog eyes, those big brown puppy eyes that I couldn't say no to.

"Fine, but you owe me."

"Name it. You need a date, a car, a trip to Fiji? Whatever you want, it's yours," she said with a smile that lit her up like a Christmas tree.

"Well, actually, its two things I want." My felt my lips curl up with a devious idea.

"You're pushing it Nicky." She winked at me. "What do you want?"

"First, I want a chance to photograph you again, in a real studio this time, with all the extras—wardrobe, hair, make-up, everything."

"I think I can do that for you. What's the second thing?" she asked, raising a brow.

I sat up and scooted toward the edge of the couch. Elizabeth sat back on her heels and stared at me with a questioning look. I had to do it. I reached out and touched her face with the back of my fingers. She flinched when my skin touched hers but she kept still and kept watching me.

Elizabeth Monroe was one of the strongest women I'd ever met. She kept a hard shell around her for the longest time, and I'd never forget when she let me crack it with a simple kiss. Her cheeks flushed as I took my time looking at her. Warmth filled them along with the pink hew I loved seeing. Her tongue licked her lips, wetting them and making them glisten in the soft, lamp-light-filled room. I leaned toward them, needing that glisten on my own lips.

"Simon," she said softly.

I spoke as close to her lips as I could without touching them. "Kiss me goodbye, Belle. Give me this one last kiss goodbye before I'm gone forever."

Elizabeth's head nodded ever so slightly. If I wasn't as close to her as I was, I would have missed it.

"Goodbye, Simon," she whispered before closing the distance between us.

Her lips pressed against my own. It was gentle and what we both needed. I caressed her face in my hand as she held onto my arm. Her fingers wrapped around my forearm and, as our lips began to part, we both let go. We let go of Simon and Belle. They were free now and, in some other universe, the two of them were happy and madly in love, at least that was what I was going to tell myself.

Chapter 30

Elizabeth

The farther I got from him, the more it felt like Simon was disappearing. We'd closed a chapter in our lives, and I was glad that it ended like this. I was glad I got to say goodbye. Even if it hurt, it was the right thing to do.

Nick and I caught a red eye out of Vegas and landed in New York by early morning. He took me to Charles. I was running on fumes, only catching a few moments of sleep on the plane ride back. I'd been going full steam for the past three days, and it was catching up with me. I fumbled with the key to my temporary new home. It was seven in the morning and, as I entered the condo, I was nearly blinded by what I saw.

I suddenly remembered that I'd had to announce my every move when Gia and Teddy were together, asI walked in and saw my brother's ass and my best friend's tits as he bent her over the kitchen counter. I spun around just in time to see the door close behind me.

"Jesus Christ, Beth!" Charles yelled.

I covered my eyes and attempted to peek over my

shoulder. Gia had dropped to the floor to hide behind the counter. Charles stood in all his glory, and I thanked god the cookie jar on the counter covered his pecker.

"It's seven a.m. What are you doing banging my best friend this early and over the kitchen counter that we both have to share now?" I yelled, with my hand still covering my eyes.

The cocky son of a bitch just stood there with his hands on his hips.

"I didn't expect you to be home. I rather like living alone, by the way. You're not planning on staying long, are you?"

"You're disgusting. Please make sure you sterilize the kitchen before you leave for work today."

"Sorry, Beth." I heard Gia cringe from behind the counter. She stuck her hand up in the air and waved toward me.

"I'm going to pass out in bed for fifteen minutes. When I wake up, I'm going to take a hot relaxing shower, please don't be screwing my best friend when I walk in there."

I saw Gia give the universal sign for okay followed by a thumbs up before I walked away. I kept my hand over my face but spread my fingers wider so I wouldn't walk into a wall.

I needed to lie down for just a few minutes. I needed to close my eyes and let the quiet of the room flood my senses. When I opened them back up, the room was still magically quiet. I rubbed the sleepiness from my eyes, knowing I needed to get up and at least shower before I passed out for good. Filth from traveling covered my skin. I could feel it as I rubbed my cheeks to help wake myself up. My hair was way overdue for a washing. The roots were slick with days of grease and currently matted to my cheek with drool.

I didn't want to move from the dark and cozy hole I'd made in the covers, but as I became more aware of things, I noticed I wasn't huddled under a cover. It was dark in the room, really dark. I turned over and nearly lost my shit. It was six o'clock at night and the lights that lit New York City and kept it hustling through the darkness were streaming in through the window.

I got out of bed, grabbed a change of clothes and a towel, and headed for the bathroom. I'd told Nick that I was going to call him in the afternoon. We were supposed to meet this friend that owed him one at the hospital today. I'd left my bag with my phone in it at the door. I had to call him and tell him I'd overslept and that I hadn't dropped off the face of the earth.

I ran out of the room with my new clothes and towel in my hand. I'd turned the corner to go into the living area and grab my bag, when I saw a silhouette sitting on the couch, looking at a computer screen. The rustle of my feet got its attention, and Nick turned from the computer screen to see me standing just outside the hallway with drool on my face and hair going in every which direction.

He smiled over at me. "Good morning or I guess it's good night now."

"How long have you been here?" I asked, adjusting the clothes and towel in my hands.

"When you never called this afternoon, I decided to come over and make sure that you were okay. Natasha's gone off the deep end and is posting all sorts of shit about you that isn't true, but I still had to make sure just in case."

I made my way to the couch and plopped down next to him. He immediately leaned away from me and made a face. The oh-my-god-you-stink-like-three-week-old-garbage face.

"Oh, it's not that bad," I said.

He covered his nose and mouth with his hand but I could still see the smile in his eyes. "It's pretty bad."

He cringed. I hit his shoulder before leaving him on the couch to take a quick shower.

Steam filled the bathroom and, as I stood under the scalding water, I replayed last night over in my head. I'd kissed Nick. No, not Nick, it was Simon I'd kissed. It was tender like him, soft and comforting just like I remembered Simon to be.

I was in the middle of shampooing my hair when there was a rap on the bathroom door. "What?" I yelled as water spilled over my face, sending soap right into my eyes. "Fuck that stings." I wiped at my eyes and shoved my face into the scalding water.

"Are you all right?"

I opened my stinging red eyes when I heard Nick from the other side of the glass shower door. I covered my body with my arms and moved back from the glass. Only the beads of water on the glass and my sorry excuse to cloak myself kept Nick from seeing my naked ass.

"What are you doing in here?" I said from the corner of the shower.

"Our way into the hospital just called. We got the go ahead but we have to get there and get out in an hour," he said with what looked like a smirk on his face as he tried not to look at me, but I knew he was.

"Okay, let me finish up real quick and we can go."

"All right," he said, not moving.

"Nick?"

He looked up from the floor and through the water beaded glass. "Yeah?"

"Get the hell out of the bathroom," I screeched.

He laughed at me. Then put his face up to the glass, like he was a little boy peeking into the girl's locker room.

"Are you serious, right now?" I yelled.

"What? It's not like I haven't seen it before. Have you been doing squats?" he asked.

His devious smile spread across his face as he wiggled his eyebrows at me.

I threw the wash cloth I had in my hand right at his face. He backed away when it hit the glass and slid down. *Bad idea, Beth.* As it skidded down, it collected the water beads in its path, making an almost perfectly clean shower glass. I quickly ran my hand through my soapy hair and slopped it over the glass, making a new soapy barrier between me and my peeping tom.

During the ride over to the hospital, I couldn't look Nick in the eye. He had this cocky grin plastered on his face, and I still felt naked, even though I was sitting next to him, covered head to toe in clothes. I didn't have time to dry my hair so I did a quick braid and shoved one of Charles's hats on.

"Will you stop it?" I finally said.

"Stop what? I'm not doing anything," he said, all innocent, from beside me in the cab.

I gave him a questioning look back. He knew what he was doing, and he needed to stop. He was gloating about seeing my bare ass in the shower.

"Stop looking at me like that," I clarified.

"Like what?"

"Like you've seen me naked," I stated.

"Well, I have—"

I covered his mouth before he could finish. "Don't, just don't. Try to keep the right head in charge tonight. Can you do that for me?" I asked.

I felt him smile behind my hand. He nodded in agreement so I let my hand fall from his mouth.

"Let's go over this one more time just so we're clear, and our cover doesn't get blown, I'm Jack and you're Jill, and we're looking for our long lost brother. Got it?" he asked as we pulled up the back entrance of the hospital.

"Jack and Jill, brother, sister, and we're looking for our long lost brother. Got it!" I repeated. "You're sure about the name, Jill? Isn't that just a little weird, ya know Jack and Jill nursery rhyme and all?"

"It was the first thing that came to my mind, and, besides, we can't change your cover now. I've already talked to her and she thinks you're name is Jill." Nick smiled. "So, nursery rhyme wins."

There was a young woman standing by one of the side doors. Her foot was stuck in between the doorjamb, holding it open. We made our way to her, and it was obvious she was a knock out, even in her scrubs and pulled back hair.

"Thanks for doing this, Regan," Nick said, reaching out to give her a hug.

I watched as she lingered on him. Her eyes closed and her hand gripped him tighter than necessary for a casual hello.

"It's the least I can do," she said, pulling back and staring up into his eyes. She glanced around him and saw me standing there with a poor excuse for a disguise on. Along with the hat I swiped I also put on a fake pair of glasses. Nick might not have been noticed out in public, but I sure as hell would have been. A disguise was a must if we were going to get past her. Nick had informed me that she was a budding actress and itching at the chance to get famous. That was how she got into the mess of owing Nick in the first place.

"Jill, right?" she asked, addressing me.

I jumped at my imposter name and quickly got into character. "Yes. Jill, Jack's sister. Our mother has a wicked sense of humor," I said, trying my best to put on a fake smile, and held my hand out to shake hers.

"Wow, you look really familiar. Do I know you, or maybe—have been in the hospital before?" she asked, gauging me skeptically.

This is it, our cover's been blown. Of course, she's seen my face around the hospital, I was on every freaking magazine cover known to man.

"Nope, I don't think so," I said, trying to change my voice and make it deeper than normal.

"Regan, how long do we have?" Nick asked, saving my ass again.

"The file room is all yours for the next hour. The woman who works in there is going on break, and I found out she's running to some restaurant to grab food and bring it back for a few people so you have at least a solid hour, if not more, but I'd stick to an hour. If she gets back sooner, I'll come by and get you."

We both nodded and followed her down the winding halls of the hospital.

When she opened the door to the room, I expected to see file cabinets lining the walls and stretching as far as the eye could see. Thankfully this hospital had gone digital. The nice woman who was on break getting dinner for her co-workers was in charge of putting all files, new and old, into the computer system.

Regan gave us a quick lesson on how to search and what to look for before she left us there in the vacant room. There were no windows, no way to tell if it was daytime or nighttime. It was kind of depressing. It was no wonder the woman who worked in here jumped at the opportunity to get dinner for her co-workers. It was like being in a dungeon.

When the door closed behind Regan, we both looked at one another, nervous and anxious that maybe we'd done all this, and we weren't going to be able to find anything. We sat down at the computer at the same time.

Nick put his fingers on the keys then turned to me.

"What should we put in?" he asked.

"Well, as far as I know, he's been Spencer all along. What if we put in Spencer and the year he was born because we know that, and look at birth records?"

Nick nodded in agreement.

In the year Spencer was born, there were also twenty eight other Spencer's born in New York. Public record had Spencer being born in July, according to Wikipedia and numerous gossip sites. But when we narrowed it down to July, there was one Spencer born and he was African American, definitely not the Spencer we were looking for. *Another cover up from the mysterious, Spencer Salvatore.*

"We need to change gears," Nick said after going through ten of the Spencer baby files. "We're never going to find anything this way, and we don't have enough time to whittle it down. How old did Camilla say he was in that picture?"

"Eight. She said it said age eight on the back."

"So that would have been…" Nick did the math really quick and put in the correct year and then Spencer's name and hit search. Again a ton of Spencer's popped up, not only from the year that he put in but from years past, all with the same birth date but different last names, four to be exact. They kept repeating with every visit Brown, Black, Smith, and the last one Phillips.

"Try that one," I screeched in excitement.

I had a feeling we were getting close. The first one he clicked on was Brown. A one year old Spencer who had posterior rib fractures. The next Spencer had a cut and fifteen stitches on his eyebrow. There weren't pictures, obviously, but I quickly remembered the scar over Spencer's eye. The next one was a broken nose, again I thought of the slight shift to the left down Spencer's nose.

A five-year-old Spencer Smith was sent to the ER to get a busted lip stitched up. Immediately, I saw the small white scar on Spencer's lip behind my closed eyes. The last was Spencer Phillips who had a buckle fracture on his arms, both of them.

It was too much of a coincidence that all these Spencer's had the same birthday but different last names. Something wasn't adding up.

"This is him," I said out loud.

Chapter 31

Nickolas

A re you sure? How do you know—wait a minute, look at this." I opened up three of the files at once and each one was from a different, smaller hospital. "They're all from different hospitals too."

"Why would—"

The door to our dungeon flew open before she could finish her thought. Thankfully, it was just Regan checking in on us.

"Did you find him?" she asked, walking over and standing next to me. She placed a hand on my shoulder and peered into the computer screen from beside me.

"We think we did, but all the last names are different, plus why would they have taken this child to—three—wait, four different hospitals around New York?" I asked, sitting back from the computer so she could get a better look.

Regan did a quick once over of the few files that I had opened. She pulled back from the computer and her face fell, her smile faded, and her eyes got serious.

"What? What do you see?" Elizabeth asked from the other side of me.

"It looks like—I mean usually when we see things like this, on top of these types of injuries, it leads to a certain stigma." She shoved her hands into the front pockets of her scrubs and started fiddling with whatever was in them.

"What does that mean? Were they trying to get around the system or something? Were they illegal immigrants maybe?" Elizabeth asked.

"Kind of—It's hard to say," Regan answered.

"Kind of? What does it mean, Regan?" I asked, glancing up at her.

"You see this here." She took the mouse from me, scrolled to one of the files, and brought up an X-ray scan. She pointed to the bones in the arm. "This is what we call a buckle fracture and it can be a sign of child abuse. The aggressor holds on so tightly to the child that the bones buckle and fracture."

"Are you saying someone hurt Spencer Sa—our brother, to the point of breaking his bones?" I said, catching my slip up.

"That's what it looks like. As far as going to all the different hospitals and clinics, that's just another layer to it. Moms will take their children to different hospitals and use fake names so it doesn't look like abuse. What this Mom didn't know was that all these hospitals are now under one branch, one big hospital bought all these smaller ones so now we have all their files."

"So why wasn't anything done? If they knew about this—I mean, it's all here. Why wasn't it sent over to social services or somewhere like that?" Elizabeth asked.

She stood aggressively from the desk and went to go toe to toe with Regan. I pushed back from the desk myself and got between then. With my back to Regan, I steadied Elizabeth with a hand on her shoulder and mouthed. *Calm down.*

"I don't know," Regan screeched from behind me. "What year did this all happen?"

I felt her move behind me and glance down at the computer screen. I kept a calming hand on Elizabeth, afraid she'd let her temper get the better of her.

"Here's your answer. The hospitals were only joined together ten years ago. These files are from almost twenty plus years ago. A lot of nurses and doctors looked the other way back then."

"They turned their backs on a small child, clearly getting physically and, most likely, mentally abused," Elizabeth yelled.

My calming hand on her shoulder was pushed away. Thankfully, she stalked off in the opposite direction of Regan and myself.

"Listen, I'm sorry, but there's really nothing that can be done now," Regan said.

"Nothing that can be done? This is why he's the way he is! If someone would have spoken up for him—Oh, my God, this explains everything—why he wants to leave me—why he thinks he's going to hurt me—He's afraid of turning into his abuser. Ni—I mean, Jack, we figured it out," Elizabeth said with wide eyes as she spun back around to us.

"We're still talking about your long-lost brother right?" Regan asked.

She was getting too curious. Not only had I slipped a bit, now Elizabeth had, and her ranting about why Spencer left her was only making things worse.

Elizabeth stopped moving and reached in her pocket. Her phone was ringing, and I could have kissed whoever it was on the other end for getting her to shut her big babbling mouth.

We were a few choice words from getting caught, and I didn't need that right now.

"It's Camilla," she said before answering. "Hey, is everything okay?"

She turned from Regan and me again while talking to her. I tried my hardest but I couldn't make out what was being said. Regan was in my other ear, talking about getting drinks after her shift and that she missed me. I smiled politely at her and nodded in agreement, just to keep the charade up a little bit longer.

"I know it's been over two years but I—I still think about you. What about you?" Regan asked, taking me off guard.

"Umm—yeah," I mumbled.

"So you do too. I knew it was different was with you. I know we were only together for two months, but I just had this feeling, ya know?" Regan reached up and touched my face tenderly with her small delicate hand.

I stopped trying to listen to Elizabeth and actually looked down at Regan. She was a pretty girl, blonde and green eyed, a pinched nose, and high cheek bones. She was a lot shorter than me. The top of her head only came up to my neck. I felt her grab onto my shirt, pulling me closer toward her.

I licked my lips, nervous about her getting so close to me. I wanted more with someone, but I didn't think for a second that it would be her. There was too much history, too many lies, and that was not how I wanted to start a relationship, not anymore. I wanted a fresh start with someone who only knew me as Nick and nobody else.

"Don't let me interrupt," Elizabeth said from behind me.

Regan's hands left me in a rush as I spun from her to Elizabeth. She had a wicked smile on her face, and I could tell she loved every minute of this.

"Do you two need a minute?" she asked through a chuckle.

"No. What did Camilla want?" I asked, changing the subject.

"He's home."

"Home?" I asked. "Like Vegas home?"

"No, New York home. She said he was upset. Jack, I have to go to him. I have to tell him I know everything. He's at his place."

"You're just going to go over there?"

"I have to," she said with a smile a mile wide. She ran over to me and wrapped her arms around my neck. "Thank you," she whispered in my ear before pulling back and leaving a kiss on my cheek. "Pray my key still works," she shouted behind her as she dashed out of the room, leaving me there with Regan.

"Jack…" Regan said in a serious tone.

I turned back to her, expecting her to leap into my arms after her little speech, but she was sitting back at the desk and scrolling through the files some more.

"What's wrong?" I asked.

"That's not your sister, is it?" she said, glancing over at me from the computer screen.

"Of course, it is. Why would you think otherwise?" I said, trying to save my ass.

"Because that's Elizabeth Monroe. I knew I recognized her, and this little boy you're looking at is Spencer Salvatore, isn't it?"

"Regan, listen—"

"Jack, what's going on?" she asked sternly.

"How do you know it's Spencer Salvatore?" I asked, ignoring her questions.

"Look at this," she said, pointing to the files.

"I don't get it, what am I looking at?"

"This little boy Spencer Phillips died on this night, and then the next day Spencer Salvatore pops up, same age, same healed fractures, and same injuries as this one?" she said, pointing to the file of SpencerPhillips. "This is really Spencer Salvatore, like the millionaire?"

I thought about lying, spinning some sort of excuse but, honestly, I was tired. I was tired of lying to people and trying to keep my stories straight. So I just nodded yes.

"I can't believe this kid turned into Spencer Salvatore. He must be traumatized," she said in a sad, depressed voice.

I couldn't agree more with her in that moment. I didn't know what to do next, did I stay, did I go? Was the puzzle solved? Was this the big secret he had been keeping from her? It all seemed a little strange and honestly not as grim as I had originally thought.

But what I read next had my head spinning. There written on Spencer Phillips file was a name I'd seen only once before. Frances Phillips was listed as Spencer Phillips next of kin. I'd seen that name on a file on Natasha's desk months ago. I remembered her covering it up quickly. Looking back, I never did hear about a celebrity named Frances Phillips. This woman was connected to Spencer. I didn't know how, but if Natasha had a file on it, it was bad news. I grabbed my phone and called Elizabeth.

Chapter 32

Elizabeth

I tried calling Spencer as I made my way through the hospital, but he didn't pick up. I jumped into the first cab I saw and headed as quickly as I could to Spencer's place. When I got there, I ran right for the elevators. I pulled my keys out and prayed that he hadn't changed the locks. The elevator opened and there in front of me was the door to Spencer's home.

My hands were shaking. I could feel sweat beading on my upper lip. All sorts of thoughts went racing through my mind. *What if he changed the locks and I can't get in. What if he gets even more furious that I know he was abused as a child?* I threw in a few good scenarios like him scooping me up in his arms and never letting go. Him telling me he was sorry and that he should have trusted me with his secret. I decided for the benefit of my trembling heart to just stick with the good scenarios.

I let the key slide into the lock, *so far so good*. I squeezed my eyes closed as I turned it. It turned without me having to force it. The lock clicked open with ease. I pulled the key from the door and shoved it back in my bag. I knocked once but there was no answer. I knocked again and called Spencer's name. Still, it was silent on the other side of the door. I did have an idea, one that could backfire, but it was worth a shot.

I pulled out my phone again and dialed Spencer's cell number. If he was in there, I'd hear his phone ringing and know that he was ignoring me. I pulled the phone up to my left ear and placed my right ear on his door. It rang on my end first, then as if it was a flashing neon sign over his door saying, "I'm Home and Ignoring Your Call," his phone rang from the other side. *Jerk, I knew you were in there.*

I should have sat back and thought things through a little more, but this was me and I might have had a tendency to overreact and run on pure adrenalin. I white-knuckled the handle, turned it, and flung the door open. "Salvatore, you coward! Why the hell—" I had taken one step into the room, when I quickly shut my big mouth.

The room looked like it had been ransacked. Lamps were on the floor, pillows were ripped, and their feathers were everywhere. Pictures were crooked, the few decorations that sat on a nearby table were scattered and broken on the tile floor. The ringer on his phone was still going. I looked down at my own and saw that it was still calling him. I searched the room a moment and found his phone glowing from under one of the strewn pillows on the floor. I kicked it with my foot and watched as my picture lit up his screen.

Suddenly it got quiet again. Both phones had stopped ringing, my picture faded, and ultimately the screen on his phone went black.

As I stood there, that eerie feeling I had when I first surveyed the room got worse. I saw it out of the corner of my eye. There on the wall to my left was hole, after hole. Blood speckled the white paint. Thin drips ran down the wall and stopped just before it reached the molding at the bottom.

I walked over to the holes. I reached out, my hand just about to touch them. I could feel the rage that must have gone into them. It was captured in the wall, forever, to stay there as a reminder of what had happened in this room. *But* what *happened in this room? Is Spencer okay? Is he hurt? Was he in a fight?*

I backed away from the wall and, as I did, my foot slid on something. When I looked down, I saw I had stepped on a crumpled piece of paper. I knelt down and picked it up. I spread it out and saw my own handwriting. But I hadn't written anything. The paper looked like it had been crumpled up multiple times. There were water stains on it, old and knew, some still damp. My eyes flashed up to the top of the paper, and I read what someone had written in my handwriting.

Spencer,
I can't do this anymore. I can't be followed around and harassed anymore. I wish I would have never met you. You've ruined everything for me. You've stolen my trust, my love, and run off with it over and over again. I can't go on anymore, I can't be happy. I can't move on from you. You've ruined me. Tell my brothers I love them, tell my Gran I'm sorry and tell Nick I should have listened to him. You can find me finally at peace at the address below. When you see me, know that you've caused me to do it, you caused me to end it all.
~Elizabeth

Who would do this? I knew deep down who had done it. I just didn't want to believe that someone would go to such lengths to hurt another human being. But I wasn't dealing with another human being. I was dealing with Natasha and whoever else she dealt with.

This explained the mess in here and the holes on the wall. He obviously believed it, leaving his phone behind, and the place a mess. It was clear he rushed out and went to the address on the bottom of the page. I gave the place a once over just in case I missed anything else, any other signs, but there was nothing—just the aftermath of a man who was blaming himself for what was written in this letter.

My ringing phone broke through the quiet of the room. It was Nick calling.

"Nick, something's really wrong."

"Where are you?" he asked with urgency.

"I'm at Spencer's, but Nick there's a letter here and it looks like I wrote it, but I didn't. It's basically a suicide note—"

"Elizabeth—"

"There's an address at the bottom of it, I'm leaving now to go there—"

"Elizabeth!"

"Nick, he thinks I'm going to, or that I already have, killed myself. His phone's still here, I have to get there and show him—"

"Beth!" he yelled at me.

I stopped with my rant and took a deep breath.

"Listen. It's a trap, you can't go there," he said.

"What do you mean I can't go there? Nick, I'm going. I have to—"

"Please don't be stubborn right now. Just listen to me."

"I'm not being stubborn. I'm trying to get to the man I love and show him I'm not suicidal and that I didn't write that note," I huffed.

"Can you wait for me there? I'll be right over and then we can go over together."

"Nick, there's no time, I have to go now—What if it's a trap?" I said, sucking in air at the thought that this was bigger than me finding out Spencer's secret.

"That's what I've been trying to tell you. Now stay where you are until I get th—"

I hung up the phone and ran out the door as fast as my legs could carry me. I dropped the letter where I had found it. I'd committed the address to memory and, as I jumped in a cab, I rattled it off to the driver.

"Are you sure that's the address?" the driver asked.

"Yes, now go," I said, shoving my hands in a forward motion.

"It's an abandoned building, ma'am, and it's not in a good area are you—"

"Yes!" I yelled again. "I'm positive. Please just get me there as fast as you can."

He nodded in the rear view mirror and sped off from the luxury building that housed not only Spencer's home but Blue the popular night time hot spot of New York.

Chapter 33

S hould I wait here?" the cab driver asked when we pulled up to the abandoned building. In the spot next to us sat Spencer's SUV. He'd driven here himself. He'd left the lights on and the driver's side door open. He was here, which meant I would be safe.

"No. Thank you, though." I said, handing the driver a wad of cash.

He'd turned around in his seat to look at me. "Are you sure, miss? I don't feel right leaving you in a place like this so late at night."

"I'll be fine." I smiled before exiting the cab. I walked over to Spencer's car. The keys were still in the ignition. I took them out and closed the driver's side door. The cab drove away slowly, and I suddenly felt like an idiot for telling him to leave.

This is how those Lifetime movies start, with a stupid girl telling the cab driver to leave her at the abandoned building where she knows a crazy woman is probably lurking around inside, waiting to kill her and her boyfriend.

I looked down at the keys in my hand. At least I had a getaway car. The door to the building was wide open and beckoning me toward it. It was dark and musky as I walked down the hallways, calling Spencer's name. Paint was curling off the walls, windows had been smashed in. Glass crunched under my feet as I walked down the hallway. A few emergency lights were on, here and there, making it easier to see.

I couldn't have been that far behind Spencer. The water stained, fake suicide note was still damp with what I assumed were tears. He had to be somewhere in this building. I called his name again, louder this time than all the times before.

I stood in the middle of the hallway and waited to see if I could hear anything, and I did. Above me I could hear footsteps shuffling around. I ran down the hallway to the door I had passed earlier that said stairs. As I ran, I called Spencer's name. My heart was racing, and my adrenaline was pumping through my veins. I had one mission in life right then, and that was to find Spencer. The hallway was longer than I thought and, as I was about to reach the door that lead to the staircase, it swung open hitting the wall and sending dust flying in every direction.

I had been running so fast that, when I tried to stop, my feet slid on the broken glass, paint chips and dust that covered the floor. I was panting and scared that it might have been Natasha on the other side of the door, but it wasn't.

There standing in frame of the doorway was Spencer. He too was catching his breath. His chest moved vigorously as he took in air to fill his lungs.

We keep still a moment, staring at each other. It had only been a weekend but it felt longer than that. I'd learned more in that weekend about Spencer Salvatore than I had in the months and months we were together. Through all that knowledge, one thing still rang true, and it was the fact that the moment my eyes landed on his, I felt weightless. I felt those wonderful butterflies fluttering within my stomach.

The moment passed and Spencer ran at me. I'd never seen him move so quickly. One second he was in the doorway, the next he was wrapping his arms around my waist. I held on to him like I never had before. My feet left the ground and his head rested over my heart. I slipped through his hands and, as I did, he adjusted his arms up my back to hold me closer. His eyes were red rimmed, his hair fell over his forehead, and, as I reached up to move it off his face, he brought his own hand up to cover mine. Our were hands fused as one and I never wanted it to be any other way.

"Are you real?" he asked. His eyes welled up and glistened in the dim light. Mine did the same as I nodded yes. "I'm sorry. I should have trusted you, I was scared," he pleaded.

He released his tight hold and cupped my face in his hands. I knew it was stupid but, as his warms strong hands wrapped around the back of my neck and his thumbs brushed over my flushed cheeks, I forgot about everything. I forgot that we were dealing with the devil herself, the fact that I did know Spencer's secret, and, most importantly, that we had lots more to overcome.

Spencer studied me and, after a moment, his eyes narrowed in on me. He held my neck tighter and the tone in his voice changed to the one I knew all too well. "Why did you leave that note? I thought you were dead." His jaw was clenched so tightly he could have cut glass with it.

"I didn't write it," I said sternly.

"Then who—why would someone do that?" He was still in his work clothes, tailored slacks and button down shirt. He'd rolled up his sleeves and loosened his tie. He looked like a million bucks, even though he was sweating, dirty, and his hair was out of place. The man was a waking sex billboard and, most of the time, I didn't think he even realized it.

"Spencer, there's so much I need to tell you, but you have to trust me. You're in danger," I said, trying to get dirty images out of my mind while I forced my brain to focus on explaining everything to Spencer.

"I'm in danger?" he asked, clearly not believing me.

"Yes! I told you I didn't write that note. Someone— well, I know who, but they wrote that note to make it look like I was going to kill myself so that you'd come here and—"

I couldn't finish my thought because someone had started clapping their hands. We both turned in unison to see a shadow move from one of the rooms. A slender woman dressed in black, with jet black hair to match Spencer's, stepped out of the shadows. She was still clapping her hands together when she made it to her final destination in the middle of the hallway. I was standing in front of Spencer when she made her appearance. He quickly took hold of my arm and moved so that he was a half-step in front of me.

"Isn't this just—nauseating?" Natasha said as she slow clapped her hands for the last time.

"Who are you?" Spencer's voice echoed off the barren walls, filling the hallway with his deep resonating voice.

She snickered. "All in good time."

"What do you want, Natasha?" I asked from beside Spencer. He turned to me, brows pulled together in question. I squeezed his arm. "This is the woman who left you that nice little note. She's the reason everything's gone to shit," I explained.

"Oh—now, Elizabeth, darling, if it weren't for me, you would have never of met Nicky or become this modern day Jackie-O that everyone just seems to love. Let's not forget the pitiful excuse for a man next to you," she said, nodding in Spencer's direction.

"We're leaving—now," Spencer said over his shoulder in my direction. He slid his hand from my wrist and entwined his fingers with mine. I nodded up at him and made ready to leave. As we moved to pass her, a man the size of Spencer came out of the shadows, blocking our path out.

Spencer and I looked up at the man. He flashed us a smile before pointing a gun in our direction. I turned when I heard rustling coming from the left. I'd like to say I was surprised, but I wasn't, when another man stood in that direction also wheedling a gun. I squeezed Spencer's hand tighter and tried to swallow, but my mouth was dryer than the Sahara Desert. We were caged in, stuck between a sharp pointy rock and a bitch of an ice queen.

"I don't think you're going anywhere," Natasha mocked.

Chapter 34

Elizabeth

We didn't have a choice. We followed Natasha down the hall. We'd made several turns and went down a few stairs. The two men walked behind us, guns still pointing at our backs. I held on to Spencer's arm for dear life. This wasn't what I was expecting.

I knew Natasha was behind all this, but I figured the worst she could do was have the media and paparazzi covering the building. I never thought for a second that she'd be in league with men like the ones forcing us down the hall with guns to our backs.

We were ushered into a huge room. The ceilings must have been two, maybe three, stories tall. The room was vacant, except for a few huge machines off in the back. The abandoned building we were trapped in was right out of a movie. As we walked into the room, I noticed a figure in the middle, squatting down or maybe sitting in a chair.

The closer we got to the figure, the faster I wanted to wake up from the nightmare I seemed to be stuck in. I'd only seen images like this in movies or on TV, and I was terrified.

Spencer's grip on my hand tightened as the scene before us became clearer. There was a man slumped over in a chair. Spencer and I recognized him at the exact same moment. We both called his name. "T."

The bloodied face of Spencer's best friend lifted slightly from its sagging position. Dried blood made a line from his nose to his lips. A deep, nasty cut was on his cheek. One of the corners of his swollen eyes was split open. We were standing in a modern day torcher chamber. I recognized the clothes he was in and realized that this was what I'd seen him in the last time we'd talked in Vegas.

His shirt was ripped away from his body and cuts were strategically placed over his chest. His ribs were red and dark purple. He'd been beaten, and I felt guilty because it was my fault that Natasha knew who he was. She'd seen me talking with him and probably heard that he knew everything. His hands were bound behind him as he sat bleeding and broken in the chair.

"Let him go!" I yelled.

Natasha chuckled as she made her way over to T. The two men followed her and stood one on either side of him. With his head hanging again, fresh blood dripped from his nose, landing on his knee.

"Why are you doing this?" Spencer demanded.

Natasha didn't answer him but motioned her hand at T's limp body. One of the men pulled out a knife. I screamed when he slashed it behind T. I thought he was going to finish him, kill him before our very eyes, but T's arms fell to his sides with a lifeless thud. Natasha took a hand full of T's hair and yanked his head back. T hissed in pain as his head was moved about like a child's toy. She peered into his eyes and blew him a kiss. I watched in horror as he squeezed his eyes shut and tried to move his head from her grasp.

"You know your friend squealed like a little girl," Natasha said, shoving T's head away from her. He slumped back over in the chair but I saw him glance up at Spencer and shoot him a curt nod before his face fell out of sight.

"You're one fucked up lady," I called to Natasha.

"Maybe—but he's more fucked up that I am," she said, pointing to Spencer. "Just ask him—oh, wait, he refuses to tell you anything. I guess I'll have to." Natasha stepped away from T and headed back in our direction with a determined look on her face.

Before her pointy heels could click on the concrete floor anymore, T sat bolt upright. With blood still running down his face from all his cuts, he yelled, "Now!"

In a rush, Spencer pushed me hard to the left before running at one of the men who were holding us hostage. I fell to the floor and watched in terror as T stood, grabbed the chair he was sitting on, and hit it over the head of the man standing next to him. A shot was fired, the bang echoed in the empty building. T had knocked it out of the man's hand after a short struggle. I watched the gun slide across the floor as T beat the man who was holding it.

A second shot was fired, and I turned, hoping that Spencer wasn't in the line of it. He too had managed to get the gun away. I didn't see how he did it, but there were no more shots fired. Spencer had the man by the shirt and was punching him in the face over and over. The man went limp, slipped through Spencer's hands, and fell to the floor. It all had happened so fast, both T and Spencer were fine and standing over the men they had taken out. They were across the room from me now and the closest thing to me was Natasha.

I scrambled to my feet, took in my surroundings, and saw that one of the guns had been tossed right at Natasha's feet. I didn't think she saw it until I glanced down. She did the same. Her brow rose and her lips curled as she knelt down ever so gracefully. She rose back up, gun in her hand, gleam in her eye, and a smile on her face. She immediately pointed it at Spencer.

Spencer held his hands up and began to take a step in my direction, but he had to step over the unconscious body in front of him.

"Don't move!" Natasha threatened.

Spencer froze and placed his lifted foot back on the ground. T placed a hand on his shoulder and the two friends exchanged looks, before T's legs gave out. Spencer tried to catch his friend, he tried to hold him up, but it was clear that T was in bad shape and any adrenaline he'd had in the fighting had gone. He fell to his knees before falling over next to the man he'd disarmed.

"T!" Spencer called as he fell to his knees with his friend. T's eyes rolled to the back of his head and he passed out like the men around him. I could see the steam coming off of Spencer's body. It was cold in the room and the heat that Spencer was putting off was escaping all around him. He laid his friend's head down carefully before standing back up.

His eyes bore a hole into Natasha, but she didn't flinch. Me, I would have been scared shitless. "What the hell do you want with me, woman?" he roared.

Natasha stood holding the gun at Spencer. "You killed him, you son of a bitch! And now I'm going to finish you the same way."

He went to take a step and I yelled out, "Spencer, please. Don't move, she's crazy."

Angry, scared tears made my vision blurry. Turning to me, Spencer nodded and kept still, but it only made me more nervous. I was terrified about what he was going to do. The look in his eyes told me he was sorry, sorry for bringing me into all of this, sorry for hurting me.

I watched as he turned back to Natasha and began to walk closer to the loaded gun.

"Stop!" I yelled, but he wasn't listening to me anymore.

"Take one more step, Salvatore, and I will end this right now," Natasha threatened.

I felt myself begin to fall. I was slipping. I lost feeling in my legs as they turned to rubber and I expected to hit the concrete floor. I never hit it, though. Something held me up right before I landed.

"Elizabeth, you have to pull it together. We're all going to get through this, trust me, okay." Nick's comforting voice sounded in my ear, like a beacon calling me back.

Steadying my feet, I turned to him. "Nick! W—What are you—" My plea was cut short by a cackling laugh.

"How typical, Nicky boy to the rescue. Don't you get it, you fool? She'd rather be with an abusive, raging killer than with you. If you ask me, they deserve each other." Natasha's evil voice echoed within the empty building. "Don't move!" she yelled at Spencer when he tried to advance. She shot a warning shot just to the left of him. He kept still and held his hands up higher. "Next time, I won't miss," she threatened.

"Natasha, please stop this. You don't want to do this," Spencer said calmly, changing his tactics.

"The hell I don't." she snapped back.

"He's your family, isn't he?" Nick said from beside me.

My head whipped around as this new information swirled in my ears, and, from the look of it, Spencer's as well.

"What are you talking about? She is *not* my family. I've never met her in my life." Spencer's jaw tightened. I could do nothing but look between the two men I cared for and the woman who was hell bent on destroying everything I loved.

"So you figured it all out? And now you know that this excuse for a man, this pathetic boy killed my brother, his own father! He deserves exactly the same fate."

Spencer turned back, glaring at Natasha. "Your brother?" he repeated.

"Yes, you sick fuck. Your father was my twin brother, and you put a bullet between his eyes. So now I'm going to do the same to you—or—maybe I should just let you see what it feels like to lose your other half."

I heard the cock of the gun and watched as Natasha turned it on me. My eyes moved to Spencer's. Worry replaced anger as he stared back at me. Too far away from me to do anything about it, he stood there as helpless as I was.

I glanced back at Natasha. Her eyes were wild with rage and revenge. She gripped the gun tighter and took two steps as she pointed it straight at me.

I stood frozen in front of the gun. Spencer was across the room, and Nick was by my side as Natasha fired the silver gun. She barely moved from the kick back when it fired. She was strong and had clearly fired a gun before.

The shot rang loudly in my ears. I prepared myself for the blow of the bullet. Drawing in a deep breath, I closed my eyes and came to the realization that this was it. I was going to die. It was like a nightmare I had once. I was being chased down an alley and had finally gotten caught at a dead end. I knew it was coming, the force of the bullet leaving the gun, the power of it pushing me back, making my body concave around it. The way it stung as it ripped through the different layers of skin, muscle, and bones. The agonizing burn that soon began to fade as I slowly woke up clutching at my chest, which was pounding a mile a minute. But then I realized that it was all a dream, and I was safe in bed.

It was like that but a million times worse. My eyes flew open at the raging hot sensation that rippled through my arm. First thought that went through my mind as I looked down at my bleeding arm was that she missed. There was a pressure that squeezed just below where the bullet had entered my flesh. I could feel the hot blood running down my arm the moment the pressure was gone. I glanced down and saw that it was a hand that was once wrapped tightly around my arm.

When I glanced up, I was staring into Nick's warm brown eyes. We both watched as he adjusted his hold on me. He placed his hand tightly over my wound to help stop the bleeding. When our eyes met again, he smiled at me before grazing my cheek with the back of his knuckles. The serene look on his face comforted me. Maybe we were going to get through this. Natasha had missed and only got my arm, which throbbed beneath his tight grip.

In some strange way, I knew there was more going on behind me. I could hear the shuffle of feet and muffled voices yelling, the flash of blue and red lights. We were going to be fine, all of us.

A simple cough brought all that hope to a halt. Dark red blood spilled out of Nick's mouth.

"Nick—Nick!"

I pressed my good hand over his chest before moving it to his face so I could get him to look at me, but his eye's drifted closed. I tapped his face then placed my hand back over his chest. Heat radiated from it and spilled onto my hand. Blood seeped between my fingers and down the back of my hand. Blood was pouring from his chest and flowing down my forearm. I looked back up at him.

His eyes were open. "Belle, I—I—"

Cupping his face, I shook my head. "Shhh, Nick, don't talk. It's going to be fine. You're going to be fine." I was saying that more for my benefit than his.

A chilling cough came from the depths of his chest, as more blood escaped his mouth. The color was draining fast from his face, and soon his legs gave way.

Chapter 35

Nickolas

I'd made it, was my first thought when I saw Elizabeth, Natasha, and Spencer standing in the huge abandoned room. Three men were on the floor, and Natasha had a gun pointed at Spencer. I'd called the cops as I made my way over to the abandoned building, knowing that Natasha was going to hurt someone, if not everyone in her path. I'd snuck in without anyone seeing me and stood beside Elizabeth. I held her up and told her we were going to get through this, all of us.

I still didn't know what was going on and why Natasha was ready to blow Spencer's head off, but I had to assume that the name on the file at the hospital and the name on the file in Natasha's desk, had to have a connection. They were related, family. Hell, maybe they were the same person. I was right of course. When I called out to her and said that Spencer was her family, she let it all come flowing out.

When Natasha turned the gun from Spencer to Elizabeth, my heart sank. I saw the crazy in her eyes, and I knew she would do it, if only to get back at Spencer for killing her brother. I turned my back to Natasha and tried to cover Elizabeth as best I could, but I wasn't fast enough. She'd gotten both of us but only got Elizabeth's arm.

I sank to the ground with a thud. Elizabeth went with me and held my head in her lap. She stroked my face as hot tears slipped down her cheeks. She was beautiful—even crying, she was beautiful. Reaching up with what strength I had left, I covered her hand and stilled it on my face. "I still love you. You know I never stopped, right?" I asked. Tears ran down her face when she nodded, I sighed. "Maybe—maybe in another life."

I wasn't sure if she heard me. It was so hard to get the words out. My chest burned with every word, but I had to let her know.

"Nick, stop it, just—you're going to be fine, okay? You're going to be just fine."

Good, she heard me. I still had more to tell her. I coughed again and dug down deep for the strength to continue. "I'd choose you every time—even knowing it would come to this—I'd still choose you. I'd do it all over—as long as—as long as I knew you were happy."

I couldn't take my eyes from her face as I gasped for the air that just wouldn't fill my lungs anymore.

"Stop! Stop it, Nick, don't talk like this. You're not dying! Not yet, not until you're old and gray," she said sternly.

I knew she didn't mean to be harsh—but it was comforting to hear her stubbornness, even as I lay there with the taste of copper on my lips and a searing pain in my chest.

I smiled up at her. "I'll—I'll see you soon."

Peacefulness began to wash over me, I felt warm and comfortable. Suddenly the pain was nothing. It had vanished and all I could feel was calm.

Chapter 36

Elizabeth

No! Nick, don't close your eyes, stay awake—please, don't go to sleep, don't die."

I shook his shoulders back and forth, giving up when his body went eerily still beneath my touch. His eyes were still open, but nothing was behind them. They weren't warm anymore, they were cold. He was gone. The pain in my arm was gone, with all the adrenaline that was coursing through my veins. I folded my body over his and tried to hold him tighter.

Sensing the presence of someone next to me, I pulled myself off of Nick's motionless body. Through my tears, I saw Spencer hovering over us. Kneeling down, he looked over Nick's body. I watched as his hand covered Nick's eyes. I stared at him, before glancing around at my surroundings. Police were everywhere. Lights were flashing but there was no sign of Natasha.

"Where is she?" I asked urgently.

"She's gone, the police fired on her. She's dead, Elizabeth."

I didn't know whether to be relieved or pissed. I wanted to be the one to kill her. There was no doubt in my mind, I was going to kill her after what she had done to all of us.

"She tried to kill me, Spencer." As everything rushed around in my head, the pain in my arm began to come back. I held on to it, putting pressure where I felt the blood trickling down my arm.

"I know, baby, but she didn't. You're going to be fine. Nick saved you."

Nick saved me. My eyes flashed down to his bloodied body lying across my lap. A fresh wave of tears came to my eyes. Nick had taken a bullet for me, and there was nothing I could do for him now. There was no way for me to repay him for saving my life.

"Excuse me, miss, were going to need you to step back. The medic would like to take a look at your arm, if that's okay."

Turning to the voice behind me, I nodded up as two more men moved Nick from my lap. I sat on a stretcher, only a few steps from where he lay on the ground. One of the men checked my vitals while the other checked my arm. I didn't dare take my eyes off of Nick as the men worked on my arm.

Suddenly something became clear to me as I took in the scene. No one was helping Nick. They just left him there on the cold, concrete floor. I stood up from the stretcher and tried to break away from the two men. "What about Nick? Why isn't anyone helping Nick?" I called out in hysterics.

The men fought against me as I tried to get to Nick. But they were stronger and I was placed back on the stretcher and strapped down. The monitors they put on me were making an awful racket as I struggled to get back to Nick.

"Elizabeth, he's gone. There's nothing they can do,"

Spencer said as he did his best to hold me and keep me calm. When I was properly strapped down on the stretcher, the two men left me and made their way over to Nick. Then I watched as they covered him with a sheet and left him there on the ground.

"Don't leave him there alone," I shouted. I fought against the restraints on the stretcher, I kicked my feet and thrashed my arms best I could. A nearby EMT and Spencer had to hold the stretcher so that it wouldn't topple over. "You can't just leave him there. He's all alone. I'll stay with him—let me just go over there with him." I begged, changing my approach. "Please just let me stay with him until…until…" *Until what, Beth? He's not coming back.* I was so mad at myself for letting this happen. I reached out for Spencer's arm, gripping it tightly, I made him listen to me. "Please, Spencer, can you stay with him?"

"Elizabeth, please try to calm down. I'll stay with him, but you need to get your arm looked at. I need you to be strong and let them fix you up. Please, lie down and let them look at you. I'll stay with Nick."

A wave of relief rushed through me as I fell back on the stretcher. I kept a tight hold on his arm, but pain shot through my own. It spread toward my shoulder as I released my grip on Spencer. The medics came back over and put something into the IV they had placed in my arm. My head swirled and I saw spots all around me.

"I'm going to lie the stretcher all the way down," the man over top of me said. "You've lost a lot of blood, and you're getting lightheaded. The bullet didn't go all the way through so we need you to lay still. You're going to have to have surgery."

The last thing I remembered seeing was Spencer kneeling over Nick's body, his hands in a praying position as his head rested on them.

Chapter 37

Elizabeth

Had Spencer really killed his father? That was what Natasha was accusing him of.

When I awoke in the hospital, the room was dark. My brothers sat close by, and, even though I couldn't see her, I could smell Gran's perfume. Gia was huddled close to Charles, their hands intertwined with one another's. Teddy was on his phone, no doubt making plans to get me home where they could coddle me to death. The only person missing was Spencer.

Shifting as quietly as I could to adjust my body in the strange bed, I glanced down at my bandaged arm. *Shit— not quiet enough.*

Everyone in the room turned to look over at me.

"Beth, you're awake, are you in any pain?" Teddy asked, rushing over to my bedside.

"I'm fine, just really sore," I said to ease the concern on my brother's face.

"I'll go get a nurse. I'm sure they're going to want to know you're awake."

I nodded at him, as he leaned over and kissed my

forehead. Once he was out of the door, I turned to Charles and Gia who had gotten up from their seats to be by my side.

Charles took my good hand in his, rubbing the back of it softly. When I looked up at my brother, he smiled back and gave me a wink. But as I stared at him, his smile faded because he had to have known what I was going to ask. "Where is he, Charles? Where's Spencer?"

"Beth, he…umm."

"Spit it out, Charles, where is he?"

Charles's eyes shot to Gia for help.

Turning my gaze on my friend, I inquired again. "Gia, what's going on? Where is Spencer? He should be here. Why isn't he with me?" By then, I was demanding an answer.

"Beth, he's gone. No one knows where he is. Teddy even called his father. They don't know where he is either," Gia told me.

The panic set in fast as my mind worked over what she was telling me. "Get out! Everyone get out now!" I pulled my hand away from Charles and crossed it over my body. I wanted to be alone. Not only had Nick died in my arms, but now Spencer was playing Houdini again.

"Beth, please let us help you through this," Charles pleaded.

"No! I just want to be alone. You can help me, by leaving me alone." I turned away from them, looking at the monitors that were beeping with my elevated heart rate.

"Fine, but we'll be a phone call away. Do you hear me, you stubborn little brat?" Charles said, eyeing me up.

After both Charles and Gia gave me a kiss, they exited the room. The quiet was what I thought I wanted. But once they were gone, all that was left was the sound of my own breathing and the beeping from the machines.

The effects of what had happened in the last twenty-four hours were hard to even believe.

Spencer was MIA and Nick, the man who only wanted to love me, was gone. *How had I screwed things up so badly?* I was on the brink of giving up. Every time something got good in my life, it was only a matter of time before it went to shit. I was so mad at Spencer and even madder at myself. After everything we had been through, I thought that when I found him last night, it was over. I thought that we were going to put everything out in the open. I was in love with Spencer and, after last night, I knew he still felt the same.

That night, I dreamt of the two men who had consumed my life for the past year. I woke up with a wet face and pillow. The last thing that crossed my mind was holding Nick's body and Spencer walking away, never to be seen again. The feeling of being totally alone jolted old wounds that I thought I had buried deep down.

I went to wipe the wetness from my face but found my hand held down. I was unable to move it. I opened my eyes and someone's head was resting on the bed, their hand held tight over mine. All I could do was stare down.

Spencer's dark hair fell over his forehead. His breathing was steady, as he slept beside me.

Even though it hurt like hell, I moved my bad arm so I could brush the hair off his forehead. He hadn't left me, after all. He was there with me. I knew deep down he wouldn't really leave me again. We loved each other, flaws and all, and nothing was going to tear us apart, not if I had a say. He stirred under my hand, his eyelids fluttering open. Sitting up to look at me, he took the hand on his face and kissed it tenderly.

"Hey," I whispered to him.

The strain on his face made him look older. But he managed to give me a half smile. "Hey, back."

He lifted his head from the hospital bed and, in one swift motion, he was up out of his chair leaning over me. His warm hands cupped my face. His full lips, lips I thought I would never feel against mine again, came down in a rush. My face was damp again but I didn't know if it was from my eyes or his.

"Where were you? I thought you left me," I said against his lips.

He pulled back from me and the bed. The hands that I had come to love dropped from my face as he brushed them through his own hair.

"Spencer, talk to me. You're scaring me." I sat up straighter in the bed as Spencer turned away from me, his hands resting on top of his head.

"I can't do this, Elizabeth."

The monitors around me went off like crazy. "You can't do what, Spencer?"

"This. I told you I can't be with you. Look what I've done to you. If you would have—if she would have—I can't put you in danger like that. If you're with me, then you're in danger."

"Then I'll be in danger. Spencer, you didn't do this. That psycho bitch did, and she's gone now."

"If it's not her, there will be someone else," he said, still too far for me to touch him.

"I don't care. As long as we're together, we'll be fine. I love you—"

"I killed my father, Elizabeth," he yelled at me. "I beat a man within inches of his life. It's in my blood. Jesus, my aunt tried to kill us, my father tried to kill my mother, and it's my fault your parents are dead. Don't you get it? This is all my fault."

I sat there in the bed, more confused than ever. I had a few pieces of the puzzle but, clearly, there was a lot more I didn't know about. "No, you didn't kill my parents.

They died in a car accident, Spencer, I told you this already. Either way, I don't care. You don't get to walk away from me anymore. We'll get through this together."

"Elizabeth." His voice rang in the air as he tried to get his point across. "Your parents are dead because of me, my father, my mother, my deranged aunt—Nick, everyone—everyone is dead because of me."

"Spencer, my parents were killed in a car crash," I said again, hoping that it would sink in. "You were like eight year's old when they died. Are you telling me you drove a car on a highway at eight? It doesn't make any sense. Please, just sit down. Talk to me, tell me everything you've been holding back. It's obvious you're drowning. Let me help you, let me in."

Taking a deep breath, Spencer walked back over, sitting in the chair that was flush against the bed.

"Fine, I'm tired of lying to you. You want to hear the truth, here it is, all of it. And when you hate me at the end of it all, I'll be able to say I told you so."

Chapter 38

Spencer

Against my better judgment, I sat down and told the woman I loved every horrible, brutal thing that had happened to me or that I had done.

"It started when I was born. I was supposed to be the strong son of Nathan Phillips. I came into this world weak and frail. I was almost four pounds when I was born, but not for a lack of my mother trying. She did everything right. It was my father who made me enter this world as a premature baby. He tossed my mother down a flight of stairs because she forgot his beer one night. That was the night I was born. I spent the first two months of my life in the hospital. They were the most peaceful days of my young childhood. I soon realized that hospitals would become my safe haven, my refuge from a man who I was supposed to call Dad.

"I watched as my father beat my mother then turned and beat me. He was a rough, stern man. When he told you to do something, you did it. I couldn't tell you what he did for a living. He would come and go as he pleased. But he must have made good money because he would always threaten my mother that he would take me and put her out on the streets.

"The worst night of my life was the night I spent hiding under my bed. What else would a scared almost-eight-year-old do when his parents were fighting? Something was different about this fight, though. I had to help my mother. It was the only thought that crossed my mind as I covered my ears and curled into a ball under my bed. I decided that night that I wasn't going to let my father hit her again.

"I thought that I could stop it, that I could stand up to him. Even though he scared the shit out of me, I had to try. The arguing became louder as I walked to the stairs. They were standing in the kitchen. My father had my mother by her arms and he was shaking her. Her head looked like rag doll. I yelled for him to stop, and he did, but not before back handing my mother across her face. He threw her limp body to the floor and laughed when I ran to her. He was so evil. How could someone have so much evil in them? He ripped me from my mother's arms. Her scream for me was heart-wrenching and still echoes in my mind.

"My father sat in a chair and took me over his knee. He beat me, just as he had my mother. I screamed as each blow hit me harder than the last. I kicked my feet and tried to get away. My mother hit my father in the back and begged him to stop. He laughed again, back handing my mother even harder. When she fell to the floor, her hand covered her face and, when she moved it, blood ran from her busted lip, and her eyesbegan swell.

"She fell to the floor as my father's attention came back to me. 'You see that, Spencer, that's how you deal with a woman.' I can still hear the evil pleasure in his voice when he said it. 'It seems as though your mother wants to leave me and take my only boy with her. Guess what?' The liquor on his breath smelled horrible as he sat me up on his lap and spoke inches from my face. 'You're not going anywhere unless I say so.' He patted my head and let me down to stand on my own feet. He took the bottle on the table and drank some more. I hated my father for hurting my mother and me. He should pay for all the times he'd hurt us.

"My mother sat up and cursed at him. They started yelling at each other again. She was telling him that we were leaving, and it didn't matter what he thought. She was in love with someone else, someone that was going to take care of us. That sent my father over the edge. I heard the sirens getting louder. I prayed that they were coming to save us. T was my best friend and his father was a cop. I thought that if I could run over fast enough, I could get him to stop my father. I knew there wasn't enough time. He had her around the neck, and she couldn't breathe. I had to stop him. I looked around the room and saw his bag on the chair. I knew he carried a gun. He'd let me shoot it, taught me how to aim. I was good for a kid. He even said so. I rushed for the bag, found the gun, and pointed it at my parents. He had my mother in front of him, his fingers tight around her neck. He told me to put the gun down. I undid the safety like he'd taught me. I aimed it at his forehead. He knew I was a good shot. Shit, he had taught me. With both hands steady, I took deep breaths as I eyed my target, just like he'd taught me to. He let go of my mother's neck, and she fell to her knees before him, gasping for air.

"I didn't take my eyes off my father. The sirens were just outside now. They were coming to save me. They were finally going to take my mother and me out of that hell house. I looked down at my mother for a split second, and that's when my father lunged for me. I fell back, hitting my head on the nearby table. The gun was still in my hand. The kick from the gun had made me fall back. My hand tingled from the aftershock. I got up fast to my feet, cocked the gun, and pointed it toward the body that lay still on the floor. A puddle of blood began to spill from my father's head, where he layface down on the kitchen floor. I'd done it. I'd taken on the beast, and I'd won.

"My Mother screamed and ran over to me. Taking the gun from me, she placed it on the table behind me. Out of nowhere, there was a pounding on the door. "NYPD…" The door was rattling. My mother hugged me tight.

"'Spencer we have to leave—now.' She grabbed the gun, and we went out the back door and over to T's house.

"T's house was dark. My mother banged on the back door. Mr. Thomas came to the door and let us in. My mother hugged and kissed him. T came down the stairs, and I ran over to him. I told him I shot my father. Mr. Thomas and my mother were talking. She handed him the gun that I had just used to kill my father.

"'I have to leave, I can't stay. I just wanted to tell you that I love you. I have to get Spencer out of here, before they come for him.' My mother was rambling, and Mr. Thomas tried to calm her down, but it was no use, she was hysterical. 'I can't lose my baby, I'm sorry, Connor. They will be looking for us. Please help me.'

"I stood next to my best friend and watched as our parents talked. They were in love, and it was obvious, now that I look back on it. All my mother had to do was leave my father.

"'Caroline, you have to calm down, everything will be fine. Spencer won't get in trouble,' Mr. Thomas said, try-ing to sooth my mother.

"'Connor, he shot Nathan! I have to run.' She kissed him then grabbed my arm and pulled me out the door we had just come in through. He ran after us, but went back inside. My mother threw me into the back seat of the car and got in the driver's seat. She told me to put my seat belt on, and, as she put the car in drive, Mr. Thomas came to her window, hitting it, trying to get her to stop.

"I yelled at her to listen to him. 'Mom, he's a cop. He can help us, please just stop the car.'

"'Spencer, we have to leave. We can never come back. Do you understand? They will figure out you killed your father.' She was crying and driving frantically. I didn't know if she meant that 'they' were the cops or someone else. I know now that she meant someone else.

"The cop cars didn't take long to catch up with us. There were tons of them. 'Mom, please stop!' I yelled at her.

"'Spencer, I love you! Whatever happens, I love you, and I don't want you to feel guilty about what you have done. You saved my life, you're my hero. You are nothing like your father. I want you to forget all about him—do you hear me—' I sat in silence 'Spencer, do you hear me?' she asked again, as she looked back at me through the rearview mirror. I looked at her beautiful eyes. I had her eyes. She smiled, and all the bruises and blood disappeared, and all I saw was my angelic mother looking back at me. That's when the lights went out. She was last thing I saw.

"I was lying in the back of the car. There was a horrible smell of smoke, and my whole body hurt. I was having trouble breathing. I began to panic as I looked around me.

"Lights were flashing and men in yellow suits were talking to me, but I couldn't understand what they were saying. The roof of the car peeled back, and a man leaned over, looking down at me. They unclipped my seat belt and pulled me out of the car.

"I lay on a stretcher, looking up at the stars. 'Spencer, you're going to be fine.' It was Mr. Thomas.

"'Where's my mom? Where's my mommy? What happened?' I couldn't move my head. They had strapped me down so I couldn't move.

"'Spencer, you were in a car accident—your—your mother wasn't wearing her seat belt.'

"'No! Where's my Mom?' I felt the tears run down the sides of my face. I knew deep down what he was going to tell me, even at that age I knew.

"'She didn't make it, son.'

"'You're lying—where is she? I set us free. I killed him. We can stay with you and T now.' My mother's true love leaned over me, holding my face in his hands. He was more of a father to me than Nathan Phillips ever was.

"'Spencer, you can't tell anyone about your father. You need to keep quiet.'

"I looked up at the dark sky, as everything hit me. I had killed my parents. I shot my father and my mother was talking to me and looking at me when she hit the other car. It was my fault. It was all my fault. I killed my parents.

"'Spencer—Spencer, look at me—' Mr. Thomas called.

"I couldn't. My eyes became heavy and I just wanted to sleep, so I closed my eyes, intent on never opening them again."

Chapter 39

Elizabeth

*W*hat does one say after hearing a story like *that?* I sure as hell didn't know. He'd killed his father, hurt people, but underneath all that, he was just a frightened child, wanting nothing more than to feel safe.

"Was that the night you met the Salvatores?" I asked.

"No, I'd met Ellen and James multiple times before that. They were kind, and they knew the circumstances. Together with T's father, the three of them made it look like I was killed.

"It turned out my father was high up in a mob ring. There was an ongoing case and the cops were following him to the main boss. That's why it was so important for me and for everyone to keep this secret. If it got out that I was alive and that I had killed my father, they would have come after me, and I don't even want to know what they would have done. These weren't the men on *The Sopranos* or other mob movies. Nothing mattered to them, not even killing an eight-year-old boy. T's father knew this so he covered everything up. The Salvatores adopted me and quickly took jobs on the other side of the country."

"What about now? What about Natasha, did she tell them, are they after you again?" I asked frantically.

"I don't think so but, Elizabeth, this is what I've been talking about. I can't put you in danger like this. I knew that from the beginning. I should have listened to my head instead of my heart." Spencer sat back down in the chair next to the bed. With his head in his hands, he exhaled a deep breath.

"Spencer—" I called to him.

He looked up from his hands. He was scared but, most of all, he was hurting. His eyes had seen so much, so young, and it was clear that he was tired of pretending and tired of keeping everything so closed in all the time.

I knew he was damaged, maybe a lost cause, even dangerous. He was a product of his past, a product of an abusive upbringing. He had anger issues, he had serious trust issues, and now I knew why. I always knew there was more to his story, more to the man that made me forget how to speak and think logically. The fact of the matter was that I still loved him. He hadn't killed my parents. He was a child, he was an innocent. Fate had taken my parents from me and, in return, had given me Spencer.

I thought back to all the times we'd passed each other in our lives. Meeting in a nightclub that I swore I'd never step foot in, but remembering now, a feeling I had about taking a chance, giving in, and going out for the night. Or when I ran into him on the street outside of the club he'd bought with my brothers. The coffee shop, the park, all of it was fate pushing us toward one another.

We were meant to be together, we were made to take the other's pain. He took away my insecurities and gave me a confidence I only dreamed of achieving on my own, and I was going to take on his guilt and accept him for everything that he was—good and bad. I was going to love him unconditionally, the same way he loved me. "You know you can't get rid of me," I declared.

It took a second, but his smile spread to his eyes. "I can't promise you, things won't get worse. If Natasha told anyone from the past who I really am, they could blackmail me or they could come after you. Elizabeth, I don't know what I'd do if—" He stopped there and hung his head.

"The only thing I want you to promise me is that you love me, that you'll tell me the truth, even if you think I shouldn't know it. Spencer—" I said, adjusting in the bed so I could sit up and look him in the eye. I gestured to my arm. "—this is nothing. I'd endure a hell of a lot more to be with you. You mean that much to me."

There it was—his smile, the one I found myself living for. "You're insane, and stubborn as hell," he said, shaking his head at me.

"And you're a control freak with a slight temper problem. I think we were made for each other. You make sure I don't go into the insane asylum, and I'll put a lid on your temper." I winked at him, reached out, grabbed his shirt, and pulled him closer. He had to stand from the chair as I brought him over top of me. "Now, kiss your girlfriend like you mean it," I said, as I yanked on his shirt again.

"Okay."

My eyes shut as he closed the distance between us. The room went darker, but not for long. For, the moment his lips touched mine, colors erupted behind my eyelids—beautiful colors of bright reds and clear blues, lime greens and daisy yellows, sunset oranges and stormy purples.

Whatever pain I felt in my arm disappeared as those colors danced around my head. I held on to him, gripped the back of his head by his dark hair with my good hand,

and kept him close. He left my lips and kissed my neck but the colors remained.

"Don't you ever let go of me," he breathed in my ear.

"I won't," I whispered back.

Chapter 40

Spencer

I'd never understand why Elizabeth loved me so unconditionally. She was everything I needed but nothing I deserved. I was the monster in this story. I was the reason why so many people had been hurt.

I was given a second chance at life, a second chance with a family that loved me, and I'd taken it for granted. I spent the first year with the Salvatores, silent. I didn't talk to anyone, not even my best friend T. My mother had told me not to blame myself, she told me I was nothing like my father—turned out I was.

I had no other family, or at least I didn't know I did. It was always just the three of us, my mother, my father, and me. I never met any grandparents or aunts and uncles. I never knew my father had a sister, let alone a twin sister. It all made sense now, the resemblance between her and my father, the way she laughed at things that weren't funny, the evil she was willing to inflict on others.

With her dead, and the men T and I fought arrested, I was terrified that, at any moment, I was going to be next.

If she was in contact with the same people my father worked for and if she'd told them the truth, my days were numbered. On the flip side, if the police found out, I'd be in jail for killing my father and posing as someone else. But I'd been living with that hanging over my head since the day I shot my father, and I didn't regret doing that for one second. What I did regret was missing out on everything my mother and I could have had together.

Everyday of my life I woke up, wishing I would have been killed in the car with her, that way we'd be together. I'd lie in bed until Ellen or James came and got me up for school. As an adult, I turned on a robotic part of me. I woke up, went to the gym, and went to work. I put on a show for everyone around me. I acted like I was enjoying my life but, in reality, I wanted nothing more than to open my eyes and see my mother again.

I never dated after the incident that happened in high school. That time in my life scared me to the core. I was acting like someone my mother would have despised. I played the part of the rich boy. It made my skin crawl when I thought about how I treated people back then. I was jealous and became violent when I'd heard that my girlfriend at the time was cheating on me. I went off the rails and, when I looked in the mirror at the police station, I saw my father looking back at me. So I changed that night. I swore I wouldn't be put in that situation again, the robot turned on, and I simply followed him around.

I'd always attracted women. One good memory I had when I was young was being in kindergarten and being stuck in the middle of two classmates who were fighting over who was going to be my girlfriend. It was harmless back then, and I didn't really understand or care. But as I got older I was able to use my looks to persuade girls to kiss me. In middle school, I was Romeo and the number of Juliet's lined up and waiting at the balcony was astounding. As a man, I had desires but I went into everything telling the women that I was with that it was strictly a one-time thing.

I grew up, knowing that, at any moment, someone could find out who I was or what I had done. Thankfully, I had a group of people around me who protected me. In the beginning, there were five people who knew. With T's father gone, T took over for him. He'd had an ear to the ground and was as good, if not better, than his father at making sure anything that might arouse suspicion was taken care of.

The night I met Elizabeth Monroe, it was like the robot started to malfunction. I felt alive when I was near her. I felt my heart rattle against my chest for the first time in a very, very long time. I found myself smiling when I was around her. I didn't know how to talk to her. I was rendered as speechless as she was. So I'd send her notes, but it wasn't enough, and she was with someone else. She'd pushed my buttons and brought me back. I was terrified because I could feel the jealousy and my temper rise with every touch and every kiss. I pushed her away and then pulled her back for my own pleasure.

She should have hated me, she should have kept clear of me, but fate had other plans. She was right about us. We were made for one another, and we fit together perfectly. For a long while, I believed we'd be able to get through it all. Hell, we had so far, but the moment I heard the story about her parents, it started a downward spiral.

T and I found out that it was her parents car my mother hit. We had to open files that had been sealed and, when we did, someone saw my father's file, and I had a feeling it was Natasha. She was watching my every move and must have had me followed.

When I got a call from T that someone had opened the

file after we had, I panicked. Again I pushed Elizabeth away.

I couldn't tell her, even though I wanted to. I tried to push her back to Nick, but that backfired and, when I read the note I thought she had left me about ending it all, I broke down and prayed that, if I could make it to her, I'd tell her everything and trust in her love for me. Because if there was one thing I knew about Elizabeth Monroe, it was that she loved me as much as I loved her, and I was a fool for thinking otherwise.

As I walked out of her hospital room, I stopped just outside the door and looked back in at the woman sleeping. She was my new angel. She was my reason for waking up. She'd destroyed the robot. I might not have been the most even-tempered man but she made me want to be better, and that was all I needed.

Epilogue

Elizabeth

"Nick, I'm not going to tell you again. Stop throwing the football in the house." His cheeky little smile made it hard for me to yell at him, but enough was enough. I wasn't cleaning up another broken picture frame.

"Mom, I have to practice, tryouts are only a week away," the brown-haired, brown-eyed little boy huffed.

I rubbed my aching back and rolled my eyes before flopping down on the couch. "Fine, you can tell your father when you break another one of the picture frames, or vase, or windows." I peeked at my eight-year-old and had to stifle a chuckle as he stomped his feet and mumbled under his breath. *We might have created a little monster. Sometimes, I think he can be worse than his father. Okay, so maybe I played a little part in his stubbornness.*

"Mommy—Mommy, look at this. Daddy got me a new doll."

I sat up and braced myself as a blonde four-year-old with clear blue eyes came running right to me. "Oh, Caroline, it's beautiful."

It was a fact that the little girl sitting on my lap was going to be spoiled rotten because her father kept buying her every little doll he could get his hands on.

"Why don't you sit here?" I said, moving her so she was sitting on the couch next to me. "Now, play with your doll. I need to talk to Daddy for a minute."

Next, I began the painful process of getting my pregnant ass off the couch. My motivation—yelling at my husband.

I stood at the entry way to his office. He was sitting in his high-backed chair, looking out the window. The tall glass book shelves lit up the room as the sun danced off them. He was talking business, something about one of the hotels that we owned winning an award or stars, I couldn't really tell which. Once he said goodbye, I watched as he hit a button on his ear piece then took it out.

He stood from the chair and walked closer to the window. His large-suited frame still took my breath away. Maybe it was because I knew exactly what was underneath it, maybe it was just because he was the most handsome man alive, and all mine. Either way, I won.

Clearing my throat, I took a step just inside the office. "Mr. Salvatore," I called to him.

He turned from the window and that devilish smile spread across his face. He moved from behind the desk and leaned against the front of it. His hips rested on the edge as he crossed his long legs in front of him. "Mrs. Salvatore, how can I help you?" he asked, placing his hands on either side of the desk.

I crossed my arms, resting them on my round belly. "We have a problem."

"A problem? What might this problem be?"

Oh, he knows damn well what the problem is. The jerk doesn't listen, that's the problem.

"A certain little girl just came running to me, ever so excited because her daddy just bought her *another* new doll. Do you know anything about that?" Raising a brow, I shifted my weight to the other foot and waited for his response.

He confidently shook his head. "I have no idea what you're talking about."

I shifted my weight again. "Really?"

He shrugged. "Nope, I have no clue what that little girl is thinking, saying I gave it to her. Maybe she found it."

Unfolding my arms, I moved them to my aching lower back. "Spencer, I told you, you can't keep buying her dolls."

"Relax, Elizabeth, it's not a big deal. I told you before, if I want to buy my children things, then I'm going to do it."

His sexy blue bedroom eyes could usually do magic and get me to back off, but not while I was pregnant. Then they didn't work at all. "Don't tell me to relax, Spencer! If you keep buying her things, she's going to be a spoiled brat. Now, we don't want to deal with a spoiled brat for a teenager, do we?" I asked as if I was addressing one of the children.

"She's four, Elizabeth. If I want to buy her a baby doll, then I'm going to do it."

I took a deep breath and tried to calm down. The doctor had warned me to keep my temper in check while I was so far along. He feared it would bring on early labor. Too bad my doctor didn't realize that that was nearly impossible. "Spencer, you can't buy her everything—"

A tinge of pain shot across my lower abdomen. I reached my hand under my stomach to try and ease it. Sucking in a hissing breath, I curved my body around my stomach, thinking that might help too.

The moment it happened, Spencer was up off the desk and by my side. "Are you trying to have this baby four weeks early?" he asked, rubbing my stomach.

"Well—" I panted and glared up at him. "If someone would just listen to me, I might be able to keep my temper in check."

"Come here," he said, pulling me over to the desk. Leaning against it, he placed me between his legs. I rested my head on his chest while he rubbed my back. His strong hands relieved the ache from standing.

"You're a jerk, you know that?" I tried not to smile because I was mad. This was all his fault, the baby dolls, the aching back, all of it, but I couldn't help it. The man still made me weak. So my lips curled up in an unwanted smile, like they always did.

He smiled back before leaving a kiss on my nose. "So you've told me."

"Mom, Dad. Uncle Chuck and Aunt Gia are here. Can I go outside and play with Thomas and Luke? We want to play football in the backyard."

"Yeah. That's fine, but tell your cousins not to break anything this time," Spencer yelled, in hopes that our energetic son had heard him. "Those boys are terrors," he said in a serious tone.

"They're ten, and boys, and a little wild. I don't think they're that bad."

"Say's you. They broke the fountain last time they all played 'football.' I'm not sure how dish soap is involved with football, but those boys found a way to get the whole fountain covered in bubbles."

I kissed his cheek and began playing with his shirt. "They're good boys. They're just a little mischievous, I mean look at their father."

Spencer nodded. "Good point."

I pushed myself off his chest and pointed my index

finger at him. "Seriously, Salvatore, back to why I came in here."

"You mean you didn't come in here to kiss me and tell me how much you love me?"

I smacked his chest and gave him my best angry face. It didn't have any affect, except to make him laugh at me and pull me closer. So I resorted to pouting up at him.

"Okay, Okay I'll only buy her a few dolls a week."

"Spencer—"

"Fine, fine, you win for now, but once this baby is out, we're going to have a real conversation about it, and you know how I love our 'conversations.'"

"Yes, I do, Mr. Salvatore, yes I do."

Worlds will collide in

Opposite

HEARTS

Coming Soon

Turn the page for a brief preview

Chapter 1

Teddy

I'd just gotten off the six hour plane ride from New York to LA. No need to go to baggage claim, I only had time to grab an overnight bag, which I kept stored in the office in case of an emergency, and what I had just went through was pretty much the worst emergency a man could go through.

I hopped on the first direct flight they had available and rushed to the hospital. I sat in the busy waiting room with my brother and ex-girlfriend. Talk about feeling awkward. The two had made it public and I was happy for them, but it didn't downplay the fact that I was tired of everyone getting what I so desperately wanted in my life. As we awaited the news about our sister, I kept busy on my phone, sending e-mails, checking my calendar, and watching stupid cat videos thinking that maybe it would take my mind off the real reason I was there.

My baby sister had been hurt. It was my job to protect her, and I didn't. I was the oldest, I was the one who was supposed to keep her safe, steer her in the right direction, but I left her because I couldn't take seeing my ex with my younger brother.

With both our parents dead, I took it upon myself to become theirs. My brother Chuck and I were only a year apart but anyone could tell I was mature beyond my seven years when our parents died. I grew up fast, focused on school, helped out my grandparents when it came to my siblings. I skipped all the things teen boys usually did. I didn't play sports, I didn't have a girlfriend. I just studied and looked after my siblings.

I finished college early and took over our father's business and soon my brother followed suit. Together we expanded it beyond what my father ever expected it to be. He was in real-estate and soon my brother and I were dabbling in night clubs and other ways to expand.

Now that my sister was healthy, safe, and in love, and my brother had a handle on his own life without me breathing down his neck, I was left all by myself. I'd spent so long focusing on them, I forgot about me.

I stepped on the moving walkway in the airport, letting it take me on the slow monotonous ride which was much like the life I'd been living. I laughed aloud at the irony. People beside me, in front, and behind all turned and stared at the over tired, overworked, shell of a man I'd become. I smiled at them and put my head down in embarrassment. *How did I get here?*

I felt the vibration before I heard the ring of my phone in my pocket. I scrambled for it, thinking the worst, but was relieved to see it was only my secretary. "Please tell me something good." I said, answering my phone.

The sweet female voice of my secretary Kelly came through the receiver, delivering on my request. "I do have good news," she declared. "Your team found the next big thing."

"And what exactly did the team find?" I asked skeptically. My LA team had been begging to do the same thing as the DC team did. The DC team managed to convince Chuck to open a night club. I wasn't thrilled about it in the beginning but it was doing good, and you couldn't deny the green that came with it.

"Well, there's this already existing bar that just went on the market. The owner doesn't want to be bothered with it anymore and just wants to cash out. The current manager wants to keep running it so, you'll just be a silent owner, unless you—"

"Send me the specks, I'll look it over."

"Well here's the thing. Bradshaw is trying to beat us to the punch."

Bradshaw, the realtor equivalent of an arch enemy. "Why's he interested it?" I grumbled.

He was a fifty-four year old jealous jackass. Until Chuck and I came to LA, he had the market locked down, but people didn't want the old man anymore. They wanted young and fresh. So, now he did everything we did with a fake tan; facelift; and spoiled, paid-for, twenty-something-year-old girlfriends.

Kelly sighed from the other end of the phone. "Because he's seen how much success you're having and wants to jump on anything you're even considering."

I stepped off the conveyer and made my way to an empty seat. "How fast is this happening?"

"Bradshaw put an offer in but the owner supposedly knew your father and wants you to come check it out ASAP. His words not mine, 'I'd rather sell it to a Monroe. They have more integrity in their pinky finger than Bradshaw does in his whole body.'"

I laughed aloud again but, this time, no one gave me a second glance. "All right, I'll go down and check it out tomorrow."

"Umm—" Kelly said with a nervous tone.

"Umm, what?" I countered.

"Paul, Jim, and Veronica are on their way now and they want you to meet them. I have a car waiting for you outside the airport," she squeaked.

"You're killing me, Kelly." I rubbed my tired eyes and got back on the conveyer belt that was my life. "Tell them I'm on my way."

"Great! I'll call them now!"

I hung up with Kelly and continued on my way out the airport. There, waiting for me was an SUV and a man holding a piece of paper with my name on it. I'd been gone a week and, during that week, I'd barely had a full night's rest, so adding on the time difference, I was a few hours away from being the walking dead. I got in, laid my head back on the head rest, closed my eyes, and fell asleep.

I awoke when the car came to a stop. I could hear the pounding base of music seeping from the building we were parked in front of. I didn't know how long we'd been driving but it was light when we left and now it was pitch black. I checked my watch for the time—nine-thirty. I approached the bar noting that the parking lot needed to be repaved, and the roof looked like it needed repairing, but other than that it seemed to be a solid building, a packed solid building, and it was only a Wednesday night.

I swung the door open and was hit with music. Not bad music but catchy, rhythmic music that just made you nod along and pay attention. Inside was your typical bar, but the stage they had was legit, and the band that was playing was really good. I'd like to say that I was current with music but I wasn't. That was Chuck's job, mine was more book keeping. I spotted my team at a table and made my way over to them.

"Guys, this couldn't wait?" I asked as I approached.

Jim slurred and stuck his hand up for a high five. "Hey! The boss man's here!"

Veronica grabbed the hand Jim had in the air and pulled it back to the table. "Sorry, it was happy hour then this band started playing and, well, one drink led to another," she said, apologizing for them.

Paul flagged down a waitress. "Can we get another round and add one more on."

He smiled at the beautiful girl. She nodded and turned to the bar before I could tell her I wasn't drinking anything.

I pulled out the empty chair and sat. "I guess we're not talking business tonight?" My three best exchanged a look before giggling. "I expect you all to be on time tomorrow morning. We do have to work. It's only Wednesday."

Veronicas face sobered up quick. "Of—of course Teddy, we know."

The waitress came back to the table with four beers and four shots of lord-only-knew-what. "Here ya go!"

I made eye contact and smiled at her since the rest of the table was busy signing and laughing. "Thank you."

"All right, everyone get your drink." Veronica spoke.

I sat back from the table, "I'm good. Someone can have mine."

Jim leaned across the table. "Boss man," he pleaded. "You've had a hell of a week. Take the drink and let's celebrate the fact that your sister's doing great, your brother is—well, he's Chuck, we'll just drink to his good health—and, lastly, and this is the most important, let's drink to getting you laid."

I wasn't offended. These guys were not only my most trusted employees but since moving out to LA, they'd become the closest thing to best friends that I'd ever had. I grabbed my shot and thought, *Fuck it, what do I have to lose.* "To loosening up."

"That's the spirit!" Jim hollered.

The next time I looked down at my watch it was midnight. It was refreshing to sit back with them. Our waitress had brought round after round, and I quickly lost count. Not being a drinker, it went straight to my head.

I'd gotten up to stretch my legs and, as I surveyed the bar, I saw it had no signs of slowing down. If anything, it seemed as though there were more people milling about.

I was making my way to the bar when the crowd parted and there, standing at the end, was a woman the likes of which I'd never seen before. She was in a tight, short, black dress with boots that went up over her knees and a heel so tall it had to add a good six inches to her height. She was fair-skinned, but had tattoos covering most of her arms and chest. Her dark, jet black hair fell down around her bare arms. I had to blink to keep my eyes seeing straight. She was exotic and for some reason I couldn't take my eyes off her. She was talking to someone but as, they walked away leaving her standing at the bar alone, she turned and reached over the counter. Her dress rose, giving the slightest peek of what was underneath.

I was being drawn to her and, before I knew it, I was standing behind her. It was like my legs walked me over there without my head's knowledge. Once my head caught up with my legs, it was too late to pull back or turn around. She whipped around. Her hair hit me in the face, and then her hand hit me.

"Ew! Back up, drunky," she snapped.

I stammered back a step, not from her slapping me but from her beauty. "I—I'm—I didn't mean to—" I couldn't talk.

The exotic woman stared at me with her icy blue eyes, bright red lips, and fair skin. Her expression wasn't one that any man wanted to see. She looked irritated and disgusted but then her icy eyes widened and she covered her mouth. "Oh fuck!" she said beneath her hand.

I took a step back, apologizing as I did before turning around. "Sorry."

"No! Wait!"

I stilled as I felt her hand on my shoulder. I turned back and was greeted with a pleasant smile. "You wanna get out of here?" she asked as her lips curled and her icy eyes sparkled.

I couldn't remember the last time I'd done something like this, especially with a woman as extravagant as the one standing in front of me. *Oh, right, I never do anything like this.* I nodded my answer and followed her out the back door. She guided me to a large bus. With each step up the bus, I lost a little bit of the control freak in me. I was doing exactly what I'd always lectured Chuck about. I followed her as if she was a siren, beckoning me. She pulled me to the back of the bus. I watched as she closed the door behind her. Biting her red plump lip, she looked up at me through hooded eyes, and I couldn't take it any longer. I needed a release from everything, and this woman was going to give it to me.

I approached her. Toe to toe, we stood. The music coming from the bar made my head swerve as I let myself take her in. I smelled her neck and felt her breath as she sighed beneath my leisurely perusing of her. I was relaxed from the alcohol and crazed by the lust I was feeling.

"Why don't we move this to the bed?" The woman suggested. She tried to push me back, but I held us where we were and shook my head. "Come on," she purred.

I laid a single finger over her lips silencing her. She swallowed hard and turned her icy blue eyes on mine. I wasn't sure if it was in her nature or not, but as I let my finger slide and smear the red on her lips, I knew I had won full control of the situation. I took my time drinking her in, feeling my way around her body. My hand ran up the back of her neck and my fingers raked through her jet black hair. Her eyes closed and she moaned as I kept on. I dragged my hand from her hair and found the zipper of her dress. I slid it down, letting my fingers dance across her shoulders before sending the fabric down over her chest. Again she moaned. Her chest had a bouquet of brightly colored flowers tracing the curves of her breasts.

I traced them with a finger, and I watched as goose bumps appeared all over her body. I gripped the fabric and pulled it, freeing her completely. I went to my knees and continued to pull the fabric with me. The dress fell to her feet as I released it. I looked up her lean, tone body, with nothing but a pair of lacey black underwear and knee high boots. I stood, feeling my way up her fair, soft skin. I took her face in my hands and pulled her to me. Kissing those red stained lips was the final thread of up-tight Teddy. I let her rip at my clothes, and I finished ripping at hers.

We fell to the bed and, within moments, I was over her, doing what I knew I needed but knowing deep down I wanted more than the lust I was feeling for this nameless girl. Her cry and my moans rang out over the pounding music from the bar. We found a rhythm and didn't let it falter. We flipped over and I watched as she cried out on top of me, gripping my chest, while never missing a beat. I sat up, grabbing her by the neck and burying my face in her perky bouquet. I splayed my hands across her back and held her warm body against mine. As tight as I was holding her, she was holding on even tighter.

Sobriety hit me a moment and I slowed our rhythm. I let my forehead rest upon hers "I don't usually do this," I breathed.

She exhaled. "I don't usually do this either."

It was then she caressed my face and kissed me tenderly. I held her down on me finding the rhythm again. Her head fell back and I kissed her chest as she found her release. Following her lead, I ground out my pleasure but never stopped holding her. We sat there a moment, me with my head on her chest and her with her arms around my neck and her head resting on mine. I listened to her heart race within her chest and felt the cool air as it chilled my damp skin.

My moment of sobriety quickly vanished and the room started spinning. I pealed my head off her and lay back on the bed. She climbed off me and laid by my side pulling a cover up over both of us. My arms were over my head, I'd heard once from Chuck if you did that, the room wouldn't spin as much, I was going to put that theory to the test. A dark head of hair found its way onto my chest and a hand wrapped around me along with the warmth of a body. "I don't do this," she stated again.

I let one arm curl around her as she snuggled up against me. "I'm Teddy," I said, hoping to put her at ease and also hoping that it would give her the idea to tell me her name.

"Oh, I—I know who you are," she stammered.

I stilled the hand that was rubbing her back. The room was spinning faster, and I knew I was a few short words from passing out. "Do I at least get a name?" The words slurred off my lips. The only sound I could hear was the thumping of the music or, on second thought, that could have been my head pounding. Either way, she didn't speak up. "Oookaayyy. It's fine. You don't have to—"

I felt her squeeze me and snuggle farther into the crook of my arm. "Chloe, my name's Chloe. Now pass out before I break any more of my rules."

"Chloe—" I repeated. "I like it," I said before the darkness took over and I passed out.

About the Author

M. E. Gordon, was born and raised in Maryland, where she still resides with her husband. She is a stay at home mom to four children, three boys and one very, spoiled, little girl, all under the age of seven. Growing up Gordon was an avid journal writer. She wrote her first romance novel at the age of fourteen, and it was pretty bad, but over the years and through all the kids she honed her craft. When Gordon doesn't have her mom hat on, you can find her reading, working on her next story, or watching guilty pleasure television.

www.ingramcontent.com/pod-product-compliance
Lightning Source LLC
Chambersburg PA
CBHW070221260626
47160CB00002B/636